£ 2.50

£1-50

THE BITTER LOTUS

Richard Beilby

ANGUS & ROBERTSON PUBLISHERS

Published with the assistance of the Literature Board
of the Australia Council

Angus & Robertson Publishers
London . Sydney . Melbourne . Singapore
Manila

First published by Angus & Robertson Publishers, Australia, 1978

National Library of Australia
Cataloguing-in-publication data.
Beilby, Richard, 1918–.
The Bitter Lotus

ISBN 0 207 13638 6

I. Title.

A823'.3

Photosetting by Thomson Press (India) Ltd., New Delhi
Printed in Hong Kong

I wish to express my gratitude to the Australia Council (Literature Board) with whose support this book was written.

I also wish to thank Richard Barton of the Buddhist Society of Western Australia for his generous assistance and patient explanations; Graham Watson, who provided me with some special information; my son Marc who also helped me, although he doesn't know it; and the two Joans in my life, my wife and my sister.

Lotus, a name of a flower . . .
Nelumbo nucifeea, sometimes called
the "East Indian lotus" or "sacred
bean", which has been associated
with aspects of Buddhist worship.

Collier's Encyclopedia

As upon a heap of rubbish thrown
on the highway, a sweet-smelling
lovely lotus may grow, even so
amongst worthless beings a disciple
of the Fully Enlightened One out-
shines the blind worldlings in wisdom.

The Dhammapada

PART ONE

Grey, Green and glorious Lanka
was like the garden in the Sky.
The Ramayana

Warm night air, spiced with a trade wind's exotic aroma, filled the aircraft's exit compartment. Stepping out onto the platform of the airport's mobile steps I paused, breathing the sensuous humidity. I had almost forgotten the smell of the tropics: the night pungency of flowers and rotting vegetation, the fragrance and fetor of growth and decay, and the womb-like odours of the greedy earth avidly absorbing everything back into itself and giving forth equally avid new life. It is the smell of fecundity, rank and seminal and uniquely equatorial.

Beyond the blue lights of the runways I could see the silhouettes of palms with moonlight smearing their fronds and I glimpsed the shapes of distant hills, brooding, romantically humped, against the stars. Excitement lifted me out of my tiredness, and stripped away the staleness of intervening years.

Behind me the other passengers were jostling wearily, clattering their cabin luggage, and I caught a whiff of perfume from the American woman who had been seated across the aisle from me. The stewardess was backed against the railing, solidly filling out her British Airways blue, her straw hair and peaches-and-cream Englishness alien in this tropic night as she murmured through her British Airways smile: "Goodbye. Thank you for travelling with us." I smiled at her, tempted to say "Thank you for bringing me back," but that would have sounded silly, a man of my age babbling like a romantic boy. Just then the American woman nudged me with her vanity case, destroying my euphoria, so that I bolted down the stairs, disconcerted, resenting her, footsteps ringing on the diamond grating.

Reaching the ground I was annoyed to find her overtaking me, that rose-red vanity case held at the ready as though she was prepared to batter her way past me, her small, dark head lowered, sharp chin tucked, almost pugnaciously I thought, against her throat: I had an impression of fiercely independent femininity, aloof, vaguely defensive. As we passed through the blaze of lights under the aircraft's wing, where thick, black hoses pulsed spasmodically and technicians talked loudly through the whirr of generators, a gust of engine-heated air ruffled her hair, whipping the cuffs of her slacks around her ankles: I noticed small feet in expensive shoes stepping out with dainty urgency. Then she was past me, moving out of the light without a sidelong glance, impersonal, unreachable in her chic remoteness, which seemed to be compounded of impatience, high fashion and a boundless American worldliness. I was left with the shuffle of feet behind me and the voice of the belly-heavy Englishman who had sat beside me on the flight peevishly assuring his wife: "Of course I'm not tired, but you know I never sleep on aeroplanes." I quickened my pace, finding myself noting the shape of the woman in front of me. A nice, trim shape for all her disconcerting briskness, as sweetly contoured as a piece of wheel pottery and now silhouetted for my inspection by the lights of the airport buildings. Suddenly I noticed that she had halted.

Reaching her I saw that a figure had accosted her out of the darkness, a dark uniform, a dark-skinned face with splendid teeth under the light-reflecting peak of a cap, a rolling voice with an upward lilt, an arm uplifted, directing.

"All transit passengers this way, mem."

"I'm disembarking," the woman told him, which interested me because I also happened to be disembarking.

Without pausing I altered course, taking heed of the official's directions and headed for a part of the terminal which — made up of glass panels flooded with aqueous light in which dim, distorted figures swam — looked rather like a tropical fish tank. It appeared to be under construction still, the black serrations of unfinished walls sawing the soft night sky, scaffolding and skeletal shafts of reinforcing steel protruding nakedly everywhere. There was a smell of new concrete and dust, while piles of builders' litter had been raked back from the entrance.

A blur of movement greeted me — a girl coming through the out-pouring light, the mist of her apricot-coloured sari fluttering like the trembling of butterfly wings. Her features were narrow and Eastern, making me think of a nautch dancer's face, its delicate, caramel-coloured planes burnished by the amber light: lustrous eyes smiled up at me and I heard the tinkle of bracelets as she offered me a paper-covered booklet. Anula, I thought wildly,

4

and my heart lifted, wishful thinking snatching at memories in that startled instant. The likeness was purely illusory, I knew, youthful, racial and improbable in time. Anula would be long married and matronly now. Yet this girl was like Anula as I remembered her.

"Welcome to Sri Lanka," she greeted softly. I accepted the booklet, looking down at her, seeing a vision from a turbulent time of my youth. "It is a tourist's guide to our island," she was explaining sweetly. "This is South Asia Tourism Year '75. *Ayubowan*. Welcome."

I was conscious of the booklet, dry and stiffly new in my hand, reminding me that this was 1975. Sri Lanka they called this island now, but I thought of it fondly, nostalgically, as Ceylon. Just as I thought of Anula. The girl's likeness haunted me and I wanted a moment to rid myself of its spell, but just then I became aware of the American woman at my elbow, watching me staring at the girl.

"Thanks," I muttered, clutching the booklet and hurriedly turning away, shoving blindly at the heavy, pneumatically boosted, airport doors. I resented the woman: she was hustling me deliberately, allowing me no time to savour my return. As the pressurised resistance gave way before me I heard the girl behind me saying: "Welcome to . . ." Then came the baleful hiss of closing doors.

Inside, the airconditioning soon cooled my irritation, dousing me with its dry, unnatural chill. Why do they always turn the airconditioning so low in Asian countries? Just coming through that door was like being transported twenty degrees of latitude southward. Shivering, I joined the queue of passengers who shuffled meekly past the Health counter and straggled across to the Immigration desk. They were mostly a German tour group, clannish, loud-voiced, robust folk who had filled the forward section of the plane. They were distinguished by their unsunned, European faces and their abundance of photographic equipment. Already the first of the luggage was coming in, hefted by barefooted, brown-legged porters who slung the suitcases into some sort of line. Piped music dribbled languorously, soaking into the babble of voices. I smelt perfume and knew that the woman had caught up with me again.

She stood beside me at the Health counter, waiting her turn while an official conducted an assiduous scrutiny of the record of my vaccinations. It was the first time I had been able to look at her openly. On the plane we had exchanged the usual travellers', too-casual glances, blank-faced, pretending disinterest. Once, when our glances had met for the briefest of instants, her gaze had passed over me so coolly that I had almost imagined the hoar frost building up on my face. Now, as she listlessly watched the official perusing each rubber stamp on my certificate, I risked another peep. Seeing her from this angle I could discern an imbalance in her features—a wide forehead with arching brows blackly pencilled; large eyes, eye-shadowed and shaded by fatigue; a thin, straight nose; the whole upper part of the face tending to make the pointed chin and red mouth, with its slightly curling underlip, appear weak. Not pretty, but an attractive face, petulant perhaps, certainly sensuous. I declined to speculate on her age. There was a sparkle of bright stones on her left hand as well as a thick band of wedding gold: for some reason its opulence daunted me much more than its significance.

The official closed my Health book and shoved it back at me, thereby rousing the woman, who turned and caught me studying her. This time her reaction was much more positive, stiffening, eyes widening and emanating hostility like laser beams. Abashed I hurried away again, glad to be able to lose myself among the Germans who were milling around the Immigration desk. In my haste I nearly fell over a large tripod notice which greeted: "South Asia Welcomes You"—with a daffodil-like asterisk in fluorescent pink—"The Tourist is an Honoured Guest, especially in South Asia Tourism Year '75. A Sri Lankan smile is worth a Thousand Words."

"Good evening, sah. Welcome to Sri Lanka. Your passport, please."

The Immigration officer was plump and affable with a smile like a rising moon curving across the darkness of his features. He wore his good humour determinedly, like a garland over his uniform. He leafed through my passport, humming and ah-ing softly as though he was reading music in it.

"You have your immigration form, please?"

Fumbling in my pocket I brought out the piece of printed pasteboard which the stewardess had given me on the plane: its questioning dotted lines were still blank, its tiny interrogatory squares unticked, all those public secrets without which official-dom would be unable to officiate as yet undivulged. I apologised for my oversight but the officer merely smiled indulgently, waiting while I took out my glasses and bent over the card. Mason, David Charles, I wrote, underlining the surname as requested. Nationality: Australian. Date of birth: day, eighteenth; month, seven; year, 1921. Then followed a column of tiny squares bearing the legends "married", "unmarried", "divorced", "widowed". Smiling I ticked the square marked "unmarried", reflecting that, quite ironically, much of the reason for that state could be said to have originated on this island, give or take a few subsequent factors. If it hadn't been for Anula, and if Eric hadn't written that letter to Janice . . . Old history that it was, it was having its consequences now. Vocation, the next question asked, and I wrote "Author". The next one wanted to know my address while staying in Sri Lanka so I wrote "Hotel Serendib, Galle Face Centre Road, Colombo". Then followed "purpose of visit", with more tiny squares, this time marked "business", "holiday", "returning citizen". Again I paused, dallying on the edge of sentiment. There was no square marked "sentimental journey" or "laying old ghosts" or "searching for a delinquent ;on" so I ticked the square marked "holiday".

"You are from Australia, I see," the officer remarked with a light in his eye like a collector turning up a rare find. "That is good. We do not have many visitors from Australia. Is this your first visit to Sri Lanka, sah?"

Smiling I shook my head, removing my glasses and putting them away. "I spent four months here during the war."

"How nice!" Interest flared brightly. "What year was that, sah?"

"Nineteen forty two." I wondered whether that long-ago year held any significance for this man and couldn't resist adding: "I arrived here the day before the Japanese raid on Easter Sunday."

"Oh my God! The Easter Sunday raid!" His rounded eyes and awed tone gave that event a Saint Bartholemew's Day significance. "The fifth of April, 1942! My God, yes! What a day. But our Spitfires dealt with them very efficiently, sent them running off with their tails between their legs. Twenty-nine downed out of fifty-two. Very creditable, don't you think, sah?" He leaned forward, eager to disburse another thousand words with his Sri Lankan smile. "I remember you chaps. I was a boy at the time. I used to see you marching along the roads and I admired your fine hats. Did you know our Sri Lankan police now wear Digger hats?

7

Oh yes, very suitable hats, very functional. And where were you stationed, sah?"

"At Bentota for a while." I was aware of unrest in the queue behind me and I imagined the slightest whiff of scent, but names were crowding my memory, making me reckless. "Nerboda. Mount Lavinia. Panadura . . ."

. . . and Anguruwatota with mats of scarlet chillies drying in the street and piles of golden king coconuts and yellow hands of thick bananas and people and dogs and splashes of blood-red betel nut spittle in the dust and little, mournful trotting bulls pulling tinkling taxi carts.

And Ratmalana, or was it Moratuwa—it wasn't easy to sort the names out of the mass of intervening years—but there the long, tired Indian Ocean rollers spread their foam on the coarse, pink sands, clutching at the roots of leaning palms. And there were hollow-log fishing boats and lines of chanting, naked brown men hauling bulging nets out of the sea's salty dawns.

And Horana, where Headquarters Company had been camped under the rubber trees while the Sections went out and toiled like navvys, building bridges and coconut-log fortifications because the Japanese had just taken the Andaman Islands and sunk the aircraft carrier *Hermes*, and so it was feared that Ceylon would be next.

And there had been a spell in the jungle, slushing through the rotting mush on the jungle floor, hacking through crackling bamboo thickets, being driven mad by leeches and the fine, irritating hairs of the bamboos that fired the skin like dhōbi-itch. Hunting for downed Jap pilots, with that scrawny, boy-sergeant interpreter, in his ill-fitting uniform of the local volunteer corps, hectoringly questioning puzzled villagers. And finding a pilot, bits of putrefying cadaver strewn around, identifiable only by rags of flying gear, the guts chewed out—by a leopard, the interpreter had announced portentously, leopards always went for the soft parts first—finger bones gnawed clean as knitting needles by rats, and a boot with the foot still in it: there had been no sign of the head.

And that camp on the edge of a tea plantation where we had been asked if we were doing "penal servitude" because nobody in

Ceylon had seen Europeans with their shirts off, swinging axes, pushing shovels. The locals had given us a wide berth, the women particularly, chattering and scuttling away with speculative, backward glances, until the day when the Burgher Dutch manager had come down and discovered for himself that Australians weren't brothel-burning bushrangers as had been put about by the British residents of Ceylon. Thereafter the troops had been escorted over the tea factory, their big boots crunching awkwardly as they solemnly tramped around the machines while the manager explained about Broken Orange Pekoe, Soochung and Fannings while the Tamil women workers watched, giggling, white-eyed, white-toothed, brown skins as dark as if they had been steeped in tea themselves.

Then had come rumours of a possible uprising. Army Intelligence had reported that the Japanese were calling on the people of Ceylon, as fellow Buddhists, to rise against their British oppressors. The Buddhist monks had always been unapproachable, shaven-headed, serene in the faultlessness of their faith — "canaries" we called them because of their yellow robes. Troops had been put on the alert and orders had been issued that in the event of emergency all Buddhist temples and monastries were to be secured first since it was believed that the priesthood was sympathetic to the Japanese call and might very well be hiding some of the downed pilots. The order had been translated to us by a forthright sergeant as: "When the blue starts we shoot the canaries first." Fortunately it had never come to that.

And then there had been Udugama. A pleasant assignment, locating the stumps of coconut palms which the army had cut down, marking their locations on a map to verify compensation claims. Our interpreter had been old man Jayasakewa, courtly, aristocratic, speaking faultless English, always immaculate in collar and tie and striped sarong, his silver hair impaled in a knob by a silver-studded tortoiseshell comb. His home had been a fascinating impasto of West on East, snowy napery on the table, batiks on the walls, biriani followed by plum pudding, tea in delicate Wedgewood cups served by obsequious servants who issued, soft-footed, from behind wooden screens. He had been a man of substance in Udugama, deferred to, greeted with palms pressed to palms and bowing, a Justice of the Peace, owner of a plumbago mine and father of Anula . . .

9

". . . oh, splendid," the Immigration officer enthused. "So now you have come back to see our country again."

"Something like that," I admitted, thinking of Janice and her wayward son and my commitment to them which had brought me back to where it had all begun. Then I was aware of the reproachful faces behind me and I edged away, murmuring harassed "Thank yous" to the officer's parting good wishes.

Once clear of him I went looking for my suitcase in the lines of luggage. I found it slewed around, overshadowed by a large, upright portmanteau of the latest type that is fitted with tiny castors which enable it to be wheeled as well as carried. A portable typewriter, also of the latest type, had been laid on top of my suitcase. As I bent to remove it there was a peremptory hissing behind me and a little brown man in khaki shorts slipped under my arm and snatched the typewriter: almost in the same movement he grabbed my suitcase and marched away, spring-heeled and looking pleased with himself.

Going after him I grabbed his arm, feeling its stringy, poorly-fed sinewyness. He wheeled, a scrawny, pigeon-chested man in what might have been a uniform if it hadn't been so shabby, with splayed bare feet, big ears spreading under a thatch of black hair and haunted eyes in a walnut face imprinted with the age-old wants of Asia: he clung to his load as though he couldn't afford to have it taken from him. There were other Singhalese around us—an airline official, secure in the prestige of his uniform, some big-bellied men, darkly sleek in well-cut suits, and their women in rainbow saris, bodices well filled out, swathes of bare, brown belly flesh extruding plumply—they all looked so prosperous, superior and indifferent, in no way part of the little man's impoverished world.

"Taxi, taxi," he was gabbling and there was desperation in his eyes as he waggled the typewriter in the direction of the entrance.

Shaking my head I explained that the typewriter wasn't mine, but he merely nodded brightly and smiled uncomprehendingly, baring protruding teeth browned by betel-nut chewing. Beginning again I pointed to the unclaimed baggage and while he stared at it puzzledly I whipped the typewriter from his grasp. Evading the surprise and reproach in those doggy eyes I went back to the line of luggage. I was almost there when I saw the American woman standing with one hand on the wheeled portmanteau, looking

10

searchingly around. Oh hell, I thought irritably, of all the pieces to take why did it have to be hers?

"Is this what you're looking for?"

I held the typewriter at arm's length. She wheeled, bringing that disturbing face back into my view, suspicion flaring.

"Thank you." An appreciable pause while she examined my face and motives, then a belated glance at the typewriter and back at my face, her American voice suddenly flat, drawing the vowels out sardonically. Still aloof, she took the typewriter: the carrying handle wasn't wide and our fingers brushed during the exchange, that massive diamond ring lightly rasping me with its hard-edged glitter.

"My porter picked it up by mistake."

Feeling obliged to explain I gestured towards my porter who was watching and responded with laudable promptness, giving a buck-toothed smile and a vigorous nod. The woman looked at him and then back at me. Again I sensed, under the surface of her sophistication, that fiercely independent femininity ready to repulse me. I looked at her wedding ring, wondering, but at that moment a movement distracted me, a touch on my arm, somebody moving into the edge of my consciousness. Looking around I found myself confronted by a youthful, dark brown, handsome face, dark eyes and a winning smile. A well-dressed young man was standing with arms slightly spread, like a guardian angel unfolding protective wings. I had the feeling of a professional persuasiveness being concentrated on me.

"Good evening, sir. Good evening, madam. *Ayubowan*, as we say in Sri Lanka. Welcome. Is somebody meeting you?" He paused expectantly, dark eyes switching alertly from the woman to me, a whole barrage of charm being held in reserve.

"No," I admitted warily, steeling myself to resist that charm.

"Ah! Then I can help you." Beaming he closed in on us, arms opening wider as though to herd us away. "You are going to Colombo? I will take you in my car. These taxi chaps are very expensive. One hundred rupees they will charge you. Too much! I will take you to your hotel. Which is it? The Ceylinco? The Galle Face?" Again those astute, umber features, Aryan-fine and indubitably comely, homed in on me as the male and therefore the decision-maker of the pair of us, willing me to surrender to him unconditionally.

11

"Thank you but I don't think . . ." That was as far as I got, my refusal aborted by another swift rush of eloquence.

"Of course, you do not know me. Permit me to introduce myself. I am Horace Larga. My daddy owns Taprobane Tours — branches in Kandy and Galle. We are government travel agents. We can arrange for you to tour Jaffna, Trincomalee, the ruins . . ."

"Did you say government travel agents?" the woman interrupted and I couldn't help noticing her accent, hard-edged, slicing through the young man's buttery flow.

But only for a moment. "Government approved, madam." Liquid eyes dwelt on her momentarily with a sort of hurt-dog reproof before returning to me, according me the male right of precedence and appealing to me to assert it: his voice resumed unctuously, expunging all trace of the lapse. "You wish to see the ruins, Anuradhapura, Polonnaruwa, Sigiriya or the game sanctuaries, Yala, Wilpattu . . . ?"

"But you're not a government department, are you?" the woman insisted doggedly.

This time he acknowledged her, his splendid eyes languishing on her while he conceded: "No, madam, but we are government licensed. Twenty-five years my daddy has been in the travel business. One quarter of a century. That is a very long time, madam." And having refurbished his bona fides to some extent he turned back to me, his voice lifting persuasively. "We are also gem merchants, sir — showrooms in York Street, Colombo One. Oh yes, excellent sapphires, amethysts, moonstones. Did you know that Sri Lankan moonstones are the finest in the world? Perhaps your wife would like . . ."

"This gentleman is not my husband."

I started, feeling ridiculously guilty in some way that I couldn't define. She was smiling, enjoying her declaration of independence. Horace Larga was abashed for the first time, with the faintest moralistic gleam in his lustrous eyes, as though he imagined he had uncovered something illicit. He looked at me, then down at the woman's hand with the wedding ring prominent, then recovering he swooped on her, the spread of his arms suddenly no longer quite including me.

"Perhaps you would be interested in a tour, madam." His tone was soft, enticing. "The beach resort at Tangalla Bay, the coral

12

gardens at Hikkaduwa. See the stilt fishermen at Weligama—very clever, those chaps, sitting out in the sea on their poles. And Ambalangoda where the devil-masks are carved. And the moonstone mines at Ratnapura. We provide a car and an English-speaking guide, all expenses covered, Rest Houses, meals, no tipping . . ."

"Now hold on a moment!"

She fell back a step, a raised hand fending off his rush of words. Imagining that she glanced appealingly at me, I roused myself. "Let's leave it till later. If this lady is as tired as I am she won't want to think about anything until she's had a few hours sleep. But I'll take you up on your offer of a ride to town." Without waiting for his reply I turned to the woman. "What about you?"

"Sure." She nodded briskly, eyes thanking me.

Outmanoeuvred, Larga capitulated. "Which hotel, madam?"

"The Serendib."

"Ah yes. Galle Face Centre Road. And yours, sir?"

"The same." Out of the corner of my eye I saw the woman glance quickly at me and I managed not to smile.

Larga was looking from one to the other of us—probably estimating the difference between our ages. It would be about twenty years at a rough guess, I imagined, give or take a few years to allow for the magic of modern cosmetics: a formidable difference, enough to render me vulnerable to the father and daughter gibe. The thought of that possibility chastened me.

"Come, please. My car is this way," Larga was saying and between that and hissing and clicking his fingers at the porters he was beckoning us and edging his way through the crowd. My man hefted my suitcase again, while another porter picked up the typewriter and began trundling the wheeled portmanteau away, and all of a sudden we were moving off in safari order. I resisted the impulse to take the woman's arm, falling into step behind her instead.

"I guess he figures we're together," she confided over her shoulder and somehow I was beside her before I realised it. "Did you see his face when you said you were at my hotel?"

"It rocked him, didn't it?"

"Just the same, he's dishy, isn't he?" she whispered surprisingly, swaying closer, her arm brushing mine.

"He's an urger," I declared stoutly. "His daddy sent him here to waylay the likes of us."

13

"His daddy. That's cute, isn't it? I wonder if he can do his buttons up yet."

"Don't be fooled. He'd make a buck where we'd starve."

She didn't answer because by then we had reached the entrance where Larga was supervising the loading of our luggage into his car. Tipping both porters I ushered my companion into the back seat, realising as I settled myself beside her, that I was very tired. Through the car window I could see the silhouettes of palm trees mushrooming under a full moon and I had an eerie sense of having come back. I was silent until the car began to move.

"Since we're in this together, my name is Mason," I said, wondering whether I ought to offer my hand, deciding against it.

She didn't answer at once, huddling in the shadows.

"Just Mason?" Then she laughed. "My name is Gale."

"Just Gale?" I mocked gently.

"Missus Gale."

The Galle Road runs out of the Fort area of Colombo and follows the coast, passing a large, grassy common where races were held and the army staged ceremonial parades in the days before Independence. This is called the Galle Face Green and our hotel looked across it out to sea. Except for a single light spilling weakly from its entrance the place was in darkness when we arrived, yet I recognized it from those times when I had travelled this road before after evenings spent dancing in the Colombo Town Hall, helping the patriotic people of this island to raise money with which to buy Spitfires for Britain: in those days it was called Echelon Barracks or Green Barracks. Now it was the Hotel Serendib. Yet in the moonlight it still looked like a barracks, rambling, double-storied, a whitewashed mass with a driveway passing under its porch and ancient cannons flanking its entrance, so indubitably British and military and out of date. I heard the rapping of halyards on tubular steel poles and saw a file of flagstaffs across its front. As I followed Mrs Gale into its lobby I recalled having read that Serendib—the ancient Arab name for Ceylon—had given its variant to the English language "serendipity", "where good things might be come upon by chance".

Inside, the place was indisputably British, very high ceilings, parquetry floors, a broad staircase with a wide handrail of age-blackened teak curving grandly upwards, the feeling of gracious immensity all around harbouring memories of Empire in its shadows. The rest was post-Independence and Singhalese: the fan-backed chairs, the devil-masks and batik paintings, the posters extolling Sri Lanka, the "Resplendent Isle". At the foot of the stairs stood a tubby, mythological beast of mottled porcelain—an elephant's body with gaping dog-like jaws and an upraised trunk that appeared to end as a peacock's head—in its hollow guts a ruby light glowed gruesomely. Also Singhalese was the long-haired youth who admitted us without rising; signalling to the bare-footed servant who had brought our luggage from the car, he produced two old-fashioned keys with plastic labels attached. Standing beside Mrs Gale while she signed the register I glimpsed the numbers on the labels. Rooms 7 and 8. Larga stood behind us as though he intended to accompany us to our rooms: I turned, glad of the opportunity to be rid of him.

"What do we owe you for bringing us here?"

"Do not worry." He wasn't to be dismissed so easily, exuding more charm. "I will come tomorrow. Will nine o'clock be convenient?"

"My God!" Mrs Gale wheeled, mock appalled. "I hope I'm not even out of bed by then. Not after tonight."

"Make it some time after lunch," I directed. "We should be out of bed by then."

As I spoke I realised I had answered for both of us in a way which might very well revive his speculations, but I didn't care. Nodding curtly I followed Mrs Gale up the staircase.

We ascended to a wide veranda that looked down on a quadrangle of buildings with tall, narrow windows and crenellations: I was reminded of pictures of Cawnpore before the siege, all so historically British-Indian. Then, high in the sky above the city, I saw the neon outline of a tubby elephant advertising Elephant Cordials. The dark mass of a tree, starred with the blur of white flowers, leaned inward to the veranda, rubbing the railing with its boughs: the night was heavy with scent.

"Beautiful," Mrs Gale murmured, inhaling deeply.

"Frangipani," I pronounced. "I have it growing at home."

"I bet your wife's crazy about it."

"I like it myself," I said unhelpfully, wondering why I had bothered to avoid the truth.

15

She didn't answer, for the boy had halted outside two adjoining doors, rattling the keys. Rooms 7 and 8. I motioned her to enter the first door as it opened but she delayed, both of us staring into a huge, empty room where the boy was padding around, switching on lights. Mrs Gale's voice roused me, faintly ironic.

"Goodnight, Just Mason."

"Goodnight, Mrs Gale."

The fan woke me. It was ancient, creaking loudly, dangling from the ceiling above me like a twentieth century Damoclean sword, its blades as wide as a helicopter's rotors, churning cool air. Still clogged with sleep it was some moments before my mind cleared, wakefulness spreading slowly from the somnolent core of my comprehension . . . lying naked in a welter of crumpled sheets . . . in the Serendib, the serendipity hotel, with Missus Gale probably still asleep in the adjoining room . . . in Ceylon at last because I had always planned to come back . . . which was why Janice had commissioned me to look for her son . . .

. . . or I should say, our son . . .

Oh David, you have been the pride and the frustration of my life! Olive-skinned, dark-eyed David Coleman, bearded like an apostle, twenty-one years old and searching for himself with an apostolic fervour despite a Diploma of Fine Arts and a "father" like Eric. Or because of them. Perhaps because of Eric most of all.

I shifted uneasily in the bed. Maybe that wasn't a charitable thought now that Eric was dead—but to hell with charity! His death didn't alter the fact that he'd had a parlous relationship with his "son".

If anything Eric's death had precipitated an avalanche of new maternal pressure upon David. "Now he'll just *have* to go into the business," Janice had insisted with that bland relentlessness which had played a major part in driving David away. Janice, widowed and moneyed and getting the feel of her power? So long as Eric had been alive, she had defended David's artistic aspirations, but now that Eric was dead . . . "Eric spent his life building Australasian Industries so it's David's duty to keep the family name in the business. He owes it to his father." Father—Eric! Oh Janice, he's dead, so you don't have to go on pretending—not with me! To hide the trembling of my hands as I heard her outline her plans for

16

him I had swallowed my whisky—Janice's whisky now, like everything else which had once been Eric's: the controlling interest in Australasian Industries, the beach house at Mandurah. Everything except David. Half of him was mine—the thinking, questioning, indomitable half. As for duty—try talking duty to a recalcitrant young man who has turned to religion, contriving to put four thousand kilometres of ocean between himself and that duty which he is so obviously determined to evade.

At first I had refused her request, arguing that I hadn't made up my mind to go to Ceylon just yet, and that David was in no way answerable to me, that he would remind me that his mother had a competent board of directors and that he knew nothing about business anyway, or more simply, he would tell me to mind my own business. But Janice had out-thought me, easily demolishing my objections. Hadn't Eric always been my friend—my very good friend, she didn't need to remind me. Which, of course, she had been doing and not as subtly as she imagined, reminding me that I owed Eric a debt of the most primary order. Hadn't we talked about Ceylon so often and hadn't I always said that one day, very soon, I would go back and write a book about the island? And David would be unlikely to rebuff me because we'd been so close from the time he'd been a little boy, the cricket matches I'd taken him to, the fishing trips we'd been on when Eric had been away on business or too busy. And hadn't David always called me "Uncle Mase"? "Besides"—she had brought out the clincher then, blue eyes suddenly disconcertingly hard, eyes in which I had once believed I could lose myself for the rest of my life—"you're to blame, in a way, for David defying his father and going on with his painting."

To blame! That made me sit up straight. From Eric I'd had that reproach many times, but never from Janice. To blame for David not venerating Australasian Industries? That I confess to without a vestige of shame. But to blame for him being in this world at all? Ah, that's what I'd like to hear you say. But of course she didn't and never would. Yet she had a right to ask this thing of me, not only because of my love for David but also because Eric had been my very good friend, as she had been at pains to remind me . . . he had pulled me out of a sticky spot at a place called Bishitarbu during the Owen Stanley campaign in New Guinea. That's why I had never been able to turn my back on him, any more than I could turn my back on Janice and David. We were four people enmeshed by associations of the past. Of us all I was most sorry for David.

Wide awake now I sat up on the pillows and reached for my pipe. Oh Eric, I thought ruefully, I am in debt to you on two counts—your heroism and my treachery. Yet you took her from me. All's fair in love and war, and our relationship had been the product of both.

When I had first known him he had been an artificer, not yet out of his apprenticeship and two years older than me, a lusty, thick-set swarthy young man with black eyes and a white smile and tightly curled black hair. Even then he had drive and a willingness to toil, business acumen and an overpowering determination to be his own boss one day, while I—I had only a gift for words, an awakening interest in the human condition and a lot of half-formed inclinations that drove me to put pen to paper. In my more despairing moments I had often wondered what had drawn us together in the first place. Perhaps it had been the attraction of opposites, but ultimately it had been the war that had bound us inextricably together.

Ours had been an odd friendship, me a clerk at the time, reluctantly learning the insurance business, more drawn to Hemingway and Steinbeck, more ready to scribble disgustingly amateurish stories than to apply myself to the dreary writing of cover notes and renewal notices. At first Janice had been my co-worker—a comptometrist, daintily punching her lumbering, archaic machine—and then my girlfriend, making it a threesome, never coming between Eric and me—not in those years before the war, anyway. While we were in the army she had written to both of us, scrupulously maintaining a ratio of two letters to me to every one she wrote to Eric. We would have married if he hadn't written so carelessly from Ceylon. Careless? As it was, it was Eric who had married her during the leave when we returned from New Guinea the first time. And after the war, with his deferred pay and rehabilitation allowances, he had set about building a back street fitting and turning business into a flourishing company that produced castings and bearings and intricately turned parts for engines. Coleman's Engineering he had called it then. It was cruel that almost a year before his death he had bullied a lucrative contract out of Indonesia that would make his company a nationwide name. By then, of course, big money had been injected

18

into it and it was Australasian Industries.

Also by then I had several books to my credit and was becoming known, but to Eric that was a phenomenon as incomprehensible as the march of the lemmings. Art, music, literature? To him they were activities only indulged in by those fortunates who lived on private incomes, or by retired celebrities, hobbies at best. No practical man imagined that he could make a living at them. Which explained why he was so baffled and outraged when David had announced his intention of becoming an artist. "An artist, for Christ sake! You think I built up this business for you to go off painting naked sheilas? Like buggery I did!" Which, of course, was the nub of the matter.

Tragic as it was, I had expected Eric's death to resolve everything. I thought Janice would put a manager in the office and take her place on the board of directors, while David would go on painting in that draughty studio he'd rented in Fremantle. It hadn't worked out that way.

David had fled to Ceylon to become a Buddhist!

I was astounded to say the least. I knew that lately he had been attending an *ashram* to study yoga with some friends, but I had assumed that that was one of the in things for his group, like surfing, health foods and transcendental meditation. But not Buddhism! Then Janice had produced a postcard from him. It was postmarked Sri Lanka and bore a date stamp nearly three weeks old. And the picture was of Colombo, one of those streets of dowdy old Victorian facades and little shops whose weathered tiles look as though they might be Dutch, or even Portuguese, and which make up the city's Fort area and have such thoroughly British names as York and Chatham and Flagstaff. It showed an intersection where a mounted policeman directed a hotch-potch of Asiatic traffic—cars, a bullock cart, huge wooden-sided trucks, a man with a carrying-pole, a rickshaw, saronged pedestrians scurrying hazardously, and cyclists, perched like stylites on their flimsy machines, pedalling serenely. A building in the background caught my eye, its raw umber colour familiar, now faded to a powdery rose, with an arcaded pavement where people, arrested in mid-stride by the camera's shutter, stepped out between the ruddled arches . . .

19

. . . bustling, gesticulating, swirling in and out of the mid-morning heat and the curving shadows of the red brick arches, cutting across my path, sarongs, furled umbrellas, the graceful swing of women's hips, bright saris and bracelets, tourists in sunglasses with coveys of begging children in tow, women beggars suckling babies, beggars performing tricks, shopkeepers beckoning from their doorways, strident sounds and sibilances and bicycle bells and the smell of sweat and coconut oil and all the while brown faces entreating me, brown hands offering me ebony elephants, lottery tickets, ballpoint pens and batik scarves, shell necklaces, road maps, woven hats, carvings of wood and bone and stone and regiments of cunningly corroded brass Buddhas. "You buy . . . you want . . . you give me . . ." At a street corner a sign proclaimed in English and Singhalese: Scavenging Time—7 p.m. to 2:30 a.m.

Halting I looked up the sloping cross-street to the clock tower: one of the clock faces was missing, the aperture where it had been now boarded up, staring like a sightless eye. I recalled that somewhere up that street there had once been a Combined Services Canteen in a brightly lit basement in which tired but resolutely cheerful matrons had laboured over steaming urns, dispensing tea and sandwiches to servicemen, while around a piano and at little tables sloe-eyed, lissom Burgher girls had chattered and flirted patriotically. Locating it meant recovering something of myself and the excitement of those hectic times. And locate it I did, but the basement entrance was murky now, worn wooden steps, musty smells, and a gold-toothed money-changer popping out of the shadows, offering to change my dollars into rupees. Shaking my head I retreated, dodging an irately trilling bicycle. The sightless clock tower looked down, reminding me that so much can change under the blind eye of time.

Back under the arches an Indian youth with the delicate features of a painting in a Jain temple waylaid me, trying to entice me into his shop. Gemstones? Silver filigree? Devil masks? When I declined he tried to detain me, one hand lightly gripping my arm, the other fanning a deck of postcards with the dexterity of a cardsharp—postcards of the Lion Rock and the Sigiryia Maidens, Kandy dancers, the Aukarna Buddha, moonstone miners in their muddy burrows. I shook my head but his fingers tightened on my arm and he smiled a timeless, pimpish smile, producing a picture of naked Vedda women. Annoyed, I swung away, blundering into a passerby, feeling a bare foot squash unpleasantly under mine. An elbow roughly fended me off, an American voice rasping harshly. "Hey, cool it, man! Watch where ya treadin', will ya!" Wheeling, I started to apologise hurriedly, putting out an appeasing hand, feeling a boney, male hardness under the coarse cloth of a sleeve.

"I'm sorry. I hope I didn't hurt you. I didn't see . . ."

I looked into a young man's bearded face, pale eyes behind square, steel-rimmed spectacles, a domed and sun-browned cranium with a circle of untidy hair spreading down around the jaw as though Nature was compensating him for premature baldness by giving him frizzy, chestnut whiskers. His clothes looked like army surplus. He carried a pack and had a tarnished, silver peace emblem hanging from his neck. He was eyeing me churlishly, one leg lifted to rub the toes of a dirty foot that was virtually bare except for a rubber thong. Contrite, I began again.

"You all right? I'm sorry I was trying to get away . . ."

"Yeah. Yeah. I know, these shop guys, always chasing a buck," he concurred impatiently and as he straightened and moved I saw that he had a girl with him.

She was his female counterpart, that same army surplus look, a sort of uniform scruffiness, although she favoured jeans that strained to contain the globes of her young bottom and cut up into the plump triangle of her crotch, while her sweatshirt was tie-dyed. I noticed that it appeared to be devoid of anything like female contours. Her hair was mousey coloured, thick and straight, and looked as though it had been mouse-eaten at the ends—her face peered out of it like a weedy flower in a bank of reeds. She also flaunted a peace emblem, carried a pack and wore rubber thongs. She was looking at me, smirking rather superciliously, one hand holding aside a hank of hair.

They were hippies, I realised, or, as David had once informed me, more correctly called "freaks" these days. At the thought of him, something stirred excitedly in me. Suddenly I knew that I had arrived at the starting point of my quest for David and for the lost, heady days of my youth.

"You know this country then?" I offered chattily, moving closer, delaying the man when he would have moved away. "You've been here a while, I guess?"

At the suggestion of a question his eyes seemed to haze, or maybe it was the light on his glasses, then he looked away over the crowd, his gaze travelling circuitously back to the girl. For a moment I thought he was looking for someone, but the only European in sight was a woman tourist in a straw hat talking to an elderly Singhalese; it was a frivolous hat, its saucer brim fringed with ends as though the weaving was unfinished.

"We been around," the man admitted edgily.

"Then perhaps you can help me." I plunged in then, opting for guilelessness. "I'm looking for a young chap rather like yourself."

This time his gaze snapped alertly back to me and I noticed that his eyes were hazel, seemingly without substance, like looking down pale shafts into his skull.

"You his old man?" he demanded gratingly and for some reason the emptiness of his eyes was disconcerting.

I nodded silently, looking away, seeing the tourist woman and the Singhalese moving among the vendors in the shadows of the arcade. The young man was smiling unpleasantly, something murky fuming the lightless depths of his eyes. I was aware of the girl's smirk stirring animosity in me.

"What's he like?" the young man demanded.

"Dark," I began slowly. "Twenty-one. Name of David Coleman. Wears a beard. Well set-up, about five eleven. Goes about a hundred and sixty pounds." It seemed such an impersonal description for someone who had meant so much to me, then I remembered something which must surely distinguish David wherever he went. "He's an artist."

The young man looked thoughtful, eyebrows screwing, lips pursing in his beard, unwonted concentration tugging his balding scalp forward like an animal's. The girl released her hank of hair so that her face seemed to withdraw like a wild thing retiring into a bush.

"What's his gig?" the man demanded.

I shrugged, at a loss to find rational words. "Buddhism, the meaning of life." It still sounded silly, even like that.

"Buddha freak, huh?" the man laughed.

"Where do you suggest I start looking?"

"Viharas, man," he hazarded with a shrug then, seeing my non-comprehension, explained. "Temples. An' the ruins, Anuradhapura, Polonnaruwa. For these freaks, any heap of stones that has the Buddha man's face on, it's sacred. An' Kandy, the Temple of the Tooth in Kandy. Lotta freaks get there. An' the Sri Maha Bodhi Tree on full moon night. Mucho holy, that one. Maybe you find that boy—if he lets you."

"Thanks. What's your name, by the way?" I asked. "In case we meet up again."

"I'm Amos, she's Margit," he jerked a grainy thumb at the girl, who acknowledged it with all the impassivity of an Indian squaw. Beyond them the frivolous straw hat had tipped forward to examine a street-vendor's wares.

"Now we gotta split, man. We gotta make that bus to Negombo or we're on the thumb. Ciao."

Mockingly he performed the Buddhist gesture of reverence, the *anjali*, palms together, tips of the fingers touching the brow, bowing. When he straightened those empty pits of eyes were grinning, seeing right through me. Hitching his pack he began to move away. His partner clawed hair from her face once more and shuffled her sandalled feet in the dust and betel spit. I remembered army doctors lecturing us about the dangers of going without proper footwear in this country because of hookworm, which gets into the body under the toenails and does horrible things inside the stomach.

Alone once more I felt depressed. Perhaps it was I who was the innocent brashly venturing into their mysterious world. The traffic irritated me, so many old-model British cars—Vauxhalls, Austins and black and yellow Morris Minor taxis, many with the death-rattle of sloppy pistons and the smoke of burning oil; there was even a delapidated double-decker bus whose faded scarlet made me wonder if it had begun life in London's streets. I wondered whether Ceylon had become the graveyard of English cars. Turning away I saw the woman in the straw hat watching me from under one of the arches.

"Mason," she called.

I didn't recognise her at once, although I knew her voice by the way she spoke my name, flicking me with it. Last night she had worn slacks, but this morning she was indubitably feminine in a skirt short enough to reveal nice knees. It was the hat which had fooled me, its straw-fringed brim like a rustic halo around her head, saucy, more like Mexico or the calypso isles. I saw that she had a camera, an expensive Pentax, with light-meter and telly lens

23

clipped to the carrying strap.

"Mrs Gale," I greeted. "I thought you'd still be in bed."

She pulled a face at me and I knew then why the hat had fooled me: it hid the imbalance of her features, that rather too-full brow, leaving the lower part of her face like that of a precocious schoolgirl, cheeking me.

"Yes, you dog," she berated ruefully. "You ran out and left me to face that superannuated elephant-boy, Caspar or Lakshah or whatever his name is."

"Don't tell me he got you out of bed," I mocked, straight-faced. I found myself deriving a morsel of satisfaction from the thought of Larga's disappointment when he discovered me gone this morning—him doubtless imagining me snugly bedded in Room 7.

"Don't gloat," she reproved me and for a disconcerting instant I thought she had read my mind. "Do you know he rang me at ten o'clock, wanting me to sign up for one of his tours."

"And did you?"

"You've got to be joking!" She reared back, Yankee accent sharpening noticeably. "Can you imagine me taking an elephant ride alone with that smooth operator? I told him I'd discuss it with you."

That snapped me out of my jolly joking. Discuss it with me—a tour! Us? Together? I wondered whether she was trying to take a rise out of me. After all, at my age one is inclined to view these apparent advances with a certain cynicism. But her face told me nothing, just sophisticated, serene, the emancipated woman supremely indifferent to my more than middle-aged perplexity. Perhaps my scrutiny unsettled her for she brought out a large pair of sunglasses and took refuge behind their blackened opacity. I felt my advantage slipping—perhaps not my advantage but that lead which one must always maintain with women like her—so I nodded gravely.

"Right then, let's discuss it. But somewhere cool. And preferably over a drink, eh?"

She gave me a smokey glance that gave nothing away.

"I thought you were never going to ask me."

I took her to the Hotel Taprobane which is at the seaward end of York Street, overlooking Queen Elizabeth Quay and the Customs

Wharf and that massive stretch of masonry wall which is called the Leyden Bastion. This hotel was called the Grand Oriental Hotel when I was here before.

The G.O.H! We used to assemble there on leave, drinking in that huge, cool lounge, calling for round after round of drinks, laughing more and more immoderately, horsing around like schoolboys fresh out of class while we lusted, not very surreptitiously I fear, for every lady sahib in sight. After the Spartan regimes of tentlines and jungle camps we hungered for women, reacting hectically to their proximity. The sahibs would wrinkle their noses disgustedly, snort in their whiskies and, in the time-honoured British manner, do their best to persuade themselves that we didn't exist. I'm sure they hated us for our Australian lustiness, for taking off our shirts and working like coolies and — the most heinous of sins among the sahibry "abroad" — for making friends with the natives. All of this while we were making them safe on their island! But that was more than three decades ago and I had changed, and the G.O.H had changed, although I didn't know that until I saw its new name blazoned in scarlet stitching on the khaki chest of the burly doorman.

"It looks a lot smaller than I remember," I remarked as we settled ourselves in fan-backed cane chairs, Mrs Gale unburdening herself of camera and handbag, removing her hat with something of a flourish.

Coolness crept over us, drying sweat, leaving us limp and languid. I was slow to order drinks, suddenly nostalgically engrossed in noting the changes around me, the airconditioning and piped music and the fashionably inadequate lighting, like miniature wastepaper baskets dangling from the ceiling. Part of the lounge had been made into an American Bar, garishly lit and extravagantly appointed. And there wasn't a sahib in sight. Except for ourselves, the clientele was indigenous. Plump, fig-dark men in flowered shirts and women in saris with chocolate belly-rolls of bare midriffs, talking softly over their drinks. Lifting a finger to a youth in dragoman draperies and scarlet cummerbund I ordered drinks: Mrs Gale asked for bourbon and on being told there was none, settled for Scotch, while I chose beer. I took out my pipe. She groped in her handbag and brought out a packet of Pall Malls. It was one of those moments when two people take stock of each other under cover of trivial actions. Then we were both leaning forward, me with a lighted match in my hands, she pouting her cigarette into the flame. Then we sat back like boxers who had touched gloves and retired to their corners.

"You've been here before, haven't you?"

She was making polite conversation, establishing a starting point in our association, blowing smoke rather mannishly as she spoke, the cigarette tilted rakishly between her fingers. In the back of my mind I registered the fact that she had heard me talking to the Customs Officer last night. But I had to say something and in these surroundings the temptation to reminisce was overpowering.

"I got into the worst street brawl I've ever seen after a day's drinking in here."

I wasn't boasting, merely marvelling from a distance of sedate years at the madness which had driven us in those days. The brawl had begun out of that rivalry which exists between soldiers and sailors and a chance remark misunderstood by some *matelots* of the Royal Indian Navy. The local population had come in on the side of the Indians. I think Eric killed a man that day, not intentionally but with his usual ruthless competence while defending himself in that terrifying mêlée of humid bodies and dark, screaming faces; and the clawing hands; the flying stones; the knife which would have gutted me if my webbing belt hadn't turned it; my raw fists burning against cloth and bone; my bruised ribs aching and the blow which had made my nose bleed so that I snuffled blood and saliva like a wounded bull; my relief when the M.P.s' whistles had sounded; our escape down fetid alleys and . . . and I was worrying about David!

"How old were you then?" Mrs Gale asked.

"Twenty-one."

The lift of her eyebrows told me nothing. She was leaning back, looking small in the depths of that capacious chair with its peacock-tailed spread of wickerwork behind her head; and smiling, ready to be amused by my old-soldier reminiscing. I shrugged, regretting my garrulity. Just then the waiter arrived with her whisky and my beer, which he poured ceremoniously from a bottle of Lion Lager. They have a thing about lions in Ceylon — Singhalese, the lion race, Sigiriya, "the Lion Rock", even their national emblem is a rampant lion holding a sword. When the boy had walked away, tray under his arm, bare feet lifting, pink soled, off the floor, I raised my glass in a silent toast: she responded perfunctorily, sipping her whisky without speaking. A couple of the Singhalese women at the nearby table were studying her with that unblinking interest which women can turn on one another.

"You know," Mrs Gale began, "when I first saw you last night I thought you were trying to pick me up. Silly, wasn't it?"

"Which," I prodded, "you for thinking I was trying to pick you up, or me for imagining I could?"

"Were you?" She crossed her legs, one foot swinging lazily. I hesitated, watching that slowly swinging foot, reminding myself that although I hadn't contrived the incident last night I hadn't avoided it.

"I refuse to answer that one on the grounds that I might incriminate myself."

"Oh, smart, Mason, smart," she applauded sardonically.

"Anyway—." I couldn't resist gibing softly, for that seemed to be the tenor of our relationship, set by her out in the street a little while ago and last night in the car, her "Just Mason". "Anyway, we're here now so what does it matter who picked up whom?"

I had gone too far. I knew that by the way she stiffened, staring at me in silence while the cigarette between her fingers sent up a wavering curl of smoke. The Singhalese women were no longer watching her, but I think they were discussing her for one of the men was staring at her broodingly. There was only the murmur of their voices with the piped music trickling into it like syrup mixing with water. Suddenly Mrs Gale uncrossed her legs. The movement worked her skirt back, baring a ripple of taut, pale thigh: she tugged her skirt down but I was more conscious of her flesh than I had been all morning. It was as though, suddenly, something had been switched on between us.

"You don't let a girl get any ideas, do you?" she drawled, acid sweet. "Here's me flattering myself you were trying to pick me up and then you hit me with that. Even my husband didn't—doesn't say things like that."

So, I thought, noting that hasty switch—a husband in the past tense. I should have guessed it. Or was I meant to guess it if I hadn't already done so? Since there was nothing I could say without sounding inquisitive I puffed my pipe, drank some beer and tried to look disinterested. She drew on her cigarette, sipped her whisky and appeared to enjoy my uncertainty. It was an awkward moment, both of us seeming at a loss. The Singhalese continued to discuss her: I stared back at them but they weren't abashed, transferring their interest to me as well, no doubt remarking on the difference in our ages. Mrs Gale put her glass down and to my surprise it was empty: intercepting my glance she nodded so I signalled to the waiter. Then she leaned forward to extinguish her cigarette, silvered fingertips grinding it unnecessarily hard, I thought. In doing so she tilted a well-cut blouse into my line of vision, nice breasts modishly uplifted but not so modishly as to spoil their cleavage. Not wanting to be caught staring I looked away, up into her dark, sardonic stare. Her tone flayed me, punishing me for my peeping.

"You know, Mason, I can't figure you out . . ."

"Not even my first name apparently."

". . . except that you were here a hundred years ago . . ."

"It's 'David', in case you're interested."

". . . and you're probably married . . ."

I shook my head, smiling—enigmatically, I fancied.

"Never?"

"Never." With some emphasis, her directness beginning to annoy me.

She shot me a sidelong glance, frankly sceptical.

"Not even a little something stashed away in a flat?"

"Not even that," I averred woodenly, registering a tiny unease with the memory of Clare. She was a big, tranquil woman who owned the typing agency that did my work. Over the past three years we had developed an association—nothing serious, no ties, more like an exchange of services, which seemed to be as much as either of us wanted. She lived in a flat but it was her own and God help you if you so much as hinted that she had been stashed there by me.

Mrs Gale was smiling in a way that I have become used to. When you reach my age without having married you learn to put up with aspersions on your masculinity, especially from women. Over thirty and unmarried and they practically accuse you of being gay—it's their excuse for some unknown woman's failure. But the beer was beginning to work in me, filtering along my nerves, fortifying me, so I smiled, deciding to do a little taunting of my own.

"Better never to have loved at all than to have loved and lost."

"You think so, huh?" Defensive despite attempted nonchalance.

"I don't take chances," I murmured. "Not with things like that."

"You should"—still defensive yet adding with a note of provocation—"It can be fun."

"Even with a husband who didn't—I mean doesn't—hit back?" She smiled balefully. "You bastard, Mason!"

The arrival of the waiter put an end to that first round and we both sat back in our chairs. I wasn't sorry either. I wanted time in which to consider both her and myself—and why I was here. I wasn't sure that I liked her—not as a man may be presumed to like the woman with whom he happens to be drinking. Our relationship had become closer and harder, taking on abrasive and subtly sexual undertones which irritated yet aroused me. I was accustomed to more gracious exchanges between men and women, yet her directness, her worldliness, was like a brisk wind out of long-forgotten places, untempered by the conventions of my generation. It was a long time since I had bandied words with a young woman of her mettle. I put my pipe away: it had gone out, was cold. Neither of us spoke while the waiter set another whisky in front of her and then replenished my beer from the bottle, not tilting the glass, building a head of froth like a bubble bath. I waited until he had padded away.

"What about Larga? Do you still want me to go with you?"

As I spoke I realised that it was an open-ended question. Go with her to Larga's office, or go with her on a tour? I wondered whether she had understood its connotations. I took a pull at my beer, a trifle nervously I must confess, first getting only the tart taste of its head of froth. Mrs Gale set her drink down and looked straight at me.

"Do you want to?"

Something about her tone touched me, whispering of loneliness, of that husband in the past tense, of the emotional vacuum—no, the storm's-eye calm in which women like her must live, swept along within their private tempests. "Do you want to?" I suspected a plea beneath that faked indifference. As for myself, I realised that until now I hadn't made up my mind. Then I thought of David and what the hippie had said . . . try the *viharas*, the ruins, the Temple of the Tooth, the Sri Maha Bodhi on full moon night . . .

"I'd like to go with you very much," I told her, realising that I had answered my own question as well as hers. "As it happens I have some business in the ruins myself."

"Business?" At once she was alert, tone quizzical, the lift of her brows in some way complementing her pointed chin—a heart-shaped face, I mused fleetingly, very fleetingly, for her voice was coming back at me, suddenly very American, drawling. "Come to think of it, Mason, what is your line of business?"

I shrugged. "Much the same as yours."

"How do you know what my line is?"

"The typewriter last night. Only a writer or a journalist would lug that around."

"Oh, sharp, Mason, very sharp!"

"'David', please."

"I'll stick with 'Mason'," she pronounced airily, drinking again.

"And do I go on calling you 'Mrs Gale'?"

"'Martina' then." She made a little gesture of distaste, frowning, tone hardening. "And don't call me 'Marty' or 'Tina'. And don't try to con me it's a pretty name."

"It's not, but it has a certain flair. Are you ever called 'Martinet' for short?"

"Ha ha!" Scornful, slit-eyed like an angry cat. "And you've got a flair—for not answering questions."

Hands spread palm upward I baited her, finding that I was enjoying myself. After all it was she who had set the tenor of our relationship with her directness, her bone-hard sexuality, her refusal to use my first name. If that was the way she wanted it . . . !

"Give me a chance," I begged mockingly. "It's not every day I meet a writer or a journalist."

"You don't believe me, huh?"

Snatching up her handbag from the floor she had it open on her knees, delving into it. It seemed I had brought her to expect raillery in my every utterance, or perhaps it was the whisky. Anyway, before I could protest, she was bringing out handkerchief, passport, a sheaf of travellers' cheques, a wallet bulging with Singhalese currency and an airmail letter with barber's-pole edging. The wallet fell open on the table between us and I glimpsed a snapshot in a plastic covered compartment at one end. It was of a man, a thin, athletic-looking face, tanned to a photographic grey, with blond.hair cut short-back-and-sides. I was reminded of the faces of U.S. spacemen, that same intentness which seemed to look out beyond the norm of ordinary occupations, an ambition honed to dedication: a professional man of some sort, I guessed. The husband in the past tense? How completely did divorce break the ties of affection, I wondered. Then Mrs Gale, or Martina as I was drilling myself to think of her now, was shoving a card at me. It was small and in a transparent envelope, accrediting Mrs Martina Gale of San Somewhere, Texas—one of those romantic sounding Spanish names which have the thunder of hoof-beats and gunfire for me. Somewhat chastened I passed it back to her.

"I apologise. I'll never doubt your word again."

"Until next time," she cracked with a ghost of a smile, mollified nevertheless. "Have typewriter, will travel—that's me. I write for this mag called *Odyssey*. It's no *Time-Life* or *Harper's Bazaar*, just a few travel promoters working together. We cover the vacation paradises, Florida, the Bahamas, Acapulco, anywhere there's sun, sea and sand to be had for tourist dollars."

"And this is South Asia Tourism Year." I was still kidding, but not so zestfully for when she talked about her job her sincerity was disarming. "So you're looking for palm trees, lagoons, exotic native dancers—plus airconditioning, modern plumbing and Coca Cola."

She looked at me out of the corners of narrowed eyes, her smile thinning cynically, that Yankee sharpness edging her drawl again.

"Stop trying to take the mickey out of me, Mason. Anyway, talking of fakes—you still haven't told me what your business is."

I grinned, acknowledging the thrust. "Yes I did—the same as yours."

"A travel writer—you?"

Her tone irked me, not disbelief but condescension: I couldn't resist being deliberately smug.

"Something a little more exalted—a novelist."

"You're putting me on!" Sitting very straight she stared at me, frankly disbelieving now. "David Mason! Never heard of you!"

Her candour was devastating: I had the depressing feeling of my books dwindling into insignificance. Of course she had never heard of me. She was an American, while I wrote about the remote northern vastness of Western Australia called the Kimberleys. Indeed I was prepared to bet a deal of money that she wasn't even aware of the existence of that vast, sparsely populated, sub-tropical region where the turn of the seasons brings "the Wet" with its lashing rains, its rivers "coming down" in almost biblical inundations and its intolerable temperatures, forty-three, forty-four and on occasions, forty-seven degrees. I had spent at least six months of every year in that country. After the war, bereft of Janice and restless with that sense of loss, I had quit my job with the insurance company. I had no woman to draw me into domesticity, no overwhelming purpose such as Eric's—besides, the urge to write was working in me, converting my loneliness into creativity. It was in the Kimberleys that I was able to effect this transformation, turning my hand to any job that offered—well-sinking, fencing, driving a geological survey truck, even a few punishing months breaking horses with a crazed ex-captain of the Polish cavalry, until a bad fall hospitalised me, convincing me that my body was no longer resilient, my bones not unbreakable. In later years, with a couple of novels to give me clerkly status, I had become a book-keeper on a cattle station. Yet with the onset of each Wet I would quit my job and, like the migratory bird I had become, fly south to the city and Eric and Janice. And to David. Of course Martina had never heard of me, I was a nonentity outside my own country. I shrugged with a nonchalance I was far from feeling.

"I can't help it if you don't read anything but travel itineraries and hotel brochures."

"You're trying to take the mickey again," she chanted and then emptied her glass.

Watching her I wondered what kind of head she had for the stuff. Two whiskies in short order! I am all for women's liberation but hard liquor knows no sexual discrimination, you have to be able to stand it. And if she couldn't . . . I thought of the photograph in her wallet, that lean, intense face, austerity somewhere in its intensity, and I wondered if there was any connection between him and her empty glass. There were quiet small sounds around us, piped music, soft movements, the scrape of a chair. It was the Singhalese leaving, the women bosomy in billowing saris, gliding past us in line like floats in a pageant, the men less graceful, slouching behind incipient bellies. Their departure seemed to signal the end of something for Martina and me. The end of our first round? I recalled my thought when we had seated ourselves at this table . . . like boxers who had touched gloves and retired to their corners. Certainly it had been a suitable thought, we had sparred ever since.

"Okay." Suddenly I'd had enough, finishing my drink, slapping my glass down rather noisily. "You tell me I don't give anything away, but when I'm honest you won't believe me."

She stared at me for a long moment, morosely, assessing: then a shrug, a twist of her lips. "So you write books. I'll buy that."

I bowed exaggeratedly. "Thank you. And I apologise for doubting you. Does that make you happy?"

"Wild," she applauded dryly, then smiling, eyebrow lifting questioningly, "Friends?"

"Bosom pals," I tossed off unthinkingly and promptly wondered whether, in time, there would be anything pertinent about those words.

She didn't appear to share that thought, but then she was reaching for that raggedy hat at that moment.

"So what are we doing here?" Jauntily slapping it on her head. "We should be talking to the elephant-boy and his daddy right now . . ."

Taprobane Tours occupied a tiny office, not much more than a cell, in a dense, tired mass of old buildings. It was in a quarter of tired, old buildings of Dutch or British colonial design. Across the street was a grimy, grey building that looked like a cross between a railway station and the Coliseum, where big trucks were backed up while scrawny, brown-skinned men swarmed over them, unloading sacks of something heavy. The sickly smell of copra came to me overlaid by the tang of hot tar from a blackened boiler around which men with brooms and buckets of tar were languidly filling potholes in the street. People drifted along the footpath and across the street with that apparent aimlessness which you see in Asiatic cities. And of course there were crows. They are everywhere in Sri Lanka, fusty black, audacious brutes that strut insolently, eyeing you with birdy cynicism, ready to thieve anything they can fly away with.

We had to climb a flight of stairs, picking our way between the bare feet and backsides of a number of men and women who were sitting there. Nothing appeared to be happening among them and I couldn't imagine what they were waiting for, but our arrival provided them with a diversion, Martina in particular. The women looked her over critically, the men speculatively, but except for a few perfunctory glances I was ignored, until a willowy youth with a dazzling smile stood up to announce that he was a student and willing to conduct us wherever we were going. I declined his offer politely but just as politely he ignored my refusal, wading knee-deep through hunching shoulders and vulnerable toes to lead the way, trailing Martina and me in a wake of interest and lively discussion.

The commotion must have alerted the Largas for when we reached the top of the stairs, where a stout wooden grille barred our way, I saw a tiny office crammed with massive furniture, with two men at a desk, staring expectantly as we hove into view. I recognised Horace Larga and assumed that the big man on the other side of the desk was his "daddy". And Larga recognised us, gabbling something at his father, whereupon both of them shot out of their chairs like jet pilots ejecting from a stricken aircraft. They came together in the office doorway, Larga senior using his bulk to bump his son aside. Thwarted, Larga junior returned to his chair to brood handsomely. His father came on, greeting us effusively.

"Good morning, good morning. Welcome to Sri Lanka. Taprobane Tours welcomes you. I am Abdin Larga. Please . . ."

He had seen our student conductor who had his hand out, asking for money. At once that professional affability faltered, seeming to choke in his throat, bursting out in a thick, glottal rush of angry Singhalese that concluded with a contemptuous wave and a word which I recognized from the past, "Yanni, yanni! Go away!"

Daunted the boy backed away, alternately darting sullen glances at Larga and rolling his large, liquid eyes imploringly at me, muttering hopefully. Martina went for her handbag while I plunged a hand into my pocket but Larga senior intervened, thrusting a fat fist through the grille, plump fingers waggling urgently.

"Sir! Madam! Please, no money or he will never go away. These boys won't work. They call themselves students but really they are beggars!" He was fumbling with the latch of a little gate which blended cunningly with the grille: his jowly chin lifted arrogantly, pursed lips projecting something proprietorial over the crowd on the stairs. "These people want to work for me so they come here and wait. I have a hotel, a gem shop. Sometimes I give them work. But these boys—they are parasites, sir, leeches!" Having delivered himself of this denunciation he resumed his welcoming spiel as though nothing had happened, wrenching the gate open and dragging us through like an octopus dragging its prey into its lair. He was fat, nut brown and as bald as an octopus, with round, remorseless, octopus eyes and a toothy smile, words swirling around him like an octopus' ink screen. "Come in. It is nice to see you. This is my son, Horace." A fat hand flashing a flashy dress ring, a gem shop owner's hand and ring, a hand which could scatter employment like largesse, indicated Larga junior who nodded morosely, rose belatedly. "You met him last night. He drove carefully, I hope. Good. Please sit down."

He also seemed endowed with an octopus' full complement of arms, shaking our hands, installing us in chairs, slumping into a chair himself, offering cigarettes which I declined, lighting one for Martina and himself and then hunching over his desk to study us alertly, all in the same unbroken sequence of movements. I could feel him willing us to part with our money, to spend, spend at Larga's. And that part of me which is concerned with my survival hardened mulishly against the man.

"You will be in Sri Lanka long?" His urbane voice rolled over me and though I listened and answered I found myself taking stock of my surroundings, that cluttered office . . . "You are American, Madam" . . . and that equally cluttered desk, papers, brimming ashtrays, telephone, more papers impaled on wire spike files and an ancient typewriter which must surely be a museum piece . . . "very nice up country now" . . . the delights of Sri Lanka and the excellence of Taprobane Tours, its quarter century of service to tourists, its infallible ability to give pleasure, all amply attested to in a ledger-like book chock-a-block with handwritten testimonials by Joe Johannsen of Clear Springs, Minnesota, Arthur Gladstone of The Hove Cottage, Surrey, André Furneaux of Basle, Switzerland, of France, of Germany, of all over the northern hemisphere . . . "you are from Australia, sir" . . . . as though I was a geographic oddity whose compliments must be added to his collection at all costs—my cost . . . "this is not the season for the perahera procession at Kandy but you will see the Temple of the

Tooth" . . . more small talk, softening-up talk, those predator's eyes focussed on me, sensing my resistance and setting out to overcome it . . . "You will have tea? Sri Lanka for good tea, that's our motto. Horace! Tea for the lady and gentleman" . . . Horace, disgruntled, sauntering as far as the grille to shout to someone on the stairs who hoped for a job in Daddy's hotel or gem shop . . . "eight days, car, driver, English-speaking guide" . . . those knowing eyes swinging from one to the other of us, knowing what eight days, eight nights . . . "the day after tomorrow, I have no car free until then" . . . those greedy, brown hands with knuckle-duster ring pawing over papers, producing a map of Ceylon, unfolding it as though unfurling a sail . . . "Chilaw, Negombo, Anuradhapura, Polonnaruwa" . . . a woman's voice at the grille, Horace answering loftily, then cups of tea touching down on the papers beside us, heavily milked, and I never take milk . . . "Sigiriya, Kandy, Yala—that includes hire of a jeep at the game reserve, you must take the Government jeep and a ranger" . . . those hands scribbling figures . . . "four thousand seven hundred rupees, all expenses paid, no tipping" . . . Martina flicking ash from her cigarette, one of Larga's Bristols, the dry, papery smell of the things permeating the office . . .

"We want separate accommodation"—a pause in which I was aware, not only of Martina but both Largas watching me like inquisitors waiting for me to blurt out incriminating protests, then—"don't we, Mason?"

I almost murmured a sanctimonious "Of course," biting it back to lie stoutly: "That's right!" I caught Larga and his son exchanging surreptitious glances so to distract them, to get their minds back to the one thing they really understood, I brought out my travellers' cheques.

"How much?" I demanded crisply, gratified to see that I had their instant attention.

"Hold it, Mason." Martina laid a hand on my wrist. "We agreed to go Dutch-treat—remember?"

I tried not to look surprised but I couldn't remember any such agreement. Martina had her handbag open by then, bringing out her travellers' cheques, looking at Larga.

"Four thousand and something rupees, you said. How much is half that in U.S. dollars?"

After that there wasn't much more to do but extricate ourselves from Larga, which wasn't easy.

"You are staying at the Serendib. Ah yes, the government hotel." A shrug, thick, purple lips pouting, fat hand, ring twinkling, subtly depreciating. "My hotel is the Shalimar. Very comfortable. Perhaps when you return from your tour? . . ."

No chance, I thought stubbornly, declaring politely but firmly that I was satisfied where I was. Fortunately Martina concurred with me and to my surprise Larga released us gracefully.

"Horace will drive you into town," he beamed genially.

Horace drove us to his daddy's gem shop.

I should have expected it: it was probably the Larga routine. Even when I had alighted from the car in York Street and saw the name on the shop, The Oriental Lapidary Emporium, I didn't realise I was being conned. Then I heard Horace working on Martina, that soft, persuasive tone beseeching her to come in and look, not buy, just look.

It was a little, old fashioned shop, fusty, with a peculiar, brown dimness in which the gems in their gold and silver settings, arrayed on black velvet trays, looked more like butterflies on collectors' boards. The main source of light was from the street through the display window, but on a glass cabinet which served as a counter there was a goose-necked lamp, curled like a cobra rearing to strike. There was a musty, spicy smell as though people slept and cooked on the premises. Emporium, I thought derisively.

At our coming several softly spoken men in native dress seemed to rise from nowhere, like genii materialising from the jewelled shadows, closing around us, ushering us to the counter, gently but resolutely pushing chairs behind our knees. Somebody must have thrown a switch for overhead a neon tube flickered and tinkled and blazed into stark radiance. Then fingers clicked imperiously and bare feet scuffled to obey, bringing cups of tea followed by tray after tray of brooches and rings, all slipped temptingly, for closest scrutiny, under the goose-necked lamp. Having delivered us into their clutches, Horace Larga drew back to watch proceedings with moody eyes.

Emporium it mightn't have been, and that they actually were lapidaries themselves was questionable, but they certainly were salesmen. Fawning and persuading they hung over us, whispering

37

enticingly, taking turns to sit in front of us, their nutmeg faces with tourmaline eyes hypnotically fixed on us, willing us, not merely to buy, but to submit to their desire to part us from our money. Their persuasive voices rubbed insidiously at our resistance while clusters of gems passed before our eyes: brown hands, with strangely delicate, backward-curving fingers displayed amethysts, moonstones, star sapphires, garnets and even a cardboard box of unset stones.

Martina was enthralled. Until then I hadn't fully understood the fascination which gems have for women. To me they have always been stones, admirable because of their cold, baleful beauty but stones nevertheless, torn from the earth at risk to some man and invested with a soulless, artificial worth. Seeing Martina handle them made me realise that such stones are precious because of women's pleasure in them, because women can transform these least worthwhile products of the earth's bounty into objects of beauty which also beautify. Perhaps that might explain what I did later.

For the present, however, I enjoyed watching her hold a pair of ruby drops to her ears, rejecting them in favour of an amethyst pendant which, in turn, she passed over for a sapphire ring. I noticed the way she worked its oval setting over her wedding ring as though she was laying a new experience over the old. I felt an impulse building gently but irresistibly within me so that when one of those raffish salesmen brought out the moonstone pendant I knew that a moment of significance had arrived between us.

It was a lovely little piece in a flower setting of silver wire, the gauzy petals upturned at the tips. The stone appeared perfect to my untrained eye, taking the light into its cloudy depths and refracting it as a softly blazing star, six-pointed and as symmetrical as the Star of Bethlehem on a Christmas card. Carefully the man lifted it out of its satin-lined box, holding it by its neck-chain, letting it hang over his knuckles. He was a sharp-faced, elderly man, wearing the skull cap of a Moslem and his English was as good as mine, precise, yet with an upward intonation.

"It is the lotus, Mem, the flower of enlightenment," he explained, his vowels rolling beguilingly, and he moved his fist, making the moonstone swing on its silver chain, giving off diffused, creamy flashes. Reaching out, Martina lifted it on the tips of her fingers and at once the flashes shrunk back into the stone, becoming a perfect six-pointed glow. The man was in full flight now, positively warbling. "It is the Buddhist symbol of purity for it is said that although the lotus grows in the mud it is never dirty." "Did you hear that, Mason? The flower of enlightenment and purity. Isn't that a beautiful thought?"

Martina was leaning forward, gazing covetously at the pendant. Watching her the man smiled indulgently, confidently, glancing expectantly at me. That glance fired me, touching off the impulse which had been building in me since before I had even laid eyes on the stone.

"Do you like it," I asked carefully.

"Oh yes, very much!" She turned impulsively, her rapture pleasing me, making me pleased with what I was about to do. Then she swung back to the salesman, demanding breathily: "How much?"

The man shrugged, his lined, brown face suddenly composed and very Asiatic, ready to haggle. "One hundred and thirty rupees, sir." This time he looked straight at me, opening negotiations in the natural order of such transactions. "It is a very fine stone, sir, best quality. Mem will look very . . ."

"Not him," Martina cut in sharply. "Me! I'm buying it!"

Nonplussed, the man glanced from one to the other of us uncertainly but I nodded to him, very faintly, winking conspiratorially and he began putting the pendant back in its box, stowing the chain with it. Martina started to open her handbag, but I had my wallet out and three fifty rupee notes passed over the counter without a word. The man took them and also without a word, handed me the little box.

"Hey! What's this?" Pocket-book out, Martina stared at me.

"Something from me," I said lightly, offering her the little box. In the cone of light from the goose-neck lamp it looked large and significant . . . the symbol of enlightenment?

Martina hadn't spoken, her gaze shifting slowly, suspiciously, from my face to the box, the pocket-book open in her hand: I glimpsed the photograph in one end of it and had the feeling of that grey, professional face watching me coldly. I was also aware of Larga's handsome face watching avidly.

"Uhuh!" Martina shook her head emphatically. "I pay my own way. That was our agreement, remember?"

"I don't, but I won't argue with you. Anyway, agreements are made to be broken." I smiled, trying to twist the tail of the joke.

"For you, maybe." Her face set mutinously, then she must have remembered that for all her emancipation there were still niceties to be observed for she smiled fleetingly, unconvincingly. "Thanks all the same, Mason, but I don't break agreements."

"Couldn't you—just this time?"

I suppose I shouldn't have been surprised but I was, and also piqued in a male way, beginning to feel silly standing there holding out the little box with Larga and his minions looking on. Martina's chin lifted uncompromisingly.

"No, I couldn't. And don't hassle me."

"Why not?"

"I can't, that's all!" Irritably, hands jerking distractedly.

"That's no answer," I argued doggedly, no longer smiling.

"All right—because I hardly know you, that's why." She dropped the pocket-book into her bag, closing it with a savage snap.

"Very well." I dropped the pendant into my pocket, shoving it down deep. "I'll keep it for a week and when we come back from our trip I'll give it to you. That make you feel better?"

For a moment I thought she was going to give way to me for she smiled, then I saw that it was a mirthless, disconcerting smile. In the sickly glare of the fluorescent light her face was stripped of all softness and femininity. I probably didn't look like Prince Charming myself, too old for one thing, and in no mood to charm.

"You've got some hopes," she jeered softly. "You think I'm easy. You think all you've got to do is give me that junk and I'll fall all over you. Well, let me tell you something, Mister Mason—I wouldn't have it even if I knew you a hundred years!"

"I think you're being difficult." I made an effort to restrain my temper, to sound unruffled and tolerant, even faintly amused but without much success.

"Difficult!" She laughed savagely. "I've been called a lot of things but never that!"

"I don't doubt that," I concurred scathingly.

"Meaning what?"

"Meaning you don't know when you're being paid a compliment. Meaning that you're neurotic because you're unhappy and very mixed up."

"Neurotic! Oh! You . . .!"

Fists clenched she glared at me with that stony-faced malevolence which makes women's faces so ugly when they hate you. The men around us were standing stiffly, staring wide eyed. Then I saw Larga sidling towards the door. His departure seemed to clear my mind for suddenly the extent of Martina's perversity struck me . . . she would have gone away with me but she wouldn't accept my gift. The flower of enlightenment! Despite myself I laughed.

"That's it," Martina raged. "You think it's funny, huh! Well, I'm getting out! There's nothing here I like, anyway!"

And that was it. As suddenly as that. Snatching up her bag and camera she rose so abruptly that her chair scraped loudly, would have fallen if one of the men hadn't caught it. Then she was walking away, sweeping past me without a glance, heels clacking loudly on the floor.

I didn't turn to watch her go, standing stiffly until I could no longer hear her footsteps, only the sounds from the street, shouts, a bicycle bell, the grind of old cars' gearboxes. Then somebody cleared his throat loudly and all at once there was movement around me. Turning away I saw that she had left that preposterous hat on the counter. Without a word I picked it up and walked out.

Out in the street moist heat clamped down on me and there was a smell like sodden feathers and dust. I looked around, half expecting to see . . . A buxom tourist woman was rejecting a shell necklace, angrily shoving it back at the peddler while her husband waited, rotund and well-nigh faceless behind dark glasses. Intercepting my glance he shrugged, little pursed mouth tugging wryly. Women, he seemed to be saying, and with the moonstone pendant in my pocket, I nodded. Then I saw that Larga's car had gone, and I also shrugged. So much for our trip. She had probably gone with him to get her money back. Women indeed! A ragged beggar woman accosted me then, holding a naked child in front of my face. I gave her a rupee and fled, leaving her touching the note to her brow and mumbling through hideously betel stained teeth. It wasn't until I lifted my arm to hail a taxi that I found I was still holding that hat.

I went down to breakfast early next morning. Bearing in mind what Amos, the hippie, had said I had consulted the tourist guide book, selecting a couple of the better known temples to visit in the hope of chancing on David. Also, I reasoned, an early breakfast would minimise the possibility of meeting Martina.

I was wrong. Just as I finished my papaya and was waiting for my bacon and eggs — I wasn't partial to the traditional Singhalese breakfast of *hoppas*, nor was my stomach equal to curried fish at that hour — she appeared in the entrance of the dining-room, looking poised and elegant, the Mrs Gale of our first meeting. Startled I took cover behind *The Times of Ceylon*, hoping she hadn't seen me.

There was little chance of that. The dining room was huge enough to have been a ballroom in its heyday, but now a melancholy place, its sahib atmosphere overlaid by post-Independence nationalism — batik paintings at the windows, peacock screens of plaited cane, elephant motifs on the walls. No place for a man who didn't wish to be seen. Half of it was unused, blocked off by an advertisement for the ancient monuments of Sri Lanka while at the entrance an archaic cash register lay in wait, the universal arbiter of all earthly glory. Apart from myself it was almost empty, only a young English matron with two fractious offspring, and a Singhalese honeymoon couple — they could only be honeymooners, that delirious preoccupation with each other, whispering, soft laughter, heads lovingly close together.

Having read, with spurious interest, the first three lines of an account of a "Pop and Teen Fanfare" in the Ramakrishna Hall at Wellawatta I peeped furtively, watching a waiter approach Martina. He would have seated her at one of the other tables but she let him lead off across the floor and came directly to my table instead.

"Hi." That meaningless greeting was friendly enough: I looked for signs of yesterday's hostility but all I saw was the eternal Eve, cool and composed, prettied up, I was sure, for my undoing.

"Hullo." I too could dissemble, smiling noncommittally.

"Thank you for bringing my hat back."

I felt a moment of surprise, remembering that I had left her hat at the reception desk, then I managed a trite "You're welcome." She gestured to one of the vacant chairs at the table.

"Mind if I join you?"

"Be my guest." Shoving the newspaper aside I rose too late to help her with the chair. Nor was that a dazzling rejoinder but I was wary, not wanting to sound eager or reluctant, just polite, added to which I can never be suave so early in the morning.

She seated herself, laying her handbag on the table, smoothing her skirt, touching her hair, all with that deft, woman's preoccupation which I enjoy watching: it reminds me of a soldier checking his equipment before going into battle. The waiter, having discovered that she wasn't following him, had altered course to begin fussing crossly with the knives and forks in front of her. For some moments he came between us, diligently clashing cutlery. Martina smiled up at him, ordering grapefruit without so much as a glance at the menu, then settling her chin on linked fists she regarded me steadily, unsmilingly, over her wedding ring. I noticed that she was wearing eye-shadow, green as the Nile, that gave her eyes a look of late nights and regrets; her lipstick was also dark, the shade of venous blood, faintly blue, intense. She seemed to have a talent for the dramatic.

"Is it any use saying I'm sorry," she asked wistfully when the waiter had gone.

"Not a bit." Attempting levity, I smiled.

"I don't blame you." To my dismay she seized on my words like a penitent clutching nettles. Leaning forward she laid her hands flat on the table, fingers interlocked, nervously turning her wedding ring. "I want you to know that I don't blame you one little bit if you're still mad at me."

"Hey! Hold it!" Now it was I who leaned forward, hands on the table, tempted to touch hers, placating, reassuring. "I was only kidding. You don't have to apologise for anything."

"Oh, but I do," she insisted earnestly. "I was a bitch."

The word jarred me: it always does, especially when I hear a woman apply it to herself. But she was of the honest generation, candour at all cost, call a spade a spade and a bitch a bitch. And deep down I was inclined to agree with her: she had been a bitch yesterday. Meanly, ungallantly, I wondered whether this was a genuine act of contrition of whether she had the moonstone pendant in mind. If so she was out of luck—until I was sure, anyway, until I knew I liked her. Suddenly I desperately wished that my bacon and eggs would come. I needed something to occupy my hands, something to look at instead of into that troubled, sophisticated face. I began methodically folding the paper. Martina interpreted the action as rejection: perhaps my movements were too stiff, my concentration too deliberate.

"Don't brush me off, Mason, please!"

Suddenly what had been doubtful and touchy and slightly comic was pathetic, moving me. I must have pushed the newspaper aside for I heard it hit the floor with a little papery crash.

"If there's anything I can do . . ."

It was the worst of responses, stilted, tardy, but I was so much older than her, held back by a web of painfully instilled restraints. I dread being rebuffed, being made to look silly, particularly by younger women. What can be gallant in a man of thirty is often ludicrous in a man of my age. Martina was looking at me, her face closed up, hurt.

"Thanks, Mason," she said rather too briskly, blinking, and her hand came out touching mine, withdrawing at once like a timid thing. I had the feeling that I had missed the opportunity of sharing a human moment. "It's just that I've got troubles," she confided, not looking at me. "Such troubles you wouldn't know. Woman troubles." She laughed brittlely, upturned hands juggling embarrassment. "You didn't think women could trouble women, did you?"

She had withdrawn from me again, superficial, cynical. And again I missed an opportunity, unsure of myself, fearful of appearing to make advances. Trying to match her manner, trying to keep it light, I said: "No, but I've got a feeling I'm going to find out."

"Not from me," she promised wryly. "You've seen enough of my neuroses. I guess a guy can't have a woman slam a present back in his face and not wonder what's screwing her up."

"You've apologised for that," I reminded her.

She shrugged, looking away, and for some reason I was glad to have her gaze off me: it was as though something intense and demanding had been diverted. Feeling more than ever ill at ease I looked around, wishing that my bacon and eggs would come, but the waiter was nowhere in sight. Bending I retrieved the newspaper from the floor, hearing the noises of the dining-room; the Singhalese couple were sharing a newly wed's joke, the soft salacity of bedroom confidence in their laughter. I heard the children murmuring fretfully and the young English matron chiding tartly, "Judith, pull your skirt down, please. Don't play with your food, David." David! That name never failed to catch my ear and despite myself, despite Martina watching me across the table, I looked around, half expecting in the hopeful way of wishful thinking, to see him there.

We were like that, David and I. Close. Uncle Mase. "My other daddy", was how he had once identified me as a little boy. Almost like father and son. What am I saying—almost! My name might not be on his birth certificate, but heredity had a few things to say on my behalf for I am somewhat black-avised myself, with a skin that takes the sun easily and in build "a fair lump of a bloke" as they say in the bush. And David is nearly my height, dark-complexioned also, like a southern Italian, with hair as black and as straight as an Indian's, while Eric had been thick-set, tubby, all that hard-muscled toughness when he was young, softened by booze and lack of proper exercise, broken blood vessels reddening his cheeks.

And there was something more than a physical similarity. David and I thought alike, or at least when he was young he had the kind of mind which was receptive to my philosophies. Writers are primarily concerned with the human condition and most men who have lived in the isolation of the bush have a down-to-earth awareness of the workings of nature. I think—in fact I know—that the romantic aspects of my lifestyle gave me a unique status in David's estimation. And I admit that I exploited it, each year bringing him something from the north, something that Eric's money could never buy. Usually it was Aboriginal artefacts: a lozenge-shaped shield incised with zig-zag patterns, or carved boab nuts, or a pair of singing-sticks, or boomerangs fashioned out of the bend of a bloodwood bough and decorated with ochres that had been mixed with saliva and bird-flower gum. It was his response to bark paintings of totemic animals and birds which had first alerted me to his artistic inclinations.

Eric was quick to perceive my growing influence in David's life and to register his disapproval. "What do you want to fill him up with stuff like that for? He's not going to be a university professor. He's coming into the business with me." To my surprise Janice had defended me. "Don't be silly, Eric. David is helping the child. There's other things in life besides business, you know."

David was sixteen when he first flew the flag of revolt—or grew

45

his hair down to his shoulders. "I ought to throw the young bugger out till he gets it cut," Eric had blustered. I had returned from the north that year to find the Coleman household like a city riven with civil strife, David sullen, adamant that he was going to study for a diploma of Fine Art, Janice by turns distraught, pleading and bitchy, Eric threatening furiously. It was then that I had come under the concentrated fire of his abuse. "I blame you for the boy's crappy ideas. You're a no-hoper yourself and you'll have him the same way." From Janice I got: "Of course Eric's very upset. You know how hard he's worked, but that doesn't give him the right to decide David's life." From David I got: "The business—yuk! I've got to hang free, Mase"—the "uncle" bit had disappeared by then, I was plain "Mase", man to man, no more kid stuff—"A man's got to be himself. You know that. I've got to make this art thing on my own, just my own talent, not the old man making a cushy job for me. Besides, I want to paint." And on another occasion, troubling me: "Dad's a Depression-thinker, that's his trouble. If you don't get blisters and raise a sweat it's not work to him. Why can't he be like you. You took a punt at creative work and that's what I'm going to do." I wasn't sorry to return north that year.

So David had hung free, been himself, took his punt at creative work, more than ever passionately committed to revolt. Who hasn't heard the catch cries of the young these days? The world a mess . . . the Bomb . . . profit motive . . . materialism . . . pollution, and so on. You could set those words to their own wrangling, jangling music and have the anthem of this age. David took part in the Vietnam Moratorium March and he carried a placard in protest against the State Government's Fuel and Energy Emergency Bill and I knew that he spent evenings in smoke-hazed rooms, drinking coffee and ardently inveighing with others of his kind who were "involved". Drugs? I don't think so. I don't know. I hope not. And girls? Inevitably. There are always girls hanging around art students, either art students themselves or the dilettante in other artifices. But when I had asked him . . . "What do you take me for, Mase? You don't think I'd bring a chick here, do you? The old man would run a check on her father's bank account and Mum would vet her virginity. Honestly, the way they go on you wonder how I came to be born." "Now steady on, David," I had growled uneasily. He also went surfing—which turned out to have had a part in what followed later—going away for weekends and holidays in company with a band of muscular, semi-articulate young men whose rallying cry seemed to be: "There's a wave on at Yalli"—Yalli being their own tribal rendering of the Aboriginal name Yallingup, a beach where the surf ran wild and exhilarating. From those excursions he would return, gaunt and hungry, burned to the colour of a fruit cake, lips chapped, eyes rimed with salt, abrasions on his elbows and knees where he had been dashed against the limestone reefs. He was hanging free, taking his punt . . . at Buddhism?

I had the uncomfortable feeling that in hanging free he was also freeing himself of me. He had usually talked so freely and he was well aware of my interest in Ceylon where some of the holiest shrines of Buddhism are located, yet he hadn't mentioned his interest in that faith. Or had he? Troubled I had remembered him leading one of our conversations around from an account of a surfing trip from which he had just returned, and the "guys" lounging around a big fire of driftwood on the beach at night, discussing surf and surfboards, chicks and cars, pot and "pigs", to the meaning of life. Not Buddhism—the meaning of life. And I, failing to perceive that the youthful idealism which had fired his revolt against his "father" might very well accept the asceticism of the Buddha's Way, had answered that to the best of my understanding there was no purpose to life other than to propagate our species and make the best of our sojourn on this earth.

Why didn't you question me, David? Why didn't you challenge that assertion? Or was my negativism repugnant to you?

My bacon and eggs smelt of coconut oil and the toast had been burned; I saw that there was no pepper and salt on the table. Then I heard Martina protesting to the waiter and I saw that her grapefruit consisted of a glass of juice which, the man insisted stubbornly, was grapefruit. Catching my eye she pulled a little face and shrugged helplessly. To harass the waiter I asked for pepper and salt which he promptly filched from an adjoining table and then retired, smiling smugly. I attacked my eggs, slicing deeply. Martina lifted her glass, smiling at me falsely.

"Poor Mason, I gave you a bad time yesterday. I guess I owe you an explanation."

I shook my head, not looking up from my disembowelled egg. I had the feeling that if I didn't handle this firmly it would develop into another of her horrible auto-critique sessions, breast-beating, confessions, *mea culpa* . . . That's what she seemed to want.

"On second thoughts," I said gravely, "I think you did the right thing not accepting that moonstone. They aren't really for European women. They don't look so well on a pale skin."

"I bet you know." She perked up at once, all set to make fun of me as she had done in the Hotel Taprobane.

I nodded, still munching. "I knew a girl once who wore one."

She took that one in without comment, green-tinted, bruised-looking eyes narrowed, studying me as though she was seeing me for the first time: it was strange what the eyeshade did to her expression, the rest of her face so young. I told myself I'd have to stop this, indeed regretted having started it. To give myself time to think I bit off a chunk of toast and chewed meditatively. Martina sipped her grapefruit.

"You must have been quite a guy—street fights and dusky maidens wearing moonstones. You must have spread yourself quite a bit."

I smiled wryly. "And fell buttered side down a few times too."

That amused her for she chuckled, settling her chin on one fist, not taking her eyes off me.

"Tell me about her."

"Who—Anula?"

"Was that her name?"

I nodded, regretting that slip, feeling that I had given something of myself away, something very personal that I had never discussed with anyone before. Anula had been at the very core of everything that had happened: without her Eric . . . without her he would have found some other way to accomplish what he wanted. Martina was smiling that amused and quizzical, provocative smile that pleased yet irritated me. Since I knew there would be no stopping her now I decided to have some fun of my own.

"Somehow she always made me think of the moon with that name."

"I'll bet. Midnight with a moonstone on her brow."

"I don't think I noticed the colour of her skin, except that I liked it."

"They say they get whiter the longer you're away from home."

"Don't be bitchy. Anula meant a lot to me once."

That was an exaggeration of course: at the time I had been preoccupied with Janice and our engagement, yet knowing Anula had influenced my life, even David's life had been affected in its own way. Martina leaned forward, suddenly excited, her hand reaching out, not quite touching me this time.

"Hey! I know why you came back. It's Anula isn't it? I knew you were looking for someone."

I swallowed a partially masticated crust of toast which scraped my throat all the way down. Then I exploded in a burst of coughing; struggling to get my handkerchief out of my pocket I knocked the newspaper to the floor again. When I got control of myself I saw Martina watching me complacently. Swallowing painfully I wiped my eyes.

"You should be writing fiction," I scoffed.

"But I'm right, aren't I?" Pleased with herself she leaned forward again, so far this time that her bosom rested on the table, affording me a glance into its secrets. I was never sure whether she deliberately offered me these glimpses, certainly she didn't appear to mind.

"I'll make a deal with you," I proposed, looking up into her eyes, seeing that she knew I had peeped. "I'll tell you about Anula if you tell me about your husband."

She straightened slowly, the jubilation fading from her face, leaving it looking hurt. At once I regretted my words: there had been no need to be brutal. She leaned back in her chair, regarding me sardonically over the last of her grapefruit juice.

"Who's being bitchy now?"

Dropping my gaze I applied myself to my congealing bacon and remaining cold egg. Our conversation had looped deviously, coming back in my face: at no point in it had I said that I forgave her for yesterday and neither had she said she would go with me tomorrow. Those things seemed to have been taken for granted. Behind me I heard the young English woman reproving her offspring in precise tones: "Eat it all up, please David. Judith, sit up straight."

I found myself thinking of David and Anula and, oddly enough, of Martina. Looking up I saw her push the dregs of her juice away: she wiped the corners of her mouth, examining the serviette for lipstick, movements as dainty, as fastidious, as self-oriented as a cat.

"Well, what's our thing for today?" she asked brightly.

I noted her use of the plural. So it had been settled, yet suddenly the thought of searching for David with this young woman dogging my heels didn't appeal to me: and it wouldn't be just for today. I found myself viewing the prospect of the next eight days with a mixture of anticipation and uncertainty—not quite so serendipity.

"I'm going to look at some temples," I told her. "I thought I'd start with the Vijayaramaya and the Asokaramaya."

"Wild," she declared soberly. "I might get some material for a piece, local colour, the mystic East. It should be good copy."

"Do you know anything about Buddhism?" I countered warily.

"No," she confessed blithely, "but I will if I go with you."

The Vijayaramaya didn't impress her. Nor did it hold anything for me. The only person in sight was a monk in a saffron robe and steel-rimmed spectacles reading a book on the porch of what I presumed to be a seminary. It formed part of a quadrangle of biscuit-coloured buildings enclosing a compound of biscuit-coloured earth baking in the morning heat, containing a bodhi tree and the glaring, white-washed bell shape of a *dagoba* on a platform decorated with a frieze of sculptured elephant heads. A hallowed peace lay over everything, so hot and heavy I felt compelled to whisper.

"What's that?" Martina demanded sharply, pointing.

I explained that she was looking at a *dagoba* which was a traditional form of Buddhist shrine constructed to contain relics or to mark a sacred site, and that in some countries, Tibet for instance, they were known as *stupas*. Drawing on sketchy knowledge I expatiated on the evolution of the various shapes, the bell, the pot, the bubble, the paddi heap, the lotus.

"When the Portuguese first took control of this island they broke into many of them, looking for treasure," I concluded hastily, for I heard my own voice droning pedantically through the heat. Martina was looking up at me, shadows of the bodhi tree smudging her face. A crow alighted on the platform, black and scruffy against the stark white symmetry of the *dagoba*. It struck me that life was like that, dark and dirty against the dazzling perfection of faith.

"Go on," Martina urged.

"That's it." I shrugged wryly, wishing I was alone. "Now you know as much about *dagobas* as I do."

She nodded thoughtfully, running her thumb down the carrying-strap of her camera. I hoped she wasn't going to use the thing because I didn't know how Buddhists felt about their holy places being photographed. Somewhere a bell began to toll, reverent bronze notes resonating through the shimmer, singing to me . . . *the temple bells are ringing and I know they ring for me . . . come you back* . . . I shivered, feeling a ghostly response prickling my skin.

"You're really into this Sri Lanka bit, aren't you?" Martina queried seriously.

I shrugged, smiling, finding myself listening to the bell. "Into this Sri Lanka bit." Funny as it sounded in her jargon she was right. If I was asked to define the attraction this island held for me I could only think of one word—exotic. Whenever I thought of it, four colours always flooded the images of my mind. Predominant was green, succulent, so beautiful that I wanted to embrace it, press it to my face like a woman's breasts—the green of young paddi and banana leaves, the orderly hills of hedge-like tea, and the jungle, rank and dank, with blue-green tints in its deepest shadows, waiting like a monster to take everything back. Next was yellow, the yellow of Buddhist robes and temple paintings, king coconuts, pepper flowers and the buttery tints of frangipani. Then there was red, of the women's saris, fruits, devil masks and bougainvilia and the shining mats of chillies drying in the village streets. And lastly there was brown, the colour of its loamy earth, its teak, its elephants, and its fine-boned people. I cannot explain it more coherently than that. A sober Elizabethan savant once declared Ceylon to be the Biblical Tarshish, while other scholars claimed that it was the resting place of Noah's Ark and even Muslim legend has it that Adam and Eve, expelled from Eden, fled here. Its placenames sing to me—Taprobane, Sihalam, Serendiva, Cilao, Ceylon, Sri Lanka.

"I fell in love with Ceylon—I mean Sri Lanka—many years ago."

Hearing myself make that correction I thought ruefully—she

knows this island as Sri Lanka while I remember it as Ceylon, that is the difference between us. The bell ceased tolling, its last note drowning in the sunshine and shimmer. Martina turned away as though the ringing had signalled the end of our visit: I turned with her, both of us stepping thoughtfully as though we were treading carefully into a new and intimate seriousness, moving towards the gate.

"Funny," she remarked, "but I can't think of you falling in love with anything."

"Thanks! Do I seem that cold?"

Either she didn't hear the sarcasm in my tone or she chose to ignore it, her face down-turned, strolling, limber legs swinging straight from the hip.

"No, not cold," she pronounced sagely. "More like controlled, I guess. You just don't get involved. You're a solitary, Johnny-Walks-Alone."

I wasn't sure that I liked that—not involved, Johnny-Walks-Alone—it suggested a misanthrope. I was silent, oddly irked, not knowing what to say. We had walked through the gate and into the street now and I saw that our taxi had shifted into the nearest shade. An old woman was jogging towards us, bare footed, wrinkled face like the dark, ravaged countenance of the earth itself, a golden nose-pin in one nostril and a pile of firewood on her head. She made way for us, her fearsome burden straining the tendons of her scrawny neck. I caught the rank, sweetish smell of her sweat and chillies, heard the breathy whip of skirts around her ankles as she passed us.

"I write about people," I argued aggrievedly for the sight of the woman's toil had stirred me. "And people love," I added warmly, for Martina's assessment of me still rankled.

"That's not the same—not like being in love yourself," she asserted gravely. "Not writing about it."

"Surely it argues a certain experience," I bantered, wondering why I bothered, why I should feel on the defensive.

"So there was someone?" She looked up, face serious.

"Nobody I'd lose any sleep about," I lied blithely, feeling a twinge of conscience remembering Clare. If the truth be told I had foregone quite a lot of sleep in Clare's bed at one time or another.

"Just the same," Martina was saying thoughtfully, "I can't figure why you never married."

"I was crossed in love," I said softly, knowing that if you don't want to be believed the best thing to do is to tell the truth.

Martina looked at me doubtingly but we had reached the taxi by then and I wasted no time in opening the door for her. It was a Morris Minor, black and yellow, with ravaged, cherry-red upholstery that smelt of coconut oil and sweat, a legacy of at least a decade of previous passengers. The driver was a sloe-eyed Indian youth with a profile like those seen on old medallions. I presumed that he was a Hindu for attached to the dashboard by its magnetic base was a little grey plastic figure of Ganesh, the elephant-headed god of travellers: his wrinkled trunk was looped over his human paunch and his eyes were disturbing, of some green substance which would glow in the dark.

"To the Asokaramaya," I directed as we pulled away with something inside the engine frantically hammering to get out.

Martina was silent, staring out at the dirty street. As I pulled out my pipe I swear that I saw Ganesh wink at me with one luminous green eye.

A monk showed us round the Asokaramaya. He was an urbane, golden brown man with bare feet, a shaven head and dark smudges under his eyes: he wore a crumpled robe of that erubescent yellow which reminds me of hot sunsets or raw gold. I judged him to be about my age and I wondered where he had been during the April of 1942. Kalutara? Looking into his jaded eyes with their liverish pouches, their secrets of faith, their tired acceptance of human weaknesses, I thought of our sergeant of thirty-three years ago saying crisply: "When the blue starts we shoot the canaries first."

"Here are the Jataka stories," the monk enunciated quaintly. His English was stiff, infrequently used I suspected, and oddly phrased as you'd expect from a man who did his thinking in another language: his tongue seemed to curl around the vowels, bringing them out in the sing-song cadence of his classical Pali.

We were in a crooked passageway which angled to the right, for Asokaramaya is octagonal, with an octagonal central core, and on every face of those eight sides were dioramas. Here, in reds and greens and yellows and earthy browns, were kings, splendidly apparelled and unmistakeably kingly; queens and concubines with slender hands and the soulful features of Sistine Madonnas;

53

merchants, peasants, soldiers, artisans, beggars and gurus and even a hairy, black demon with a werewolf's visage: they swaggered or languished or sat in earnest consultation against painted or three dimensional backgrounds of field and forest and columned halls. Over all floated flocks of heavenly beings, smiling benignly, trailing blue and yellow robes, their heads bowed beneath the ceiling as though they were supporting Nirvana on their necks.

"Jataka stories," the monk said again, rolling vowels like marbles in his mouth. "All here stories of the Buddha from before." He pronounced it "Booder", crinkled lips pursing reverently around the hallowed name: clutching the shoulder of his robe he drifted away, spindle-shanked, bare feet gritting softly on the floor. Martina looked mystified so I hastened to explain.

"The Buddha was reborn a number of times. These are stories from his different reincarnations."

Halting in front of one of the dioramas the monk rubbed one bare foot against the shin of the other, staring rapturously. In this one the Buddha sat cross-legged, in the posture of meditation, on the coils of a gigantic cobra whose fearsome, diamond-patterned head was elevated, hood expanded and arched protectively: the ground was portrayed as waterlogged while the background was jungle, obscured by fine brushstrokes of rain. Flowers lay in front of the effigy, enormous waxy blossoms with white centres and apricot-tinted petals that had burst open in pale explosions.

"See, the royal naga-serpent, Mucalinda, shelters the Awakened One from the storm."

Releasing the shoulder of his robe the monk pressed his palms together in the gesture of veneration. I recalled having read that the name, "Buddha", was from the Indian word "buddh", meaning "to awake" in the sense of enlightenment. Looking up into that smooth, inscrutable face with its hooded eyes and heavy lips and its smile which wasn't quite a smile, merely a suggestion of ineffable benevolence softening the corners of the mouth, I saw dust on the divine nose. There was more of it, accumulated in the upturned palms of the hands, darkening the folds of the meticulously shaped robe and on the ritually arranged feet. I heard Martina enthusing over the flowers.

The monk smiled tolerantly, relaxing his pious attitude for the first time as he indulged her woman's frivolousness. They were the flowers of the *sal* tree, he explained, the tree under which the

Buddha had been born. Cannonball flowers they were called because when they fell from the tree they burst open on hitting the ground. Casually he reached out a skinny arm and scooped up one of the heavy blossoms for our inspection.

"See, this flower has *dagoba* and naga-serpent."

His tawny finger, with badly bitten nail, poked the flower, revealing a fleshy, bell-shaped pistil topped with a tiny spike like a spire while the anthers were a yellow fuzz edging a white central petal that curved protectingly over the heart of the flower: the thick, pinkish petals had begun to wilt, lying limply, covering the man's creased palm. Martina was intrigued, urging me to look more closely at these symbols of *dagoba* and serpent. I peered dutifully, also sniffing the flower, but any scent it might have had was drowned by the faintly acrid odour of the man's hand. When I looked up he was smiling, plummy lips parted over broken, grey teeth, an intensity in his lustreless eyes. I had the eerie feeling that I was looking at the real man under the Buddhist robes, a man I might have shot. He tossed the blossom back, back-handing it carelessly as though he was disposing of rubbish: it landed on the Buddha's foot and slipped off to lie in a sad little heap. I thought of the person who had laid it so reverently at the Buddha's feet.

When we went on the monk began telling Martina a story about a king who had been out hunting a deer when a beautiful young man interceded to save the creature's life, but the king shot his arrow into the youth instead. It was a long and allegorical story, not easy to follow because of the monk's accent, winding inevitably to a conclusion which I didn't quite comprehend. I followed, thinking of David and Buddhism, and wishing I could have a smoke. We had nearly completed the circuit of the temple and through the entrance I could see our taxi parked under a jak tree at the edge of the compound with a gaggle of children round it. With a tiny gust of annoyance I realised that I had no small change left to give them.

Outside the heat wrapped us with humid coils and in addition to wanting to smoke I wanted a drink. When we had resumed our shoes I donated ten rupees to the temple funds and the monk palmed the note expertly, dry fingers brushing mine. I felt that I was paying him off, laying what might very well have been his ghost. I saw the children watching us, holding back as though they were waiting for us to cross some invisible boundary of the temple's influence. Martina donned her dark glasses, the big, smoky rounds making her eyes enormous, like one of those little nocturnal animals.

"You know," she observed thoughtfully as we walked towards the taxi, "this Buddhism's got a lot going for it."

I smiled. "Buddhism has had a lot going for it for two-and-a-half thousand years."

"No, seriously, Mason," she insisted earnestly. "It gets you, doesn't it. And did you see all those flowers?"

I nodded, poker-faced. "I also saw a lot of dirt."

"I guess that's the difference between us," she observed quite serenely. "I see the flowers and you see the dirt."

Again I felt a stab of resentment as I had at the Vijayaramaya. She glanced at me as we walked side by side and I saw myself reflected, ridiculously distorted by the convex surfaces of her glasses. I wondered whether that was the way she saw me, distorted, cold, not involved, walking alone through the flowers and dirt. The image troubled me and I would have said something, but at that moment the children swooped on us.

They came in a scrambling rush, chittering like a swarm of little bats, impish faces, sharp white teeth and beautiful eyes, hands reaching out: some of them offered flame coloured bougainvilia and coral frangipani. Homing in on Martina they ignored me, except for one doleful lad who tugged at my arm, rolling his eyes soulfully. I tried to tell him I had no money but he wouldn't believe me.

Martina stood her ground, handbag open and held high, fumbling in it while the children surged around her, scrawny bodies, skinny arms and elfin faces, like one of those United Nations Save the Children posters. Flowers had been thrust into her hands, into the bend of her arms, even into her handbag and the front of her blouse, spilling from her as she moved. Flowers and dirt and begging children!

"You start throwing money around and you'll have a riot," I warned but she only laughed, big, dark glasses flashing ridicule.

"You're a hard-head, Mason. You don't want to see the flowers, you only look for the dirt."

And before I could stop her she was distributing coins. The children boiled around her, snatching, shoving, scurrying away. She tried to remonstrate with them, but her voice was lost in the screeching. Still smiling she fell back a pace, holding her handbag out of reach and as suddenly as it had begun the mêlée broke up, children trotting away, some of them quarrelling between themselves. Martina plucked a frangipani from the front of her blouse, sniffing it, regarding me over the petals.

"See," she mocked. "No riot. A little shoving perhaps, but no rough stuff. You treat them properly, they're all right. They're the original flower people."

Slowly I released my pent up breath. I wasn't sure what I had wanted to happen — maybe a little jostling, not enough to hurt her but enough to convince her that you shouldn't fool with these people, that there was an earthy relationship between flowers and dirt. Instead, I turned and marched to the car without a word. As I held the door open for her she put her pointed possum face close to mine and through the smoky lenses and my own reflections I saw that her eyes were dancing.

"I do believe you're sulking because they didn't mob me." She touched me, very lightly, on the tip of the nose with the flower.

My first impulse was to knock the thing out of her hand, an impulse which was aggravated by the knowledge that the taxi driver was grinning, but I restrained myself, looking away, seeing the flowers scattered in the dust.

"All right," I said firmly. "You want flower people, I'll show you." Cold, I thought grimly, not involved. I tapped the driver none too lightly on the shoulder, taking the grin off his face.

"Take us to the Pettah."

We entered the Pettah at some speed via the Beira Bridge, wheeling along a waterfront street where all I saw was aged buildings with mossy tiles and mildewed walls and the architectural furbelows of another age, for the Pettah is, as the tourist brochures state, the oldest part of the town. Signs were in Pali, Singhalese and Arabic script with English renderings underneath. The names intrigued me, reading like a roll from the island's history — Jayawardana, Van Landenberg, Thos. Smith & Son, Da Costa, Gunasekera, Fernando, Jansz. We whirled past a candy-striped mosque and once I spied a cathedral, arches, rose window, campanile spires against the sky, undoubtedly Catholic and therefore Portuguese. There was a Hindu temple heavy with the mysticism of fertility, white cows, virile gods and voluptuous goddesses swarming over the pyramid above its gateway. Without warning our driver swung off the street in a careering right-hand turn that brought Martina lurching against me.

As we righted ourselves I saw that we were hurtling into a market of some kind. Dirt and refuse and bullocks' dung and a gravel road bumpy with ruts and trolley tracks; godowns on either side where bare, brown men in dhoti rags loaded trucks and bullock carts; benches with women scaling and gutting fish; silver-grey heaps of fish, mullet shapes and salmon sizes, dappled tangles of octopus and mats of tiny, sprat-like fish browning odorously in the sun; a man with a cleaver chopping up a dolphin; crows fluttering and strutting insolently, quarrelsome little prick-eared dogs gulping offal; and people wandering everywhere.

I held my breath, expecting us to mow down half a dozen pedestrians but our driver braked savagely, narrowly missing a youth walking a bicycle with a basket of fish balanced precariously on its carrier. Grappling bicycle and load, the youth shouted indignantly but our driver ignored him. Dropping into the lowest gear he revved angrily, swerving to avoid an old man, bow-legged and jogging along with a *pingo* pole. In doing so he scattered a group of chattering Tamil women with leaf-wrapped bundles on their heads and somnolent infants on their hips. Suddenly there were children in front of us, zigzagging crazily, shrieking delightedly when our driver sounded the horn. By then the stink had reached us, fish and the smell of guts and the thin, ammoniac reek of humanity. I gagged, almost tasting it. Pulling a face Martina set about preparing her camera.

"Can we stop? I'd like some shots."

I told the driver to stop which he did, muttering, rolling unhappy, white-eyed glances over his shoulder at me, letting the car roll slowly to a standstill as though he hoped I would change my mind. I noticed that he kept the engine running. I had time to see a crow dragging a mess of fish guts through the dust before the children closed in.

For a few moments they clustered, giggling and nudging, thin legs flickering darkly, bare feet with splayed toes shuffling in the dust, then the shoving and whispering suddenly became a collective voice that swept them, chattering, against the car. Since Martina had her window down their pink-palmed hands came through or clung, little fingers folded darkly over the edge of the glass. Their sharp flesh smell filled the car. Then a woman's face appeared, tangled hair, black hungering eyes in a wasted face, betel-reddened mouth grinning ingratiatingly. She nursed a child against her shoulder, naked except for a string around its waist, little bones showing sharply, scurfy skin flaking on thin buttocks. Her skinny hand came through the window, clawing at Martina's shoulder. Leaning across I wound the window up, the childrens' fingers, the woman's hand withdrawing, thwarted. Martina reached for the door handle.

"You're not getting out, are you?" I demanded sharply.

"Why not? They won't hurt me."

She opened the door wide, sweeping squirming children aside, and alighted. Chattering excitedly the children closed round her. I followed her, suddenly regretting having brought her here.

Before I was clear of the car the children were upon me, little hands like bats' wings fluttering swiftly over my thighs, over my hips and hip pocket. Thin, clammy fingers like a monkey's paw grabbed my wrist, scrabbling hopefully in my palm. Straightening, I wheeled, but they had skipped out of reach, leaving the woman lifting her infant in front of my face, that little distended paunch with its ugly extrusion of ruptured navel, washboard ribs, tiny baby crimping of sex, a brass amulet swinging from the waist string. I smelt the sour, empty-bellied breath of poverty, the hungering Third World breathing its charnel-house breath in my face. Recoiling, I snapped "Yanni, yanni," flicking my hand at her as I had seen Larga do, and she backed away, muttering, folding the child to her tatterdemalion bosom. The crows cawed sardonically.

Looking around I saw that Martina had moved some distance away and was taking a light reading with a hand-held meter while staring children jostled around her. As I started forward I heard the taxi driver calling worriedly, "Sir, sir! Not too far." He still had the engine running. Then Martina was off again, bearing down on a squatting woman who was eating rice from a banana leaf while a naked boy-child looked on: he was knock-kneed and pot-bellied and there was a vacuous solemnity about his expression. Halting, Martina lifted the Pentax to her eye, focussing. Oblivious of her, the woman balled a pellet of rice in her fingers and popped it into the child's mouth. The camera shutter clattered, sounding as savage as the drop of a guillotine. Looking up the woman shouted something with the same backward motion of her hand that I had used. Drawing the child to her she cupped a hand over the back of his head, turning his moony face into her shoulder. Martina shrugged wryly and turned away, winding film with a jerk of her wrist. When she handled the camera there was a deftness about her movements which was almost ruthless, as though it was the instrument of her superiority.

She moved away from me towards the women at the gutting benches, the Pentax lifted, an insatiable, monster eye goggling inquisitively. The women looked up from their work to watch her, the younger ones primping, hands flitting over their headcloths, nudging and giggling, white-toothed smiles and flashing eyes; the older ones frowned, turning away. Martina caught them all in an oblique shot which took in benches, heaps of fish, a corner of the godowns and even the man who was chopping up the dolphin. When he saw what she was doing he dropped his cleaver and took up the dismembered head, holding it in front of his face, the beaked snout with those intelligent eyes looking at us with a clown's sad grin.

"Funny guy," Martina scoffed. "We'll crop him out when it's printed. This is a magazine shot. Comics we can do without."

Swinging away she wound more film, even her walk changing while she sighted and stalked a group of elderly women who were gathered around a shellfish stall. When she had manoeuvred herself into a position that would give her a frontal shot of those dark faces, bounteous bosoms and ample flanks swathed in lime-green, heliotrope and sunburst yellow, as well as the raddled hag who sat cross-legged beside her wares, the women saw her and moved away, their clothing making drifts of vivid colour in the drabness of the market place.

She had more success with a coconut seller for at the sight of her camera he strutted, a runty little man in baggy shorts and grubby singlet, Chaplin moustache and big bare feet, tapping himself on the chest, pantomiming the act of drinking from a coconut.

"Mason," she called. "What about a shot of you drinking coconut juice."

I shook my head, backing away a couple of steps. Undeterred she enlisted the services of several children, paying the vendor to open coconuts so that she could photograph the kids drinking.

They hammed it with gusto, not only guzzling, holding the nuts high and tipping milky arcs of fluid down their throats but squatting, scooping out and gobbling curds of the pearly flesh. It was good tourist magazine stuff and Martina snapped it eagerly. I suspected that one of those shots would show me skulking in the background. Looking pleased with herself she came back to me, winding more film.

"You sore at me, Mason?" Her face lifted pertly, green-shaded eyes mocking me once more, winey lips frankly inviting.

I drew a deep breath, feeling all the irritation of the morning combining sourly within me, my desire to search for David alone, my stupidity in bringing her here, her brashness, her brusqueness and that wretched camera! Perhaps if she had been softer, if she had used my Christian name once in a while instead of being so damned egalitarian and aggressive . . .

"You're bugging me badly," I grated, fighting to keep my temper in check, not succeeding. "You're so damned full of knowledge yet so bloody ignorant! Who do you think you are, ramping around amongst these people, chucking them pennies, setting them up like dolls in a sideshow? You're a woman and women are supposed to have compassion and softness and understanding. But not you! You can't even refuse a gift without turning it into a scene from Virginia Wolf. No wonder your poor bloody husband walked out on you!"

As soon as I had said it I was appalled, not only by my cantankerousness but by my desire to hurt her. Also, in that hot, crazed moment I had enjoyed humiliating her. She had gone white and rigid, the colour on her cheeks, eyes and lips standing out starkly. I had the freaky feeling of a mask staring at me in the hot sunshine amid the bustle and smells with the dark, keen faces of the children looking on. The movement seemed to last so long, with her pain sinking dully into both of us. Then a mangey little dog rushed out, yapping spitefully at a crow and the sound split us apart. I started, Martina shuddered and, for some reason, glanced bewilderedly at her camera, then she turned and walked away without so much as a glance at me. Nearby a youth laughed, staring after her, spitting, clutching his balls meditatively through his sarong.

Standing stiffly I watched her go, walking briskly between the groups of people. This was the end, I was sure: our friendship, if you could call it that, had survived the trauma of the gem shop but not this. No woman would take that. I saw her reach the road and expected her to return to the taxi, but instead she turned right, moving further into the market. Unpredictable, I thought grimly; contrary, a very complicated woman. Shaken I walked back to the taxi. The driver revved the engine hopefully but I signalled him to wait. I could see Martina some distance ahead, keeping clear of the sweating, near naked men and the bullock carts, stepping carefully over bullock dung. I should have gone after her and apologised but somehow I couldn't bring myself to do that: I had meant what I said, I did sympathise with her husband. Yet I couldn't leave her here. Leaning against the taxi I brought out my pipe and at once children gathered to watch me light it: their attention was a distraction and I grinned at them, flicking the dead match at their feet. I couldn't see Martina on the road. Motioning to the taxi driver to follow I started off.

She was photographing some women who were sitting among piles of golden king coconuts and green bananas with children standing around, squashed fruit and refuse everywhere. A little girl was urinating in the gutter. Nearby some men loitered, hipshot and grinning, while on the other side of the roadway a burly man appeared to be doing tumbling tricks. I guessed that he wasn't a professional for there was a loutishness about him, a heavy-bellied clumsiness: there was also a sly buffoonery in his patter which kept the onlookers chuckling, especially when he beckoned to Martina to photograph him.

A lane intersected the road just there, separating the godowns from a mass of ancient houses which looked as though they had been fused together by time and squalor. This looked like one of the oldest parts of the Pettah, little changed since the days of the Dutch or Portuguese except that dirt had cemented the cracks, moss blackened the tiles of the low roofs, while on the walls mildew and seeping damp had long since mapped the territories of forgotten downpours. Only a mouldering Aspro poster and an advertisement for Bristol cigarettes announced the presence of the twentieth century.

Martina heard the car and looked around, turning away when she saw me. There was nothing particularly hostile in her movement, more like disinterest, as if I was a perfect stranger. That troubled me: if she had showed anger, told me to go away.

Anything but that numbed apathy of deep hurt. The would-be tumbler had come out of a graceless handstand, his round, fool's face quizzing me with a slyness somewhere in his guileless grin: he said something jocular that must have linked me to Martina for the bystanders grinned, glancing from one to the other of us. Resuming his clowning he turned a clumsy somersault, the creased, yellow soles of his feet flashing nakedly. Then he called to her again, backing a few paces down the lane and she went towards him, cranking the camera vigorously.

As she entered the lane the man turned his back on her, retreating further, chattering oafishly. The bystanders deserted me then, following Martina into the lane. It was some sort of vegetable market, cabbages, cucumbers, baskets of radishes and knobby tubers of green ginger displayed in wretched lean-tos of *kadjan* thatching supported on rickety stacks of pinewood cases: soap cases they were, many of them bearing the faded imprint of Sunlight Soap. There were more people now, laughing, calling encouragingly to the mountebank. He was on his back, body arched belly upwards, lurching sideways like a grotesque, fleshy crab: his face hung upsidedown, ogling Martina. She motioned to him to remain still but he rolled on to hands and knees and stood up, backing away. She followed, the crowd flowing after her. Then the man stood on his hands, his rotund body wobbling precariously, legs flapping: the frayed cuffs of his trousers slid down his ankles and his soiled shirt peeled downwards, exposing a mound of mud coloured paunch. The camera went up to Martina's eye. Just then a hand plucked at my arm, a voice entreating whiningly.

"Sir, give me money!"

Turning I looked into the dark, twisted face of a weedy youth: his right arm was folded across his chest, the hand dangling limply from the wrist while his right leg was crooked, dragging as he moved.

"Sir, my father is dead. I am hungry. My mother and sisters are hungry."

That plea reached out to me, raking my conscience, and for one harried instant I hated this country for subjecting me to that age-old demand. I would have given him money if I'd had small change but I wasn't going to show my wallet here. Then I heard Martina's voice.

"Mason!"

I would have gone to her but the youth had hold of me, his thin fingers like steely clamps. Shouting angrily he shook my arm, his dusky, adolescent face twisting despairingly: he hated me because he was poor and crippled, because I was well-fed and affluent.

"Sir, I will not go away till you give me money!"

"Mason, please!"

This time there was wild fear in Martina's voice, but as I turned the cripple grappled me with febrile strength, clinging, clawing at me with his disabled hand. I shoved him away much harder than I intended for he staggered into a heap of coconuts and went down yelling. Coconuts, women and children scattering, green bananas spilling and the cripple floundering, trying to lift himself on his lame arm and leg.

Then things began to happen quickly, a grimacing face, a brown hand clawing, intercepting me. Instinctively I resorted to the tactics which had served me well in this country many years before—I stamped hard on bare toes, feeling the little bones roll like marbles. Yelling, the man staggered back. The crowd had seen me coming, faces turning, darting out of my way, only one man confronting me. Again I used my heel and for good measure, an elbow under his jaw as he doubled. Then I was into the crowd, elbowing, shouldering, the sweet-sour reek of them in my nostrils. Several ineffectual buffets beat my shoulders but I hunched, lashing out with backhanded clouts which connected with ribby thuds. Suddenly I was through, the yelling closing in around me.

The fat man had hold of Martina's bag and was trying to drag the strap from her shoulder. Fortunately it was real leather and stout, for Martina was clinging to it, tugging. Another man had hold of her wrists, trying to break her grip. At my coming the fat man turned, teeth bared, his clown's face suddenly evil. Releasing the bag, he hunched, solid and dangerous. I threw a punch but he side-stepped, hooking at me with a wrestler's grab. I had to do something fast for I was running short of breath so I fouled him in classic rough-house style, kicking his kneecap and then, as he bent, driving a fist into his belly. As he reeled backward I saw the man who had been grappling Martina swing away and reach for something on the ground. Instantly I remembered that brawl of more than thirty years ago.

"Get out—before they start throwing stuff!"

Grabbing Martina I shoved her so hard that she stumbled and might have fallen if I hadn't dragged her along. Then something struck my left shoulder, spinning me so that I staggered, colliding with one of the stacks of pinewood cases that supported a lean-to. A bench of vegetables toppled, barking my shins, cabbages rolling like footballs, beans squashing underfoot while the arm of a set of steel-yard scales nearly poked my eye out. An old woman appeared from out of the shadowy recesses and scrambled away with a spiderish thrashing of scrawny arms and legs.

Martina had an arm around my waist, shouting at me. Mumbling I looked around and saw the fat man still doubled and clutching his guts, but the people around him were scrabbling for things to throw. Something came kiting end over end through the air, hitting the ground close to Martina. I elbowed her away from me.

"Stand clear! I'll stop their bloody gallop!"

Getting a good grip on the end of one of the Sunlight Soap cases I heaved as hard as I could. Pain streamed through my shoulder, but I jerked again, wrenching the case from side to side, feeling the pinewood, old and exposed to the weather of years, beginning to split in my hands. Suddenly the end of the case tore away. The rest of the stack rocked, settled lower with ominous splintering sounds and began to sway. Stepping back I gave it a hearty shove with my foot which stove in another case. Slowly one end of the lean-to swung outward, cases creaking, snapping, folding flat: *kadjan* thatching toppled towards us, spilling rotting fragments and junk, broken pottery, rusty tins, a hen crashing down in an explosion of cackling and thrashing wings. With little more than some crackling and splintering sounds and a leafy swishing the lean-to collapsed across the lane, scattering broken cases and mouldering pieces of palm. There was a musty stench of the rot and mildew of years disturbed. Grabbing Martina's wrist I ran. Behind us the shouting was frightening.

As we reached the taxi clods of dried mud hit the road, bursting spectacularly. The driver was revving his engine madly and I could see him mouthing frantically. As I bundled Martina inside a stone clattered on the mudguard, leaving a dent with a starry flaking of paint. The driver screamed louder. I just had time to clamber in to the rear seat and lie back panting when the Morris Minor lumbered into motion, its worn pistons clattering hideously, making a racket that hammered deafeningly between the houses while the driver was yelling like a lunatic. Grimacing I hauled myself upright, conscious of the ache in my shoulder for the first time. It was then that I realised that Martina was laughing.

She was still giggling when I paid the driver off outside the Hotel Taprobane. She insisted on adding to my handsome tip with a gratuity of her own—conscience-money she called it—compensating not only for the dented mudguard but for his jangled nerves and his discretion in the event of any repercussions.

I was still excited, the adrenalin not yet dispersed in my blood, combining with a secret elation at the thought that the David Mason of yesterday hadn't been entirely suffocated by the weight of years. And it had to be the Taprobane for the place had ghostly associations which made a celebratory drink there the obvious postscript to our escapade. Inside, however, the cool of the airconditioning and the staid murmur of piped music was like a disapproving presence reproaching me for my superannuated larrikinism. That I should even acknowledge its censure was proof of how much I had changed. Martina retired to the ladies room to emerge, combed and refurbished, by which time I had the drinks set up and was meditatively sucking my pipe. She was bubbling with delayed shock.

"I've got to hand it to you, Mason, you sure are a surprise packet when you're turned on. You came on like a grandad bull elephant back there."

My shrug made my injured shoulder hurt. It was stiffening fast but I was sure that nothing was broken or I wouldn't have been able to move it at all. I was beginning to feel ashamed, thinking of the damage I had done and its cost to people who lived at the subsistence level. Nor did the "grandad" bit help. I must have looked pained, displeased, for she leaned forward placatingly.

"I'm sorry, Mason, but you did. My God! You looked like Samson tearing the temple down when you were going for that hoochi!"

"Demolition is an essential part of the strategy of a rearguard action," I murmured modestly.

"I wish I'd snapped it," Martina lamented.

"Your editor would have liked that one," I mocked softly.

"*Odyssey's* charming girl reporter making friends with the gentle natives."

"Charming?" Her eyebrows rose sardonically. "That's not what you said back there."

So it still rankled, still had to be talked out. But not now: I didn't want to spoil this amity which was flowering so improbably and tempestuously between us. Certainly our arrangement for tomorrow was an on-again-off-again affair.

"Well," I huffed, "I was under considerable stress at the time. Anyway, if you had got the picture it might have won you an award."

She was distracted, giggling. "Not for publication, that one, just something for you and me to remember."

"I've got a memento, thank you." I worked my shoulder gently. "Anyway, I'm too old for that caper now so count me out next time you start a riot."

"I didn't start that one."

"Who are you kidding? If you hadn't rushed off . . ."

"If you hadn't said what you did . . ."

Suddenly we were back to it again, our possible point of no return, both of us serious, watching one another warily. Since there could be no evading it I decided that it must be done with frankness and without tantrums or sentiment. If our friendship was to continue it must be on terms set during the next few minutes. I lifted my hands in mock surrender.

"All right, let's say that the honours are even. I don't apologise for what I said, but I apologise for saying it."

I expected that to produce something but to my surprise she took it meekly, leaning back, head tilted, looking at me rather wistfully.

"Am I as bad as that? No, don't answer. If I know you you'll say 'Yes' and enjoy it. Stephen was like that. He said I was crazy, neurotic, expected too much of him, but I didn't believe him because that was at the end, when we were breaking up, tearing each other to pieces all the time. Stephen was my husband," she concluded with a wide eyed simplicity and ingenuousness which made me wonder, for one doubting instant only, if the shrew in the gem shop had really been her. But it had, so I steeled myself.

"Stephen," I pronounced relentlessly, "must have been a very long-suffering man."

Even that didn't provoke her: as I said, unpredictable, or wily. She didn't stir, just sat, silver-nailed fingers tapping out a nervous rallentando on the arm of her basket chair. Tearing each other to pieces, she had said. I could imagine!

"Mason, I like you," she confided unexpectedly. "You do something for me. You keep me on the jump and that's good for me, but please remember I'm a woman, and a woman needs compassion and softness and understanding."

"Granted." I smiled wryly, trapped by my own words. "You forgive me then?"

Her eyebrows arched quizzically. "I'm stuck with you, aren't I?"

"Unless you want to cry quits about tomorrow."

"Are you hoping I will?"

"That's up to you."

"It wouldn't solve anything, would it? Not for me. Anyway, after today it might be better if we got out of town for a while."

"I'm glad." I was surprised to realise how much I meant that.

"And Mason," she said softly, "in case you're interested, Stephen didn't walk out on me. I divorced him."

PART TWO

I am Poyal, the palace guardsman. This is my song.
Forgive me, O long-eyed maid of the mountainside
Coming hither my mind was filled by the fair ones.
Seeing them, death no longer dismays me.
Sigiri Graffito 12, probably 9th century AD.
Translation: S. Paranavitana,
Sigiri Graffiti, Volume II.

The car arrived at seven thirty, catching us at breakfast. In the lobby I found a slim, rather battered-looking man awaiting us. I say "battered looking" because when I saw him standing there, his bow legs encased in stove-pipe trousers, his large square head with tightly curled grey hair silhouetted against the sea-bright glare of the Green beyond, I had the impression of someone who had been roughly handled by life, much used and little benefited by it, a sort of respectability worn thin by impecuniousness.

I saw a nervous, aquiline, intelligent face that was beginning to age in pouches of coarse-pored, chocolate skin, while his eyes were very dark and limpid, sadly assessing me—another client to be humoured, deferred to, satisfied. His shirt sleeves were rolled up and I noticed his extraordinarily sinewy forearms and also the fact that he wasn't wearing socks. Trivial perhaps, but it was part of my picture of his innate, but profitless, old-world courtesy now at my service.

Standing with the heels of his shabby shoes together he introduced himself as Joseph, our guide from Taprobane Tours: for an uneasy moment I thought he was going to salute me. I offered my hand, which appeared to confuse him for he stared at it, responding diffidently, his dark, boney hand briefly resting limply in mine before he snapped back to attention. I had the feeling that in my matey Australian fashion I had offended a British-inculcated reserve, unsettling the delicate client-guide relationship.

Just then Martina made her appearance, dainty in a skirt with a sleeveless blouse whose neckline was designed to afford her maximum comfort in the heat. Although it didn't exactly plunge it did lose altitude rather steeply, a style which she favoured, I was beginning to notice. I had arrived at that conclusion while sitting opposite her at breakfast. I saw Joseph's splendid eyes widen, losing some of their sadness while his punctilio became infused with a stuffy courteousness, his spare frame inclining in a stiff Germanic bow: he didn't click his heels, but I swear he was tempted to kiss her hand.

"Good morning, Madam." He pronounced it "Ma-dam".

"Hi there!" Martina's greeting was as breezy as her neckline.

Not being accustomed to having servants I turned away to pick up our luggage myself, thereby committing my second *faux pas* in Joseph's estimation. He literally bustled me aside, bobbing over our suitcases like a broody hen settling on a clutch of eggs, fumbling, straightening, our luggage disposed about his person, Martina's typewriter under his arm. Chastened, I submitted to being herded through the door.

Our car was a Holden '63, its quasi-American shape greeting me like a fellow expatriate: tropical damp was rusting through the bodywork in all the usual places but they were like familiar scars on a well-known face. The driver hustled forward, relieving Joseph of the cases, stowing them in the boot. Because I expected to spend eight days in the man's company I asked his name, but Joseph intervened, speaking primly. The driver's name was Gopal, he told me, adding rather pointedly that the man spoke very little English. Once again I had been reproved, very subtly of course, so I refrained from attempting to shake hands with the driver. I had always thought that Gopal was an Indian name, but this man was pure Singhalese, round headed, with a cheerful face the colour of tarnished copper and scored with laughter lines around the mouth. He was balding and burly, with a bulk which I suspected had once been muscle. His shirt and sarong were spotlessly white and he wore sandals that gave out a mellow clatter when he walked. He might speak very little English but when I intercepted his merry glance at Joseph I knew that I would be able to communicate with Gopal, not only with gestures and the occasional word, but with shared laughter.

Joseph fussed over Martina, spreading a cotton sheet on the seat where she was to sit, adjusting the window to her liking and taking her handbag and camera and stowing them away before motioning her to get in. He had long, elegant hands that fluttered while he talked as though he was beating time to the wild music of his thoughts. Martina thanked him prettily with no slang and only the faintest ineradicable twang. Feeling like a small boy who has fallen out of favour I followed. As we drove away I noticed that the streets were almost empty so, more to break the quiet that had settled upon us than from any real interest in Colombo's traffic, I

72

remarked on the fact.

"Oh no, sir." Joseph turned his big head, speaking with that elaborate courtesy which seemed to frost up by the time it reached me. "There aren't many vehicles on the streets today because this is *poya* day, the Day of the Full Moon, and that is a public holiday in Sri Lanka."

For some reason the words "full moon" registered in my mind, something to do with David, something the hippie had said, but I couldn't remember exactly because Joseph was saying: "Our first stop will be Negombo."

Of course Martina brought her camera out and so Negombo wasn't our first stop.

Before we were clear of the outskirts of Colombo we stopped for her to photograph an elephant working in a sawmill, picking up logs with its trunk like a man tucking a roll of wallpaper under his arm. Then it was toddy-tappers tippy-toeing along aerial walkways strung between the tops of palms; and women pounding coconut husks; a boy with a monkey; and a string of padda boats waddling along an old Dutch canal between slender betel palms, with great sun-yellowed blobs of floating weed bobbing in their wake. Once, while we waited beside a bronze-green river for a crowded bus to cross a narrow bridge, she clambered down to photograph women beating their washing against worn, wet stones.

We spent the most time at a batik factory — a collection of long, thatched huts which looked more like the film set of *The Bridge on the River Kwai* than a factory — with coconut palms trailing their delicate, fringed shadows and swathes of batik hanging between the trees, crimson, green, cerise and blue, like earthbound rainbows drying in the sun. Martina decided that she wanted to record the different stages of the batik making process which is a long and tedious one, each colour of a devilishly intricate pattern being dyed separately after the rest of the pattern has been blanked out with wax. Stalking around, she photographed grinning youths at the boiling vats, and girls hunched over benches, each with an earthenware cup of melted wax and a stylus, painstakingly blotting out segments of a super jigsaw puzzle drawn on bolts of white cotton. When I attempted to hurry her she protested. "It's all right for you, Mason, you've seen it all before." At once Joseph perked up. "This is not your first visit to Sri Lanka, sir?" And when I told him the year and the circumstances of that sojourn he offered his hand shyly. "We have been comrades-in-arms. I was a gunlayer on an anti-aircraft battery that day." I knew then that my *gaucheries* had been forgiven.

Between these halts Gopal drove hard, braking and hooting his way round corners, driving by guess and by God, or by Buddha, narrowly missing cyclists, pedestrians, goats and dogs and tinkling bullock taxi-carts. And being narrowly missed in turn by demonic red and silver buses, which had what looked like the entire stock of hardware and greengroceries stores lashed on their roofs; or by maniacal, top heavy trucks loaded with coconuts, *kadjans*, rice or wood, or sometimes with people, who laughed and chanted and pounded the high wooden sides as they whirled past.

All this for the first twenty-four kilometres of a narrow, high-crowned road that wound, with rarely a straight stretch of more than five-hundred metres, through an almost continuous village interspersed with oil palm plantations, fields of pineapples and sugar cane and ghostly aisles of coconut palms, where fallen fronds lay like browning rib bones and buffaloes browsed, tethered in pairs. Here and there we passed ornate churches of unmistakeable European design. Joseph explained that this was one of the coastal areas which had once been the centre of Portuguese settlement and in consequence most of its population was Catholic. It seems that while the British introduced tea and teak to the island, and the Dutch constructed an efficient system of canals, the Portuguese left their religion. And so it was Madonnas with the Christ Child in their arms who looked down on the road from their dusty glass cases, or saints or martyrs bristling with arrows and gushing blood. But also beside the road, although not so numerous, were Buddhas, cross-legged and contemplative, with crows scavenging the offerings at their feet. I noticed that Joseph paid his respects to saint and savant alike, scrupulously inclining his head whenever we passed them.

He was a strange man, pathetically anxious to be good at his job, and affable once he had accepted me. He had been a Forestry Officer for many years so his knowledge was both extensive and academic. He explained that the reservoirs, which I called "dams", were really "tanks" constructed during the reigns of ancient kings and still in use, although many of them were badly choked by salvenia weed which the British had used as camouflage during the war. He pointed out trees, the water-loving *kumbuk*, the scaley-barked *nedun*, the jak fruit, the *kitul*, the tamarind and the kapok, the latters' dark pods bursting with cottony fuzz. He even had Gopal stop the car for Martina to photograph a monstrous banyan. "The *ficus bengalensis*, Madam. A parasite. It grows on a host tree, strangling it. By the time the host tree dies the banyan can support itself so it puts down aerial roots and sprouts again. You may not believe it but I have seen them as much as one hundred and fifty metres in circumference." I believed him. There was a time when I had dug weapon-pits between banyan roots, using its spaghetti-like tangle of trunks to simulate what the army called "ambush situations".

It was the Ceylon I remembered, the browns and reds and outrageous yellows and the greens, the all-encompassing green, rank and dank and gluttonous, drunk with chlorophyll and forever struggling upward to the light. Yet as we waited at a checkpoint while police interrogated the driver of a truck I learned that it wasn't quite the same Ceylon that I had known. This steamy, fertile island, capable of producing three crops of rice a year, was overpopulated now. Rice was rationed and because of the black market it was illegal to transport rice over the boundary of a province. While Joseph was explaining this Martina slipped out of the car to photograph policemen dragging the protesting driver from his truck.

It was nearly midday when we reached Negombo and tramped across the warm, pink beach to watch men bringing in racey fibreglass boats powered by Japanese outboards. They were charter boats, for hire to tourists from the ritzy hotels that had staked out hectares of prime beach for their private use. The real fishing fleet had come ashore at dawn.

We strolled around, watching women pick silver sprats from the nets while men swabbed out boats and sorted the bigger fish: they didn't appear to have much of a catch, mostly mullet and parrot fish and one steely, streamlined, wild-eyed cadaver that looked like an overgrown Spanish mackerel. The sea breeze was in, so stiff that the crows had to fight it, stroking with slow, laboured wing beats. It was very *National Geographic* picturesque, the pink curve of the bay with blue sea and white wavelets, the dark fuzz of palms and the brown shapes of catamarans and dugouts that looked more like logs washed ashore than craft in which men spent nights far out at sea—one still had its purse-shaped sail raised, drying.

As we walked back to the car Joseph traced the course of an old Dutch canal to its meeting with the lagoon. There wasn't much to see, only a glimpse of murky water reflecting sunshine through the trees, but I did notice three people walking along the road towards us. They were passing under a tree, the leopard pelt of light and shade flickering over their faces so that it wasn't until I had reached the car and they had moved closer into the savage sunlight, that I recognised Amos and Margit. They looked as disreputable as ever, Amos with his baldness and messy beard, his wretched, army surplus clothes and those glasses: Margit with her mouse-eaten hair and plum pudding jeans. Neither of them had their packs. Their companion was bare headed, bearded, pale skinned and wearing a sarong: I took him to be Burgher Dutch until I saw that his feet were bare.

"Hi!"

Amos halted, grinning through moustache and beard, making a gesture which wasn't a salute nor yet a wave, more as though he was swiping at something in slow motion: it was a friendly if rather flashy gesture which I took to signify acceptance. If Margit recognised me she gave no sign, fixing me with a blank-faced impassivity which barely acknowledged me as a human being. Perhaps I wasn't by her standards, having had the indecency to outlive my youth. Their companion stared at me listlessly, the upper part of his face a pale mask above the ferocious, coppery beard; he wore his long hair clubbed behind his head like an eighteenth century seaman. There was the wasted look of recent illness about him while his ankles were speckled with the scars of recently healed ulcers. I was aware of Martina watching them interestedly while Joseph was staring without appearing to do so, his gaze angling obliquely to a crow in a papaya tree yet taking us in passing. Gopal lolled in the driving seat, watching un-ashamedly.

"You found that guy yet?" Amos demanded without preamble. "Your boy, man—you seen him yet?"

"Not yet." Out of the corner of my eye I saw Martina's attention switch abruptly to me and I felt myself flushing.

Amos' grin widened, his glance drifting over Martina, not salaciously, but critical, then swinging back to me.

"Well, he's in Kandy, man. I asked around. He'n' Red here been droppin' together."

Again he effected an introduction with his thumb, as he had done with Margit in Colombo. The boy called Red roused himself, a boney hand plucking nervously at the sarong over his thigh: his voice was moaning and sickly, American.

"Hell, Amos, we wasn't droppin'. Davey don't drop nothin'. He's a Buddha freak. Buddha freaks ain't heads."

"Are you sure it's David?"

Suddenly I was uneasy, no longer caring about Martina's interest: the word "dropping" scared me. It mightn't be David, yet—"Davey". Red shrugged, the movement drawing my attention to the gauntness of his collarbones and I wondered whether he was recovering from malaria: he had that febrile, hollow-eyed look, flesh sweated from his bones.

"Shee-it, man," he mouthed querulously. "The paintin's, that's how. Cree-ative, like Amos said. 'N'he ain't from Stateside nor no Limey so . . ."

"That sounds like him." I cut him short, perturbed by the thought of David consorting with this sickly waif: besides the ridiculous dot-and-carry-one jargon was beginning to irritate me. "Whereabouts in Kandy?"

Again Red shrugged dolefully. "Pandy's, I guess. That's where him 'n' me was rappin'. You dig Pandy's?"

"It's a pad," Amos broke in crisply. "A flop house where the guys crash. Near the Temple of the Tooth, that's why the Buddha freaks go there."

"Yeah, Pandy's," Red echoed. "That was a week ago, if he hasn't gone to 'Ruwa. He was all steamed up to see the Gal Vihara."

"'Ruwa," Amos explained again. "Like Polonnaruwa, man. Very holy. Like *om mani padme hum*."

Again he slammed his palms together, thumbing them to his brow. Red nodded, his haggard, bearded face thoughtful.

"Could be he's at Shang. There's a vihara there, not old-stones junk like 'Ruwa. For real it is. Lotta Buddha freaks there."

"Shang?" I repented blankly for something about the name sounded unreal, not Ceylonese.

"Yeah." Amos spoke flatly and I had a notion that he didn't like telling me. "Shang, the guys call it, you know, like their own name for it. Shangri-La, you dig?"

I dug and nearly laughed. It couldn't be—not Shangri-La! The Lost Horizon! The land where nobody grew old. It was too trite, a mockery, surely, of the great illusion of their immaturity: youth unending, beauty unmarred by time. Yet they had a creepy, dumb-wise humour and it might be their way of sending themselves up. Or was it their earnest romanticism?

"That fix ya?" Amos asked.

Nodding I muttered thanks. Yet what had I learned? David might be in Kandy or Polonnaruwa or Shangri-La. Glancing at Martina I had a startling thought of myself searching for my own Shangri-La.

"Anything for a friend." Grinning, Amos turned away.

"*Ayubowan*," Red intoned listlessly.

Margit didn't speak a word.

The hotel at Anuradhapura was small but modern. Its entrance was flanked by bushes of peacock flowers and elegant fans of travellers' palms. On our arrival a covey of white-coated houseboys appeared, each seizing an item of baggage, so that when we mounted a staircase and trooped the length of the veranda in single file it was like a ceremonial procession with Joseph bringing up the rear.

We had separate bedrooms at the end of the wing and Joseph made quite a ritual of inspecting them, marching into each in turn, looking around, turning on fans, knuckling the beds, of which there were two in each room, even stepping into the bathrooms to test the taps: his snapping fingers sent boys scurrying to draw the orange and black curtains and throw open the doors on to each balcony beyond. I motioned Martina to take the first room and waited while she entered and made a leisurely survey and then, as the seal of her approval, dropped her handbag on the bed: immediately she was at home, going to the mirror and combing her hair. Noting mosquito nets knotted loosely above each bed I decided that I would take a Chlorquin tablet that evening.

My room was a replica of Martina's with the added bonus of a window in the end wall which looked out over a tract of country with one of those reservoirs that Joseph called "tanks" in the middle distance: nearer, a man was driving buffaloes through the slush of a paddy field with white birds swirling around him like snowflakes. Beyond were purple hills with drifts of cloud dragged thinly across them, while away to the left I could see the perfect round of a *dagoba* swelling like a bubble against the dark trees.

"That is the Ruwanweli *Dagoba*," Joseph said, coming to stand behind me. "Very old, built approximately one sixty years B.C."

"And still in use?"

"Oh yes." He nodded in his abrupt, earnest way. "Tonight is full moon and many people will sleep there. They come from all over the country to say their prayers at the Sri Maha Bodhi tree."

Again I recalled Amos mentioning the Sri Maha Bodhi and I would have asked Joseph about it, but just then Martina wandered in.

"You dog, Mason. How did you get a room with a window?"

"Influence," I said cryptically, smiling at Joseph. "But I'm big hearted, I'll swap if it makes any difference."

"Don't strain yourself." Smiling, she sat on the bed, looking very much in possession of the place. She was smoking, legs crossed, her face tipped up at me, sure of herself.

"If Madam wishes I will have the boys," Joseph began, but she cut him short with a wave of her hand.

"He's kidding, Joseph. You wouldn't get Mason out of here with a team of horses now."

Joseph looked mystified. He wasn't used to clients who joked like this yet slept in separate bedrooms. I smiled to signify that we were joking and he nodded, looking only a little less mystified.

"Then, sir, there is one more thing." He retreated into formality, his face suddenly blank. "Tonight the full moon ceremonies will be held at the Sri Maha Bodhi. Gopal is going to say his prayers and he asks if you would like to accompany him."

"Joseph, you doll," Martina exclaimed. "We'd love to go, wouldn't we, Mason?"

I remembered Joseph scrupulously paying his respects to every Buddha and saint we had passed on the road. I imagined he might be a Tamil, in which case he could very well be Hindu or Jain. Or part of the Portuguese legacy of Catholicism? He was shaking his head, flustered yet flattered by Martina's outburst.

"It is not me, Madam," he protested modestly. "It is Gopal. For him the Sri Maha Bodhi is very holy. The oldest tree in the world, 2300 years old, brought from Nepal as a cutting from the very bodhi tree under which Lord Buddha was sitting when he received enlightenment."

"You don't say?" Martina was leaning forward and I thought she was leading him on until I saw the interest in her eyes.

"Oh yes, I do say, Madam," Joseph assured her seriously. "We must leave at sunset, so I will bring the car at six o'clock. And Madam, no photographs, please."

The crowd was quiet. That was the first thing I noticed as I alighted from the car — so many people yet so little noise, only faint sounds of movement and hushed voices as though all the ghosts of twenty-three centuries were astir tonight. It was quite dark but the moonlight was strong and I could see dark files of worshippers converging on the sanctuary, winding between the sooty silhouettes of trees and the stark, upright shapes of ancient stones.

The ruins of Anuradhapura were all around us. Black outlines that might have been terraces; clusters of pillars that had once been pavilions; columns tilting forlornly out of grassy mounds; broken stairways leading to the annihilation of centuries. They appeared diminished, insignificant, quite without meaning at night. Gopal beckoned me, a dim, burly figure in sacramental white, leading the way.

Lights blazed in front of the Sri Maha Bodhi compound — tall metal standards topped with the mushroom globes of sodium lamps. They burned with a harsh brilliance that distorted the colours of the women's saris and tinged the white of the men's sarongs with yellow. I heard Joseph telling Martina that the lights were the gift of a foreign government, German or Thai, I don't know which for I wasn't listening very carefully. The high, cusped facade of the sanctuary's entrance was outlined with electric lights like a Broadway silhouette and there were coloured lights around the gateway. The effect was garish and jarringly modern, the twentieth century's lurid touch cheapening 2300 years of devotion. Beyond the lights rose the shapeless black mass of the sacred bodhi tree, huge and ragged against the stars with somewhere, deep in its centre, a faint radiance lighting twisted, grey boughs, glossing the sheen of leaves. Overhead the moon was yellow, open-faced and huge.

As we entered the outer glow of the lights a small boy accosted me. I expected the usual demand for money but instead he offered me a large white flower. Shamed I accepted it, lifting it to my brow between cupped hands in an imitation of the Buddhist salutation. "French?" he asked, pointing to me, but when I shook my head and said "Australian" he looked so puzzled that Gopal laughed and ruffled his hair. Nearing the entrance I saw that the facade was ornately sculpted with divine beings gracefully posed and smiling benignly from their niches, surrounded by festoons of fat, chiselled flowers while above the gateway a bevy of demigods gambolled blithely: in the glare of the electric lights they looked old and stoney, something cynical about their graven smiles. I wished I could converse with Gopal for I would have asked him who these godlings were and what their place was in this austere faith; but Gopal appeared oblivious of me, face uplifted, lips moving. The crowd was much thicker here, shuffling slowly towards the steps and though they were as restrained as ever I detected a rhythm in their murmurings, like an incantation, and guessed that they were also praying. Their devotion awed me, their tranquility infusing me with an uplifting peace, like calm, cool water carrying me with its gentle flow.

Taking my arm Gopal led me out of the crowd, steering me past the flower sellers' tables with their heaps of red and white and yellow blossoms as well as sheaves of green leaves and posies of tiny flowers. Prowling sweetmeat sellers and soft-drink vendors eyed us hopefully and there were old men peddling bundles of ancient writings that looked like runes inscribed on strips of *nipa* wood. Ignoring them Gopal pointed to his feet and stepped out of his sandals. I kicked off my shoes and stripped off my socks. The ground was warm and gritty against the soles of my feet and I found myself clenching my toes, enjoying the feel of their freedom and contact with the earth in a way that I hadn't been conscious of since childhood. I saw Gopal commission an old man to watch over our footwear. Just then Martina arrived and began removing her shoes, balancing first on one foot and then the other, grabbing my arm to steady herself. I saw her working her toes and when she looked up, smiling, I knew that she too had discovered that closeness of herself to the earth. As I turned to the steps her hand touched my arm, fingers feeling down my wrist, taking mine, squeezing reassuringly. Still holding the flower which the little boy had given me I walked with her up the steps and hand in hand we entered the enclosure of the Sri Maha Bodhi tree.

There were no electric lights here, only scores of tiny, flickering coconut oil lamps set out on the ground. Their weak flames burned tiny, ragged holes in the night, seeming to make the darkness more intense, thickening it with their oily reek. Here and there I could distinguish the shapes of *dagobas* and seated Buddhas and I was aware of trees around me, boughs interlacing overhead, a great rustling bubble of foliage with the glare of hidden lights flooding upwards into the mass of a huge tree. People streamed past us down into a darkened area like a courtyard and Gopal beckoned again. Martina tugged at my hand.

Eagerly she led me forward, a subdued excitement communicating itself to me through the pressure of her fingers: the feel of the earth against the soles of my feet was quite intoxicating, warm and vital, imparting a consciousness of rejuvenation. Looking up I saw that the lights were on a terrace where a flight of shallow stairs ascended to a small porch which I took to be a shrine, for it was decorated with reds and yellows and the saffron splash of a monkish robe. People were climbing the steps and moving around the terrace where I saw more shrines. Then I realised that I was looking at the sacred bodhi tree. It looked so old and immense, its twenty-three centuries of growth rising out of the centre of the terrace as a profusion of convoluted trunks, all gnarled and deeply ribbed, fusing, becoming one, putting forth twisted grey branches which spread so widely that they seemed to become part of the night and the sky with its twinkling stars covering the earth. It was alive with the shimmer of long-tailed, heart-shaped leaves and the murmur of reverent voices. Suddenly I was glad I carried the flower which the boy had given me.

At the top of the steps we had to wait because the crowd was thick around the shrine, men and women with bunches of flowers, children perhaps with just a single blossom, waiting their turn to approach Over their shoulders I saw the figure of the Enlightened One seated in the lotus posture, open hand resting on open palm in his lap, the timeless features enigmatic, staring over our heads into the darkness. People were offering flowers and stepping back to perform their obeisances. Buddhists do not pray as Christians do for Buddha is not a god, therefore he cannot perform miracles in response to prayers, but there is a litany to be recited in his presence. These are excerpts from the principles expounded by the Awakened One during his various reincarnations: they remind the devotee that Man has the power to liberate himself through his own efforts. "One is one's own refuge, who else shall be the refuge," the Buddha said.

Suddenly a shift of bodies admitted us to the shrine and I saw the flowers. They were heaped on an offering table at the Buddha's feet, a great soft bank of living colour, delicate, exquisite, red and white lotus, lilies, jasmine, frangipani: their scent was cloying, their sheer mass and colour dazzling. Dark arms were lifting supplicatingly around us, dark hands laying flowers, flowers fluttering through the light, petals settling lightly like butterflies, flowers tumbling softly down the heap. And the murmur of voices soft as the fall of flowers. I heard Martina exclaiming rapturously and without thinking I laid my white flower in her hands. She looked at me wonderingly and I thought she was going to speak, then she smiled and in the quiet rapture of that moment I knew she was thanking me. Humbly she offered the blossom, first lifting it on the palms of her hands, then laying it on the top of the heap as though it was of special significance. As she did so a woman turned to me out of the crowd, dark, matronly, flashing eyes and peerless teeth, an apricot sari swathing her like a sunset: bangles tinkled on her wrists and rings winked richly as she placed a lily in my hands, gesturing me to offer it. I did so, aware of her at my side as I stood with palms together and touching my brow, head bowed. I heard her voice speaking for me in lilting English. "With these flowers I reverence the Buddha. May the merit help me to liberation." Without hesitation I repeated the words, surprised by the conviction in my own voice. "With these flowers . . ." When I looked around the woman had gone.

Gopal was waiting on the terrace with Joseph fidgeting beside him. Martina slipped her arm through mine and I felt a closeness to her, a sharing of this experience. This close the massive trunk of the bodhi tree was too huge to be seen in its entirety, but the limbs were spindley. I guessed that they were also brittle for some of the boughs were supported by wooden props fitted with iron saddles. The trunk was surrounded by an iron railing which had pieces of rag and squares of cloth tied to it which I presumed to be prayer flags. Inside that railing and slightly above it was a golden railing, very ornate, its tall knurled spikes shaped like temple spires.

Joseph explained that the railings were to prevent worshippers from plucking leaves and pieces of bark as religious relics. People were moving around the terrace while groups had settled themselves, cross-legged, staring at the tree, reciting the hallowed precepts. "May the merit help me to liberation."

We worshipped at three more shrines, bare footed and hand in hand. I say "worshipped" because how else can you describe it when you stand in a shrine and bow your head in genuine respect: I felt my materialism shamed, my old philosophies in need of scrutiny. Martina didn't speak while we walked around the tree but I knew by her silence and by the tranquillity in her face that she was very moved. Several times children approached us timorously, giving us flowers and staying to watch us make the offerings, their huge eyes jubilant. A young woman with a tiny baby laid a white flower on the infant's brow and then passed the blossom to Martina, smiling delightedly when she touched it to her lips before surrendering it to the Buddha. I don't know what it all meant, I don't know whether it meant anything at all except love, goodwill, fellow feeling released on a tide of religious emotion. Perhaps it was the beginning of Enlightenment, Dhamma I think the Buddhists call it.

The last shrine was much bigger than the others with six or eight pillars forming a hall and what looked like a transept where a large Buddha stood with his right hand raised, palm outward in the gesture of blessing. Here several monks watched proceedings impassively and the heap of flowers was much bigger, the crowd much thicker so that we were unable to approach close to the Buddha. Again we had flowers put into our hands and an old man with a silver comb in his knob of white hair patted my shoulder. It was as though Anula's father had approached, long gone to his grave though he might have been, but for an instant I was back in his home at Udugama and I bowed to him instinctively. He returned my salute with courtly dignity and said something which rolled over me like a benediction, then saluting Martina he walked away.

"He said," Joseph translated, "that the moon shines on us. You will benefit from tonight."

After that experience dinner seemed a prosaic affair, an imposition of the body upon the mind. During our absence there had been an influx of tourists so that the dining room was crowded and we found ouselves sharing a table with an elderly Continental couple. They were amiable enough, smiling helplessly from behind the language barrier, but their presence was inhibiting and I was glad when we finished our coffee and excused ourselves.

We emerged into a darkness that was as heavy and as humid as steamed velvet with the night scent of flowers cloying the air. Neither of us spoke as we walked the length of the veranda and by the time we reached Martina's door and waited while she searched for her key I was uneasy, not sure what to do. A gulf seemed to have suddenly opened between us, a gulf which I could not bring myself to attempt to bridge, although I imagined that she expected me to try. She settled my quandary by kissing me, lips lightly, impersonally, brushing my cheek. The closeness of her seemed to open something inside me, releasing a loneliness, that nagging yearning for a woman's company which only a solitary man really knows. Startled, I fumbled for her, wanting her to know and understand my restraints, but she twisted away from me, saying through the closing gap of her door, "Thanks a million, Mason. It was fantastic."

My own room greeted me with impersonal elegance, the decor of other people's choosing, furniture of other people's using — my life! Suddenly restless I stripped and stood naked under the fan. I was at odds with myself, my impressions of the evening still very vivid, words leaping in my mind like schooling fish, yet I was distracted, the feel of Martina's lips still on my cheek, the memory of my tardy reaction angering me. Johnny-Walks-Alone she had called me, not cold but controlled, "I can't think of you falling in love with anything." Yet Janice and David knew otherwise, and even Clare, big, slow-smiling, comfortably-fleshed Clare whom I had denied so glibly. But they were like the furniture in this room, without immediacy to me. Embittered I turned away, deciding to record my impressions of the Sri Maha Bodhi ceremony: I do that frequently, catching a mood when it is in flood, retaining the best of its spontaneity, edited and polished, for future use.

Donning my glasses, I found the notebook that I keep for that purpose and stood reading the previous entry until a mosquito savaged my naked backside, reminding me of the precautions I had decided upon. Laying the notebook aside I lit the mosquito coil on the stand between the beds and dosed myself with Chlorquin. Even that mild exertion started me sweating again so I went into the bathroom and showered, enjoying the coldness needling my face and shoulders. By then words and phrases were begging to be written . . . the humble quiet of barefoot worship, a fragile tumulus of flowers, serenity transcending all loneliness, a tree rooted in the faith of centuries . . .

There was a knocking on the door!

"Who is it?" Surprised I twisted off the chilly flow.

"Me." Faintly, but undoubtedly Martina's voice.

Thoroughly startled I emerged from the shower at a run, wet footed and dripping, fumbling a towel about my waist. Passing the mirror I glimpsed myself, a noticeable paunch, meaty shoulders and pointed pectorals, the flabbiness of advancing years inexorably accumulated, repellent. Changing direction to the door I called, "Hold on. Let me get decent." And heard a laugh as I swung away to swoop on my suitcase, dragging out my dressing gown. It was not only decent but elegant, quite Oriental, bottle green, in judogi style like the judo wrestlers wear: ironically it was a gift from Clare. As I knotted the belt I felt the wetness soaking its back and shoulders, making me feel almost unclothed. I swept the door open.

"You're decent enough," Martina pronounced, surveying me critically. I have never been so painfully aware of my blemishes and the natural inconcinnity of exposed male limbs as then, bare feet and peasant toes, lumpy shanks and knobby knees, damp hair licked thinly over my pate and brow. A trickle of water coursed down under my ear, tickling in the grizzled hair on my chest.

Martina was also decent in a manner much the same as myself, a negligee thin enough to catch the light from my room and disseminate it like a cloud around the darker shape of her body. With wrists crossed ritualistically she held a bottle between her breasts.

"I come in peace, O Great Chief Johnny-Walks-Alone," she intoned sonorously, thrusting the bottle at me and raising one hand, palm outward, in the Indian sign for peace. "How!"

"Any way you like." I was surprised, but caught on quickly, accepting the bottle, noticing that it was bourbon, very American, significant of something I didn't have time to think about just then.

"With water if you haven't got any ice, thank you."

She swept past me in a swirl of bath-salt's scent, flesh-warm and sweetly astringent. The negligee was transparent, purple, tinging the folds of night attire underneath, lying over the paleness of bare shoulders and arms like a darker tint to her skin. It had a lavish ruffle of wide lace around the neck and wrists, circling thickly below her knees. I saw that she wore no rings and that her feet were bare. She stood, looking around, seeing my wet footprints that tracked across the carpet like the Abominable Snowman's spoor.

"You were having a bath?"

I nodded. "It happens from time to time."

And she nodded unsmilingly, as though I had made a weighty pronouncement. I realised then that for all the flippant manner of her entrance she was distracted, listening more to her own uncertainties and compulsions than to me. I closed the door softly, pondering on the bottle of bourbon in my hand: it was less than half full.

"I couldn't face going to bed." She wheeled to face me as I moved into the room speaking breathily, as though in a hurry to deliver herself of the explanation. "Not right away. Not after tonight. So I thought we'd have a drink. You don't mind, do you?"

"Not at all. Sit down."

I dragged a chair around for her, but she sat down on the end of the nearest bed and crossed her legs, the pale, waxy round of a knee and tapering shin bursting through the froth of the negligee's lace. While I was fetching glasses from the night stand where they stood with a carafe of water I heard her light a cigarette and exhale the first puff of smoke wih a breathy sound like a sigh. Neither of us spoke until I had poured and passed her a drink.

"Skol," she toasted gravely, drinking at once.

"Yam seng," I responded, then imagining interest in her lifting brows, added, "That's Chinese. Loosely translated it means 'Bottoms Up'. I used to drink with an old Chinese pearl-skinner in Broome."

"Yam seng then," she acquiesced indifferently and drank again.

And I drank with her, the sweet-sour liquor flaming moistly on my palate. It was my very first bourbon and I imagined that its steely hard, masculine tang would be inconsistent with feminine tastes. Martina was staring at me with a faraway look as though I was something small clouding the greater panorama of her thoughts.

"Wasn't it wonderful tonight!" she exclaimed suddenly, her abstraction reaching its flashpoint. "All those people! They were really high, spaced out! My God! If only I could be like that! Didn't you want to give way to it and just float and float and never be hassled by anyone again, ever?"

Not even by Stephen, I was tempted to ask. For there was a connection, I reasoned, Stephen, her unhappiness, tonight's ecstasy—they were coalescing for her in a confused way. Nor was the bourbon helping, I decided, watching her drink again. And she still loved Stephen, that was obvious. Yet she had divorced him. To fill the pause between us I drank again and then, with the smoke of her cigarette hungering me, I turned away, setting my drink down and reaching for my pipe.

"May the merit help you to liberation," I quoted softly because there seemed to be nothing else to say, those words waiting in my mind to be spoken.

"That's what I mean," Martina declaimed passionately. "Liberation! Freedom! Those people were free. They were poor, yes, many of them, I guess, but tonight they were free, above it all."

My pipe alight I reached for my drink again. "Do you know what the Buddhists mean by liberation?"

She shook her head, a tiny, tense movement like a shiver, eyes quite starry and fixed on me, trusting my knowledge.

"It means freedom from evil—that's the Five Hindrances to the Understanding of Truth—ignorance, conceit, doubt, false views, intolerance. It really means freedom, or the renunciation of mortal vices if you wish to be born again and eventually attain Nirvana."

"And do you believe?" Her intensity was daunting, almost mesmeric, drawing something from me.

"That I will be born again? That there is a Nirvana? No." I shook my head gently, regretfully, for I always feel at a loss in some way when I have to admit lack of religious faith. "You see, I can accept the philosophy but not the worship. I can't pray any more. My mind has had all the piety it can take."

She made a little sound which could have been exasperation or resignation and rising, moved a few brisk steps away from me before whirling and coming back to stand very close in front of me. Again I smelt bath-salts and the ferny scent of her hair. The lace at her throat had rolled back from the tops of small, snub breasts dipping into the pink frill of her night gown, wide apart, with an intriguing cleft flat over the delicate ridging of bone between. Her gaze burned over my face, searching for what I couldn't give. Then, surprisingly, she smiled, her intensity softening as she spoke slowly.

"You're a strange guy, Mason, but I'm glad we're friends."

I shifted restlessly, vaguely irked. "Then how about using my first name occasionally? It's 'David', remember?"

"Uhuh!" She shook her head gently, smiling enigmatically. "I always think of you as 'Mason'. That's how you introduced yourself. 'My name's Mason,' you said and I thought: 'Mason what?' That sort of fixed it, I guess. Anyway —." She laid a hand lightly on my arm, giving it a little placatory shake. "I've met scads of 'Davids' and I guess I'll meet more but there'll only be one 'Mason' for me."

"I think you're conning me," I scoffed softly but she only smiled and thrust her empty glass at me.

"Fill me up again, Mason."

As I took her glass our fingers touched and I was surprised by their coldness, like clay, despite the warmth of her smile. I didn't fill her glass, doling a modest measure instead, ignoring my own.

"Tell me," I began carefully, reminded by the taste of the bourbon still in my mouth, "do you take much of this stuff?"

She pulled a face at me, petulant, wry. "Now you're going to lecture me, aren't you?"

I shook my head. "Just curious. This seems hard stuff for a woman to be drinking, that's all."

"Perhaps I've had a hard time."

"I don't doubt it but this stuff won't . . ."

I checked myself, the depleted bottle sloshing dismally as I wagged it at her. My carping, avuncular tone appalled me. Martina swung away from me, flinging a brooding glance over her shoulder.

"Don't hassle me, Mason," she warned sombrely. "Anyway, haven't you ever been lonely?"

Challenged like that I hesitated, wondering what loneliness was. That irritant lust which drove me to Clare? That restlessness which lured me into heat-smitten outback pubs to drink with some sun-cracked prospector hunching over his beer, or an inscrutable Aborigine, or a policeman, or a stockman, or a dried-up, blowsy barmaid cocking the only white fanny in 250 square kilometres? They provided me with the characters with whom I peopled my fictions, but did they compensate tor the lack of Janice and David?

"I know what it's like," I assured her soberly.

"Maybe you do." She hitched a shoulder indifferently, only half turning to speak. "But not like me, that's for sure. I married it, for better or for worse. And brother, how much worse could it be?" She drank again, recklessly, turning unsteadily, something maudlin about the way she faced me. "You think you know all about it, huh? Well let me tell you, Stephen was a construction engineer. He was always junketing around South America somewhere—Chile, Ecuador, Peru, and once in Alaska. There was always another bridge to build, one more river to cross. But there was nothing for me. D'you realise that? Nobody to come home to me at night, nobody needing me, nothing to do but clean house, go to the supermarket, take in a movie, play bridge with my girl friends. I had nobody to work for. Nothing."

The word reached out to me piteously through the lamplight, uniting us in some way. Nothing! Nobody needing her. I thought of all the nights I'd spent alone, the years of watching David grow up, unable to claim him, listening to Eric's paternal blatherings. My nothingness had been like Martina's, of deprivation, nobody needing me.

"No children?" I probed gently.

She looked at me quickly, eyes huge and almost black in the light: there was naked hurt in them, telling me that I had reached into the innermost recesses of her distress. Then she shrugged with a faked nonchalance, the toss of her head telling me everything and nothing.

"I went back to work, didn't I, got this job at *Odyssey*," she explained, defensively I thought, as though she was arguing something to herself. "It was all right for a while, new interests, new people, travel. I thought I wasn't lonely any more but it didn't help, in fact it only made things worse. When Stephen came home I was usually on an assignment somewhere. He didn't like that one little bit. So he found someone else."

So she had divorced him. So she was lonely, unhappy. The pieces had come together for me, I understood more of the shrew in the gem shop. Suddenly I wanted to hold her and comfort her, join my nothingness to hers so that together we might have something. I think she sensed that impulse for she moved close to me again, waiting. Looking down at her I felt suddenly disoriented, uncertain of myself and her, all those old restraints holding me back again.

"Poor Mason," she mocked softly, after an appreciable pause. "How come a square john like you got mixed up with a neurotic like me? You're slipping, Johnny-Walks-Alone."

I shook my head gently, not taking my eyes off hers. "Not me, Martina. You." I couldn't resist lightly, despairingly, touching the tip of her nose. "It's you who's slipped. If you weren't so lonely you wouldn't look sideways at me, let alone come away with me like this. I told you, lonely people grab at anything."

She stiffened a little, seeming to lift away from me. "And I'm grabbing at you?"

"Subconsciously, yes." I tried to laugh it off but failed dismally. "I'm sure if you got the chance you'd grab your husband back."

"Oh Mason!"

She seemed to come up at me on tiptoes, arms sliding sinuously round my neck, her warmth and woman's softness over small hard bones pressing against me. A woman hunger flared in me. For the first time in my life I felt incomplete, something apart from loneliness, as though part of me had never come to fruition: I wanted to hold and enfold her, taking in all that fulfilling femaleness that had been missing from my male existence. The stranded coolness of her hair brushed my cheek, the blood-heat burn of her face against mine. I kissed her, tasting the bourbon on her lips.

"Oh Mason! You don't know." Lips whispering dryly against the side of my neck.

"I think I do." My hands hungrily raking her back, feeling the firmness cushioning small hard bones: the hardness of her pelvis pushed against mine.

"But you don't know. It was me. I couldn't have children."

Suddenly her body was heaving convulsively and a terrible, demoralising helplessness swept over me. Through the turmoil of my longing I heard her sobbing. Desperately I kissed her brow, her cheek, feeling tears on my lips and when I laid my mouth on hers it was soft, unresponsive, babbling under mine.

"Stephen left me because *she* was pregnant."

It was a moment before the full import of her tragedy burst upon me, then I remembered her hesitation, her too nonchalant nonchalance. But it was too deep and personal, too female and far removed from my experience for me to cope with then. Yet it steadied me, making my craving less erotic. Leading her to the bed I sat down, dragging her with me. She sat meekly within the curve of my arm, turning her face into my shoulder. Taking hold of her chin I turned her face up to mine.

"Martina, you can't go on like this. You're destroying yourself. Stephen's gone. He's got someone else. You've got to face that and live with it. If you don't fight it you'll go under."

Her only reply was to bury her face in my chest again, pressing so hard that I lost my balance and sank backward. She came with me, lying on me, and for a few moments we struggled to make ourselves comfortable on the narrow bed. The negligee had opened and I couldn't ignore the nipple which showed, penny-large and brown through the crumpled nightgown, or the deep fold of her hip and further down, the dark puff of stiff hair. Then my dressing gown opened and the warmth of our inner thighs brushed intimately, the humid places of our bodies pressing together. She was no longer crying, just sobbing softly. I was surprised by my own calm.

After a while my arm began to ache and when I tried to ease it she shifted her head. When I freed my legs she didn't stir but when I lifted myself, she murmured and burrowed into the place where I had been. Easing myself out of bed I stood, looking down, tempted to lay my hand on the smooth round of her hip. She opened an eye, smiling sleepily through the fall of her hair.

"I'm sorry, Mason."

"Try to sleep," I advised softly. "I won't be far away, just in the next bed."

Unfurling the mosquito net I let it tumble over the bed. It smelt faintly of musty muslin, a uniquely tropical smell that reminded me of New Guinea during the war, mud and weariness and fear and the demoralising anguish of homesickness. That also was part of my nothingness. As I tucked the net around Martina I saw that she was asleep.

Next morning the Sri Maha Bodhi was deserted. The courtyard had been swept, every footprint obliterated, every fallen leaf reverently gathered up by the monks, even the blackened cups of the coconut oil lamps emptied and scoured and set back in their racks. The Buddhas, the shrines, the golden railings, the great, over-reaching canopy of boughs—all abandoned to the crows and a couple of old women and a troop of monkeys crashing like hooligans through the hallowed quiet. It should have been commonplace and mundane but it wasn't, not for me, charged as it was with the memory of last night.

I glanced at Martina, wondering whether she shared my mood. She looked dainty in white slacks and a blouse imprinted with dazzling, great flowers, a scarf of saffron yellow over her hair. I couldn't help wondering about her choice of the saffron scarf and flowers. She appeared to be her usual self, except that she wasn't, not to me, for when a man has glimpsed a woman's secrets she never appears the same to him again.

She had left my room some time during the night. When I woke to the sound of birds, crows of course, and a mynah and a rice sparrows and a call that sounded like a magpie's, her bed was empty, the mosquito net dragged aside, the pillow cold. I think I heard her, or at least registered the stealthy sounds of her going in my sleep as a sadness in a dream or one of those unnameable regrets that are with you when you wake. We met at breakfast, each hiding our thoughts behind greeting smiles, mine bedevilled by chagrined second thoughts, Martina's . . . What does a woman think of a man who puts her to bed and then sleeps alone? But we had no chance to talk for the Continental couple were with us again, so we spread carefully laundered small talk like our table napkins, from time to time wiping a secretiveness from the corners of our mouths. It wasn't until we were leaving the Sri Maha Bodhi compound that we were alone together long enough to talk. Joseph had gone ahead to the old man who had minded our shoes while Gopal was lolling in the car, smoking one of his ropey smelling Three Roses cigarettes.

"I'm sorry about last night," Martina began as I helped her over the high step at the entrance.

Smiling, I shook my head to indicate that the incident meant nothing: I didn't want to talk about it, not here, not now. Martina was putting on her shoes, swaying against me to steady herself.

"I really did want to talk to you last night."

"And you did." My shoes on and laced I stamped my feet a

couple of times. Joseph had moved ahead, pausing to wait for us.

"Not like that," Martina insisted. "I didn't figure to end up in your bed."

"You didn't. We slept in separate beds."

She looked up at me, vexed. "Don't try to faze me, Mason. You know what I'm trying to say."

Nodding I looked away to ease my constraint. A few people were moving across in front of us towards the ruins and there was a monk whose yellow was almost an exact match of Martina's scarf. There was also a Japanese in traditional dress —black kimono-like garment, white sash, white pantaloons, white split-toed shoes. I thought of the split-toed tracks in the New Guinea mud. I came out of the beginnings of a reverie that was ugly with old enmities: perhaps one of them lingered for when I spoke my tone was flat, equivocal.

"I think you did all the talking that was needed last night."

To my surprise she smiled mischievously, squeezing my arm.

"Poor old Mason, I must have given you a bad time."

It was the "old" that did it, that and her persistent refusal to use my first name coming when my latent animosity had been aroused by the sight of the Jap. Maybe she meant it affectionately, maybe she just didn't think: maybe I was touchy, but it stung. Shrugging I faked unconcern, matching her candour.

"A couple of times I was on the boil, then the heat went off. I think it was Stephen put the fire out."

Instantly I regretted my spite for her smile faded and what had been free and beginning to open between us closed. We were back where we had started, at odds, uncompromising, the experiences of last night like the Sri Maha Bodhi compound this morning, swept clean. Wanting to make amends I reached for her elbow but she was too quick for me, stepping out briskly to join Joseph.

"Where to now, Joseph?" she asked brightly.

"First we see the Thuparama and the Ruwanweli *Dagoba*, Madam." As usual when he was addressing her Joseph was deferential, heels together, inclining his shaggy head. "After that we tour the ruins and the museum and then we go to Polonnaruwa for the night."

The Thuparama.

"The most ancient of Ceylon's *dagobas*, built to enshrine the

Buddha's Collar-Bone Relic," Joseph intones, sneaking a glance at the tourist brochure.

The heat enfolds us and I have the uncanny feeling that time has ceased, that I am encapsulated in the hot, static present. I wipe sweat from the back of my neck and squint up at the mighty bubble of dazzling white brickwork with a frieze of elephant heads around its base and a few pitiful pillars standing like survivors of a dead forest, tall, attenuated, weather-pitted: it has a wide staircase with extraordinarily shallow steps. Obligingly Gopal poses beside one of the ornately carved guardstones while Martina's camera clicks. As she winds film she catches my eye and smiles, a casual, stranger's smile that is neither friendly nor unfriendly. Along the road behind us a blue and silver tourist bus crawls, slug-like, pregnant with European faces. Joseph sneaks another peep at the brochure and continues, his Anglicised pronunciation as crisp as the print he reads.

"Originally of the 'paddi heap' shape, the present 'bell' shape of this *dagoba* dates from reconstructions in the 1840s. The graceful, monolithic pillars once upheld . . ."

The tourist bus has parked beside our Holden. With its smooth, bloated body segmented by windows, and its goggling headlights it makes me think of a monstrous queen bee mindlessly spawning tourists out of its airconditioned womb. They are big-boned, pink-skinned, northern Europeans as yet only partially cooked by the tropic sun, the women's bosoms medium rare, the men's noses and bare knees frying nicely. They are encumbered with hundreds of dollars worth of photographic equipment and they stare at us through malevolent black sunglasses. One of the men, paunchy, not young, with a pork chop complexion, lifts a movie camera which looks as complex and as futuristic as a spaceman's ray gun, training it on Martina, pretending to pan with her as she walks. "Rudi, Rudi," a frazzled Valkyrie calls. "*Kommen zei . . .*"

We leave, walking through a park-like area shady with sal trees, mimosa and murderous banyans that dangle their aerial roots like garotting cords. More numerous than the trees are the squared shafts of pillars, upright, tilting, or fallen and scattered like spilt matches: in places they have been carefully re-erected to simulate the pavilions and preaching halls they have once been. They are all that is left of the temples and palaces of the sacred city of Anuradhapura. Now it is the corpse of a city, its stoney bones poking out of the earth — shattered stairways, broken balustrades, crumbling walls decorated with carved flowers and lions, the forequarters of kneeling elephants and bands of obese, squatting dwarfs — guardstones like tombstones where aloofly smiling, languid beings bear pots of flowers and sprays of leaves. We pass a royal bathing tank: dainty steps leading down to scummy water where a goat now drinks in the place where princesses once played. Martina's camera records it all relentlessly. We pause to stare at the remains of the Brazen House, no more than a bristle of several hundred closely set granite shafts. "Nine storeys high with a roof of copper," Joseph asserts. I look it over doubtfully, trying to imagine nine storeys: curious, I measure myself against one of the stunted pillars, finding that it is no more than a couple of feet higher than my head, and I am not tall. I picture a small, dark, very devout people living and praying among these doll's-house pillars. The grass worries Martina. It is coarse, with viciously beaked seeds that work into our clothes. Because of that it is called lovers' grass, Joseph explains. I mop my face and look wistfully back at Gopal who is climbing into the Holden which he will drive to . . .

. . . the Ruwanweli *Dagoba*. "Built by King Duttha Gamani, approximately 160 B.C.," Joseph reads. "One thousand metres in circumference and 100 metres high. The spire is seven metres high and plated with gold and that is a diamond on its tip."

Again I crane my neck, screwing my eyes against the dazzle of Joseph's "diamond" which, I suspect, is more likely to be a rock crystal. Yet despite Joseph's exaggeration and the brochure's statistics the Ruwanweliseya is imposing, a great white bell of brickwork that fairly peals with the silent clamour of devotion. Martina's camera clicks. I notice damp patches under her arms. Just then the tourist bus arrives spawning its horde. We take refuge in the Anuradhapura museum.

At least it is cool there among the Hindu brasses and Vedda artefacts and Chinese discs and the thousands of collated fragments of Singhalese history, not to mention the Roman coins. A museum attendant homes in on us but Joseph crosses his palm with something so he leaves us in peace. Martina's glance passes abstractedly over me as we drift, no longer together, among the rows of excavated Buddhas, lying Buddhas, dying Buddhas, teaching Buddhas, preaching Buddhas, standing Buddhas, seated Buddhas, Buddhas without faces, Buddhas without heads,

Buddhas, Buddhas . . .

"The Aukana Buddha," Joseph announced, and before Gopal had
pulled the car to the side of the road he was aiming a seamed,
brown finger, disconcertingly angled, at the top of a jungle hill
which was no different from all the other jungly hills we had been
winding through for the past hour. "Up there," Joseph added
trenchantly.

It was midmorning and hot, and after the soporific purring of
the car the gummy quiet that settled over us was alive with living
sounds, leaving scraping billions of insects screaming like tiny
fire sirens. Somewhere a bird was tonking or perhaps it was a
monkey: gibbons can also make that doleful noise. I would have
asked Joseph, drawing on his Forestry Officer's lore, but he was
already out, bow-legged and spry, buckled shoes treading the
roadside grass to squat at the ditch and flick water on his face.
Gopal was slower, taking time to extricate his broad backside from
the car. Martina got out without a word.

Indeed we had been rather sparing with words all morning,
distastefully flicking them back and forth like unwanted things,
compelled to a stilted politeness by Joseph and Gopal's presence:
for my part I couldn't think of attempting to placate Martina with
them as an audience. But I did try to break the ice, if that metaphor
is appropriate in such a climate.

Since Martina was a travel writer, and I expected travel writers
to show at least a professional interest in the country they
happened to be travelling through, I attempted to draw her
attention to the diversity of farming activities around us, for on
this island which knows no seasons, only the monsoon or the
"dry", and that twice a year, you see planting and harvesting going
on at the same time. Women and girls wade in the flooded paddis,
heads down like browsing cows, pushing each plant into the rich
brown mud. A kilometre further on they will be harvesting, the
paddis drained and yellowing, the women's clothes bright against
the tawny hay, the dark forms of men clambering over the *dagoba*-
shaped ricks. Or threshing on awninged scaffoldings, flailing the
loaded sheaves like birches. Or winnowing, tossing shovelfuls of
grain into the dusty breeze while around them the mud is
sunbaked, hard as a plaster cast, and buffaloes graze on the stubble:

in these places rice husks smoulder like sawdust on either side of the road. Martina had listened to me politely, questioning Joseph about rainfall patterns and farming techniques, scribbling notes that would be unreadable because of the sway of the car. I felt I had gained a certain empathy with Stephen, erring husband though he might be.

Looking up at the greenly seething hill where yet another Buddha waited unseen, I hoped for enlightenment, or at least a few private moments for our reconciliation.

The climb was as arduous as I had expected, the first part a deeply worn track, the rest an expanse of bare rock like a giant's bald cranium into which shallow steps had been chipped. It was quite dizzying to look down on all that jungle, like a gigantic parsley patch. At the summit, where rampant vegetation closed in hungrily on the rock, the ground levelled and there was a dilapidated gatehouse where an ancient custodian dozed in the shade. He requested us to remove our shoes and I donated twenty rupees to the charity box while a couple of scabrous dogs began to fight unpleasantly close to our bare feet. We started off, tender footed and craven, flinching at every soft-soled step, through a rocky dell set with palms to halt under a bodhi tree and suddenly, there was the Aukana Buddha.

More than twelve metres high, with right hand raised in benediction, he had been hewn out of the rock which formed the core and pinnacle of this hill. He stood on a lotus petalled pedestal in a small excavation which was divided by old brickwork into a complex of small, unroofed chambers. To get down to the base of the figure it would be necessary to negotiate a crumbling flight of stairs.

"I'm going down," Martina announced.

She started towards the stairs, treading carefully, bare feet brushing a bank of sensitive plants, the touch-me-not plant Joseph called it because the lightest touch would start each tiny leaf folding up. Joseph, horny-footed, as agile as a goat, skipped ahead of her, descending a couple of steps, holding out his hand. Gopal hitched his sarong above his plump knees, preparing to follow. At the head of the stairs Martina turned and looked back at me.

"Coming, Mason?"

I should have recognised the olive branch that was being held out to me, but I was hot and my feet were sore and a section of those stairs appeared to be no better than rubble. Besides I was comfortable sitting in the shade of the bodhi tree and I wanted to smoke.

"I'll wait for you here," I called, holding up my pipe.

As soon as I spoke I knew I'd said the wrong thing for she tossed her head, turning quickly, taking Joseph's hand. Gloomily I watched her stepping down, cat-footed, an arm outstretched like a ballerina, with Joseph her clownish partner, his big, rough head bobbing and wagging solicitously, stepping down backwards ahead of her, holding her fingertips. I thought of ass-headed Bottom dancing attendance on the Fairy Queen. Gopal waited a while, then plunged down the stairs like a fat Labrador dog, appearing to bounce but in reality stepping nimbly. I lit my pipe and brooded.

Without them it was quiet, a murmurous, softly stirring peace as though all that jungle and those hills were breathing deeply. Overhead a large brown bird side-slipped on rigid wings, one of Joseph's brahminy kites, trailing rasping cries. Sobered I stared at the Buddha—huge, imperturbable, rising out of his native earth—a work of men, yet ruling men, presiding, through the silent centuries, over the purple hills, the empty sky, the steaming, teeming jungle of life. The vast stone face was inscrutable, not even time effacing its smile. The clothing was ritualistic, hanging to the waist in precise folds, falling to the ankles in fluted curves as symmetrical as the fluting on the Parthenon's columns. If the pose was rigid it was the inherently noble bearing of someone who had been born a prince. If the face revealed nothing it was the enigma of life.

Martina came into view, a reduced, pale figure with Joseph bowlegging it at her side, talking, brown arm waving: Gopal followed more sedately. They passed the old chambers, crossing the brown and scrupulously swept forecourt to the feet of the colossus. The saffron of Martina's scarf seemed to bring out the muted detail of the carving, the lotus petals on the pedestal, the large, plump feet with toes as big as bolsters, on the level of her eyes. Turning aside Gopal laid something on an offering table while Joseph dawdled, watching him, leaving Martina to go alone. I saw her reach up and lay something or touch something between the huge feet. Her action seemed to clear something in my lazing mind. Suddenly I saw her as she was, small, alone and troubled, in the presence of something vast and overpowering, reaching. Then Joseph joined her and Gopal arrived to make his obeisance and my moment of perception was gone.

When they returned I was knocking out my pipe, carefully extinguishing embers, for if you have ever experienced a tinder-dry Australian summer you never leave anything smouldering: in this sodden green island, however, it was a wasted precaution, a habit, and no more.

"You should have come with us," Martina said.

"I saw it from here," I answered without thinking.

"Things never look the same from the sidelines."

Double-talk, tart of tone, eyes challenging me. I shrugged, getting myself erect on tender, bare feet.

"I prefer the sidelines."

"I'll bet you do, Johnny-Walks-Alone."

She was right. Much of my life had been spent alone. Not away from the company of other people but alone in my thoughts, always glad to escape into a world peopled by characters of my own making. Yet I was what I had always wanted to become, a writer.

For me that had meant years of seasonal wandering around the north, working hard, living hard, absorbing the sight and feel of everything, then, when "the wet" came down, returning to the city to write while my money lasted. And when it had gone, taking any kind of work and writing at night until the next season came around and I would go off to the north again. Such a nomadic existence had a lot to do with my never marrying because I was seldom in one place long enough to form any lasting associations, besides, I couldn't see the sense of marrying a woman only to leave her for six months of every year. I had listened to too many men emoting in pubs and shearers' quarters, seen the effects of too many "dear John" letters during the war to believe that absence makes the heart grow fonder.

All that time I wrote, slowly, tormentedly and intermittently, for I had a living to earn. By no means a good living by Eric's standards and never a continuous one because of the nature of seasonal work. Yet it was the life of my choosing and I had derived as much gratification from the publication of my first book as Eric had from the establishing of Coleman's Engineering. And now I wouldn't swap all my books for the whole of Australasian Industries. I envied Eric nothing except his right to call David his son.

Janice deplored what she called my feckless existence, for although she understood my urge to write she disapproved of the limits to which it drove me. I liked to think that she still felt something for me because of David and what had been between us years before, and maybe some stirrings of conscience when she thought of what she might have been to me. Eric was frankly critical, seeing my wanderings as further evidence of my shiftlessness and lack of ambition which had prompted me to refuse promotion in the army and which kept me "fiddling around trying to write books". To Eric I was always "trying to write books", never writing them, even though copies of my work were on his bookshelves, each slyly inscribed — "To Janice who believed and to Eric who didn't." He couldn't — or wouldn't — even take that point. I was the no-hoper, the indigent, the instigator of David's mutiny, so my efforts must be denigrated, my achievements never acknowledged. "You reckon you can make a living as a painter, boy," he had flung at David one day. "I tell you you'll starve. Look at Mase and this writing lurk" — it was significant that he used the old army term "lurk" which meant what it sounded like, something shifty, irregular — "he can't even make wages, he's got to go north and work like a nigger every year." Yet in the next breath he had tried to help me in his own obtuse way. "Why don't you turn it in, Mase? Going up north, I mean. Just say the word and I'll fix you up with something at the factory any time you like." But I had fixed the horns fairly and squarely on his brow and I couldn't accept his bounty . . .

. . . besides, the north and its freedom had become my lifestream — the pubs I had drunk in and the men I had drunk with, the discussions I had shared and the fights I had lost, the camps I had lived in and the dust I had swallowed, the cards I had bet on, the horses that had thrown me, the women I had slept with. They are all in my books, prospectors, shearers and bar-maids, stockmen, Aborigines and station folk and fly-by-night *munjongs* of every persuasion in a huge, silent land of red sunsets and purple hills, grey-green spinifex and chest-high pindan grass and semi-tropical billabongs where flights of birds splash down in snowy clamour and there are flies and heat and killing distances and a freedom so intense that you can become quite drunk on it. One is one's own refuge, the Buddha said.

That night, at Polonnaruwa Rest House, we dined on wild boar within a stone's throw of the ruined palace of King Parakrama the Great — 1186 A.D. according to the legend on the map of the ruins in the foyer of the Rest House — philosopher king and ardent agriculturalist who developed the natural fertility of this region until it became known as the Rice Bowl of Ceylon.

To do this he created the Parakrama Samudra, the Sea of Parakrama, by flooding a valley, restraining the waters with a colossal earth dam called a "bund", eight to ten kilometres long and rising ten metres above the surface of the water, with a roadway traversing its summit. Looking at it I pictured legions of small, brown, sweating bodies, conscripted at King Parakrama's command, toiling in ant-like files, each dumping his infinitesimal basketful of earth. At least it was an enterprise more worthy than the pyramids. Joseph ordered a detour so that we could see a statue reputed to be a portrait of the king. Cut out of an outcrop of rock about five metres high it was of an elderly, bearded man, naked to the waist, paunchy, holding what looked like a strap but was really an ancient form of book. The puffy face was not kindly, heavy-lidded eyes, broad nose, thick lips imperiously parted. I expected a face less cruel for the builder if the beneficent Sea, but perhaps kindness on that scale requires cruelty.

We found the Rest House swarming with tourists, a busload of streaky-haired women and meaty men who seemed too proud to respond to a friendly nod: meeting them in doorways the men would look right through me while the women's faces would set like fast-drying cement if I happened to meet their eyes. Signing the Visitors' Book I read some of the addresses which preceded mine — Paris, Hamburg, Rotterdam, Bruxelles. Common Market folk.

Fortunately our rooms had been reserved, once again adjoining, with a common balcony jutting over the water, divided by a low, iron railing. There were flowering bushes all around and an angular frangipani tree clutching leafy fistfulls of buttery flowers. In my room the fan had a burned-out bearing which caused it to wobble eccentrically. But the view through the french windows was superb.

It was almost sunset, the purple water of King Parakrama's Sea suffused with pink, wooded islands floating on their black shadows, the silhouettes of distant hills and a flight of pelicans coasting low like a dribble of white from an artist's brush. The cawing of the crows had taken on a quarrelsome note for their nightly contest for roosting places had begun. Were I blind in Ceylon, I would know when it was evening by the clamour of the crows. Showering, I changed my clothes, admired the view, read some of my notes and then, driven by a restlessness which permitted no inspiration, went to the bar.

I found it taken over by Common Market folk who had occupied every chair they required and heaped the adjoining tables with their photographic gear. Their clamour was not unlike the crows', raucous, demanding, generally jostling for attention: there was a good deal of overt, horsey flirting going on. Armed with a beer I retired to the patio where I found a seat at a table which held an expensive aluminium tripod, flash gear and a telly lens as big as an admiral's spyglass. Village women were bathing in the tank, knee deep in the pink-dark water, their wet hair hanging like ebony ropes, their white cotton bathing cloths clinging to the brown nakedness beneath. Some men were photographing them, fiddling with light meters or panning whirring movie cameras. I wished I had pocketed my pride and invited Martina — on second thoughts no, not in her present mood, with the Common Market folk for an audience. The dinner gong curtailed my loneliness.

I wasn't able to talk to her over dinner for by the time she joined me, bathed and dainty and distantly polite, we were sharing our table with a French couple. I assumed they were French for in the girl's rapid chatter, between outbursts of hectic hilarity, I heard words like *"oui"* and *"non"*. She had a rosebud delicacy and a fair face like an angel who had changed her mind and become a model. She postured blatantly in her cheesecloth blouse through which large, brown nipples poked smudgy studs. Her consort was a burly man, with the meaty, battered face of a veteran gladiator and curly, black hair like astrakhan. He wore a gauzy, Hindu shirt and skimpy briefs that bulged as prominently as an Elizabethan codpiece so that when he walked he paraded his testicles like a pedigreed bull. He seemed as proud of them as he was of the enormous cine camera which he brought to the table like a small boy who refused to be parted from a toy. Between courses, and some perfunctory billing and cooing with his girl friend, he played with the thing, pretending to photograph waiters and other diners, once almost wiping my face with the flaring rubber hood of the light shield. I dubbed him "Nackers". While he carried on his love affair with his camera, his genitals and his girl friend, and while the waiter hovered around, piling more food on our plates, unasked, Martina and I ate steadily, silently, like a long-married couple chewing unpalatable restraints. She excused herself first, not waiting for me, murmuring something about having to write copy. I followed soon after without Nackers or his girl friend aware of my departure.

In my room and stripped off to my dressing gown I sat down on the bed to write my notes. Overhead the fan wheezed and wobbled in off-beat circles and since someone had tied the light cord to its shaft, presumably to bring the light directly over the bed, shadows surged in dark sweeps, objects around me capering like figures in an Indonesian puppet show. Forcing myself to concentrate I wrote: "Polonnaruwa flourished *circa* 12–14 A.D. after incursions of warlike Tamils from southern India made government from Anuradhapura impossible . . ." At that point a watery splashing caught my attention and I listened to it several more times before laying aside my notebook and going out on to the balcony to investigate.

It was a fisherman—a humped, black shape in the black shape of a canoe—casting his purse net into a moon beam, netting moonshine. It was a picture postcard scene, black water and the golden reflection of a moon as big and as bright as a tray of Benares brass with sounds coming mutedly over the lake and the scent of frangipani heavy in my nostrils. As I turned to go inside I saw the light from Martina's room through the french door. Had I been younger, more adventurous, thicker of skin, I would have gone to her, brazening it out. Certainly the rail dividing our balconies would have been no obstacle. Instead I returned to the bed, picked up my notebook and tried to recall my impressions of Polonnaruwa as we had driven through its ruins that afternoon—richly ornamented sections of crumbling walls and decaying *dagobas* that had looked mouldy because of the trees and bushes growing out of them, many with great bites into their brickwork cores where the Portuguese had ripped them open in search of treasure. That was 'Ruwa, as Amos had called it in his truncated lingo. "Old-stones junk." Remembering David then, I had asked Joseph about the Gal Vihara and he had assured me that we would be visiting it the next day. Madam would like the Gal Vihara, he had predicted gravely. That brought me back to thinking about Martina. She . . .

. . . came through the french doors so quietly that I didn't know she was in the room until I heard the click of the latch.

"Good evening."

Somehow I kept surprise out of my voice, sitting very still. She didn't answer, just stood leaning back against the doors, watching me. I saw that she was wearing the purple negligee again. I was conscious of the light and the fan creaking on its clapped-out bearings: the shadows of its blades circled the room in erratic surges, lapping like dark splashes around her bare legs and feet.

"What are you writing?"

"A few notes. I always keep notes wherever I go."

"Am I in it?"

"You get a mention along with the Sri Maha Bodhi and Colombo and the elephants . . ."

"Thanks a lot! You're . . ."

". . . and the beggars and Joseph and the ruins."

" . . . so good for my ego, damn you!"

"You're welcome. I always record the weird and wonderful things because I work from my journals when I start writing."

"And what have you written about me?"

Her vanity amused me and I smiled, closing the notebook, removing my glasses, folding and laying them aside. Whatever happened I wouldn't be writing any more tonight. There was a tightness in me, like an overwound spring, each creaking turn of the fan seeming to wind it tighter.

"You know what I think of you," I stalled. "If it's any consolation to you you're referred to as 'M'."

"You're unreal, Mason! You really are the last of the great lovers," she cracked bleakly.

She shouldered away from the doors in a violent little movement that caused the lace to open, exposing a dipping triangle of bosom. Then she was walking towards me, bare feet stepping neatly through the swirling shadows: the ruffled lace rolled heavily between her legs, a bare knee, the pallid smoothness of an inner thigh breaking through. Halting she looked down at me, so close that I could see bare flesh through the negligee, no night gown underneath tonight.

"You like to make me sweat, don't you," she accused softly. "You sit there, naked as a jay bird, and kid me you don't give a damn. And so help me, I don't think you do! Not one lousy kind word do I get, just 'you're referred to as 'M'!'"

She rolled her head, mincing the last words savagely, black hair jerking about her shoulders. The negligee opened, only the sash holding it together at the waist, giving me a view up the flat, pale valley between her breasts and the creamy sweep of belly below with its springy pad of dark hair wisping between the thighs: her navel peeped me like a lone, spying eye.

"Sit down," I invited levelly, watching her face.

She stiffened, breasts lifting a little more into view, thighs tensing but standing firm.

"Sit down, for God's sake," I snapped roughly.

For a moment I thought she was going to defy me, then she closed the negligee and sat down, her hands resting limply in her lap. At once the negligee fell open again, baring her knees and tightly pressed thighs, legs with ankles crossed. Seated, back arched, bosom high, flat tummy drawn in and head half turned to stare at me past one shoulder she looked like the playmate of the month posed for the centrefold of a men's magazine. The mainspring of my excitement began to unwind, some sort of balance wheel of past experience controlling the urge to fly apart.

Without speaking I reached out and peeled the negligee from her shoulders. She neither resisted nor assisted me, sitting very still until I had her naked to the waist, but when I untied the sash she leaned forward slightly, withdrawing her arms from the sleeves. The movement made her breasts stir delightfully and I couldn't resist kissing one nipple, feeling its dryness slightly textured between my lips: her flesh smelt warm, of secrets, faintly scented.

Suddenly her arms were round my neck, pulling my face into that soft, warm cleft, her hands sliding hungrily over my shoulders and back. Murmuring, she began to rock me, but I kissed her and at once her tongue came, warm and moist, avidly working into my

106

mouth. I strained over her but she lay back, dragging me with her and when I slid my thigh between hers she promptly gripped it so that I felt her soft, wirey place beating warmly against my flesh. Suddenly we were struggling to settle ourselves in the bed, heaving, limbs tangling, and laughing, laughing and kissing, big wet-mouthed kisses like children. Vaguely I heard my notebook fall to the floor.

"Who's David?" she asked later, stirring in my arms.

Lying face to face I felt her humid body twisting against mine. For a moment the significance of her question didn't occur to me for I was drifting in a half sleep of satiation. I merely wondered with fleeting irritation why women always wanted to talk after making love.

"I asked you — who's David?"

This time she lifted herself, a brutal tearing out of my embrace, warm softnesses rubbing damply over me. Propped on one elbow she shook my shoulder. Wide awake now I resolutely kept my eyes closed: I couldn't remember telling her anything about David.

"I'm David. Don't you remember?"

"You're Mason," she pronounced dismissingly. "Who's David?"

I felt the bed dip under me, then hair brushed my cheek as she kissed the tip of my nose, honeying the vinegar of her insistence: when I didn't open my eyes she kissed my lips, the tip of her tongue working lasciviously. I opened one eye.

"Why do you want to know?"

"Just curious. I heard those weirdies at the beach that day."

Of course — Negombo! I opened both eyes then. Her face was very close to mine, blotting out all else for me. The tip of her nose nudged mine, once, twice, persuasively.

"That kid, Red," she murmured. "He was yakking about Davey, but you said 'David'. And you were so uptight. Come to think of it, that's the only time I've seen you lose your cool — except tonight."

Smiling, she placed a fingertip on my left nipple and pressed as though she was pressing a lift button: sated though I was it sent a tremor of shock through me and I reached for her, but she was ready for me, elbowing my arm aside, slapping it flat on the dished, fatty round of her bottom.

"Down, boy! Who was it, huh?"

"A lad I know. His mother asked me to look him up while I was here."

"His mother! Your wife, huh?"

"I said 'his mother'."

Scowling I grabbed a handful of her backside and she gasped, jerking, that fuzz of pubic hair scrubbing my belly.

"Do that again," I invited, grabbing again and she convulsed again, snatching wildly at my hand.

"Mason! Cut it out! You're too . . ."

Checking herself abruptly she stared at me uncertainly across the gap of years between us. It was a strained, still moment of ghosts and regrets and unspoken thoughts while the fan creaked dolefully like the world turning wearily on its worn out axis. Quickly she lifted my hand, pressed her lips against its palm.

"Too what?" I kidded bleakly for now was the time to face this thing. "Too old? There's many a good tune played on an old fiddle. How would you like another violin concerto?"

Again she kissed the palm of my hand, rather extravagantly, I thought, as though she was grateful to me for passing the moment off with no more than irony. Huddling, she snuggled my hand between her breasts.

"You're really far out. You know that? I bet you could perform like Mantovani's Strings even now."

"Even now?"

Catching the implication I had cocked an eyebrow. Even now. This age thing would always be with us, constantly cropping up in such unguarded remarks.

"I'm sorry," she whispered. "I'm nosey. I guess I'm just a bushy-tailed bitch. I hassle people all the time, Stephen said."

So we were back to Stephen: but I couldn't take much more of him, especially now, like a ghost listening to our pillow talk.

"Oh, you're bushy-tailed all right," I assured her softly. "But it's a very nice piece of tail. As for being nosey, well, there's not so much to tell. I've known David and his mother for a long time. She's worried, that's why I'm looking for him."

She eyed me steadily. "His mother—Anula, huh?"

I was surprised, then I remembered telling her about Anula at breakfast that morning, exaggerating flagrantly because I hadn't quite forgiven her for her tantrum in the gem shop and I knew that no woman enjoys hearing another woman's praises so blatantly sung. But Martina was doing her own arithmetic — one-from-two-makes three sort of arithmetic.

"You're way off the mark," I told her. "That was more than thirty years ago and David is only twenty-one. Anyway, Anula and I were just friends. Her father was our interpreter and he took us home to dinner quite often. Anula was nice, I liked her. We'd been overseas for two-and-a-half years then and it was a change to talk to a girl who wasn't a whore or a commission shark. I was engaged to a girl at home at the time, David's mother as it happened. Not that anything came of it. It was my mate, Eric, who scored."

"He was a fink, huh?"

I nodded feelingly. "And then some."

"And you missed out?"

"You could say that. I got a 'dear John' letter breaking it off."

"You mean he canned you?"

Again I nodded, morosely this time. "A remark in a letter he wrote to her, perhaps several remarks in several letters. Anyway, Janice had enough to quote chapter and verse so that was that. Funny thing though, Eric married her when we got home."

"Funny," she mocked.

I smiled bitterly. It was funny, funny-trivial when viewed from this distance in time. All the emotion, the despair, the terrible feeling of emptiness and loss which had caused me to go back to New Guinea a second time in much the same frame of mind as those lovelorn young men who joined the Foreign Legion in an earlier age. What surprised me was that I could talk about it so easily, as though it was something that hadn't really happened to me, yet was a personal experience, like the plot of one of my own novels.

"And you're still buddies, huh?" Martina queried.

"Were," I corrected. "He's dead now, killed in a road accident."

"And now you're looking for his wandering boy. Quite a scenario. Makes mine look like women's magazine stuff."

"It's got its angles," I conceded dryly.

"So I'm thinking." She twisted in my arms, craning her neck to look at me thoughtfully. "You wouldn't still have a hankering for this Janice, would you, even after all these years? Not one little lech? After all, you're still a very salty guy. Ask me if you want a testimonial. And now that her husband is dead . . ."

"Steady on." I laid a finger sternly on her lips. "I'll be honest with you, since we're baring our hearts along with everything else. There was a time when I tried to take her back. It was a long time ago, before David was born, and Janice was very unhappy. I think she would have come with me if I hadn't overplayed my hand. But that's another story."

"A bedtime story?" Her eyes twinkled wickedly. "Do tell. I love those kind of stories."

"Not for publication."

I smiled bitterly, suddenly finding that I could no longer talk about it so easily . . . my stupidity, rushing her like a love-sick boy. Taking advantage of her when her marriage had been at its lowest ebb was what Janice had accused me of doing on the only occasion when she could bring herself to talk about it. So distraught and frightened, really hating me that day. And looking back on it now I knew that that was just what I had done—watched their marriage ebb. Each year, when I had returned from the north, Eric had looked more prosperous, a little more girth, a little less hair, his laughter a little more forced, his talk more weighted with words like "productivity", "the market", "contracts", "per-unit cost" uttered in a voice ever louder with success. And always there had been a drink in his hand. Or there were poolside barbecues when fellow executives and their brassy consorts came to drink Eric's liquor and chew incinerated mutton, the computerised hum of commerce in their talk, their laughter loud with the ring of cash registers, while over them all the dollar sign had hung like a rising moon.

Frequently Eric had been away—more and more frequently—"in the East",—Sydney, Melbourne and several times to Canberra, "to see some politicians". Forever chasing contracts, setting up contacts, wheeling and dealing, changing. And Janice had changed, thinner, little lines appearing around her eyes, a twist of discontent beginning to shape her lips permanently. She laughed less frequently, watched Eric with longer, more assessive glances while I had detected the flat note of disinterest in her tone. At the pool parties she had been a competent hostess, charming, sophisticated, yet never anything more than a hostess. I had imagined that she welcomed me with warmer than old-friend kisses. That was why I hadn't been surprised when I heard that she had left Eric, going not to their holiday house at Mandurah but to a beachside motel at Cottesloe because, she had told me, she "wanted to think it out in some place where nothing belonged to Eric".

"I should have known what would happen," I said, more to myself than to Martina.

"You should have dumped her," she pronounced briskly. "Just packed your bags and walked out."

It was easy for her to say that. She was young, impatient, not yet acknowledging the habit of life's associations. Yet divorced though she might be, she still carried her ex-husband's photograph. Of course I should have walked out on Eric and Janice, but in those first years when we came back from the war our lives were topsy-turvy. Mine was, anyway. Eric's wasn't so bad, he had Janice. Most married men were the same, they had wives to go back to, homes to settle into. But not men like me. Many of us found that our old lives had been wiped out, old friends gone or married, or we found that we no longer had the same interests. Six years of war can change a man. You find that you don't think the same as the people who stayed at home. And what was worse, many of them seemed to resent us: they were defensive, as though they felt that we imagined ourselves better because we had gone through a war. Also a lot of us couldn't settle back into our old jobs. We'd seen too much, the residues of violence and change still potent in our blood. Besides, the men who hadn't gone away had been promoted in our absence so that in many cases we came back to find ourselves taking orders from someone much younger. That's why so many ex-soldiers hung around the pubs, because the pubs were the only places where they found congenial company. And that's why I kept coming back to Eric and Janice. They were my kind of people, we could talk without making each other uncomfortable, for those first few years, anyway . . . and after that there had been David.

"It was all right until Eric's business began to expand," I said slowly. "After that he was away from home a lot, chasing deals."

"Don't tell me, let me guess," Martina murmured bitterly.

"That's right. He left her at home too much. Business began to mean more to him than his home life. It's understandable I suppose. A man works for his family, but when no family comes along he finds himself working for the sake of creating something.

It becomes a substitute for a family. God knows why they didn't have children. It was Eric, of course, he couldn't . . ."

I caught myself in time. I had spoken too positively, almost giving myself away with David's birth unaccounted for. Seeing her eyes clouding thoughtfully I hurried on.

"Anyway, as he began to do well he hit the bottle, not a real alcoholic's drinking, but a good steady intake every day, entertaining clients or just stowing it away at home. Their marriage was very shaky for a while. At one time Janice left him."

"Ah, that bedtime story!" Martina perked up cynically. "I knew we'd get around to it some time."

"You want to hear the sad, sad story of my life? Well, shut up and listen," I growled. "Anyway, when David was born that pulled the marriage together. Then Eric became big enough to hire other men to do his travelling, not the really important trips of course, but he wasn't away from home so much. And he cut down on the drinking, not altogether because he'd reached the stage where much of his business was done over drinks. In fact that's what killed him, driving home on wet roads with a skinful of booze after a company dinner. And now David is here in Ceylon and I'm looking for him. End of story."

"Except for the moral." She smiled knowingly, putting her face close to mine. "It has a sting in the tail, hasn't it? And speaking of bedtime stories and tail—David's really your son, isn't he?"

I suppose I wasn't surprised to hear her say it. After all I had talked enough, and carelessly: it didn't require genius to guess David's relationship to me. Nevertheless it was a shock to hear her speak the words which I had never dared to release beyond my own thoughts. "David is your son." It was different from me faking the relationship as I had with Amos in Colombo: this was an acknowledgement by another person of the most important thing in my life. Suddenly I wanted to get up and smoke, walk around, savouring the significance of that utterance. "David is your son." Instead I tenderly kissed Martina's brow.

"It's a wise child that knows its father," I quipped jauntily, amending, "And an even wiser father who knows his child."

"And you think you know?" Ignoring my levity she regarded me gravely.

I nodded emphatically, too long convinced to doubt now.

"But how can you be so sure?" she queried.

I looked away, exasperated by her obtuseness. Oh Martina, sweet, lovely, fucksome Mrs Gale, must I tell you how, when Janice left her husband that time, I went to that beachside motel, intent on persuading her to come away with me; how I undressed her and caressed her, rousing in her that response which she has been ashamed of ever since. How we made love until our bodies seemed to burn away. That is your bedtime story. That's how I overplayed my hand, frightening Janice with my ardour. And how do I know her child is mine? Because she and Eric had been married for ten years then, nor have they had any children since. Because Eric, who could develop a back street workshop into an organisation with nationwide affiliations, who could buy and sell me over and over again, who looked on me with an old friend's fond contempt because he considered me to be a loser—and hadn't I lost Janice to him?—was himself the greatest of all male losers. He was incapable of having children!

I stirred uneasily, shocked to realise the intensity of the bitterness which had accumulated in me during the years. From time to time I had felt animosity for Eric storming up but I had always tried to be a good loser, never suspecting the growth of this thing which had burst in me now. It was as though an old ailment had suddenly revealed itself to be malignant. Martina stirred beside me, reminding me that I hadn't answered her question: still shocked by my discovery I answered distractedly.

"You wonder why I'm so sure he's my son? Well, she christened him 'David', didn't she?"

The Gal Vihara, next morning, with sunlight so bright that it scalds the eyes while the heat, like laser beams, burns through my shirt. The three great Buddhas, upright, seated and recumbent, stare through the glare of centuries, their expressions aloof yet watchful, faintly bored, like fagged-out vigilants.

I am surprised. From Amos' talk I had expected a temple or the ruins of a temple. Instead, this is a grassy vale with some twisted, fragile-looking trees, grey as lepers' scars, which Joseph calls *palu* and *kolon* trees, shading one ridge while on the other is an escarpment of streaky granite from which these three huge figures have been hewn. There is also a small cave shrine with pillars and the customary drip-ledge. The colour and texture of the stone are extraordinary, a delicate grey-green with watery striations like *verde antico* marble. Cunningly the artists and stone-cutters have followed these streaks so that the serried folds of the sculpted garments sweep naturally, leaving the exposed stone flesh looking aged and lined.

I glance around, hoping to see David, but Common Market folk are everywhere, bright synthetic colours in checks and florals and psychedelic swirls, the twentieth century's technological achievement flitting frivolously over the twelfth century's priestly skill. Yet the ancient saffron of a Buddhist monk, hunched and watchful under the trees, blazes like a sunburst, outshining all the laboratory dyes of Christendom. Occasionally he shouts harshly and waves a skinny arm whenever a photographer goes too close or a pretty girl ventures to pose on the Enlightened One's gigantic toes. On a nearby rock the tour guide—tutored and Teutonic and brought from home—hammers information at his charges through a loud-hailer: the bull-horn is eminently suited for the projection of his harsh language, hurling metallic cadences which are as sharp and as demoralising as the spears of the Kalinga Tamils who once devastated this place.

And all around is the "old stones junk" of 'Ruwa, silent in the heat and the shadows of trees. Ruins get to me, subtly eroding my complacency, chastening me with their aura of inevitability. They whisper of what we might have been and what we will become. They are a commentary on mankind. All morning we have been among them, motoring from one pile to another, walking around, awed by their magnitude, saddened by their melancholy. The Lata Mandapaya, the Lankatilaka, the Siva Dewale, the Kiri Vehera—those names tune into my fondness for this island. There is also a palace whose name I didn't catch, once seven storeys high, Joseph insisted, and certainly evidence of two storeys exists—holes where flooring joists were bedded in the brickwork—the rest a beehive of tiny, cell-like rooms opening into one another. I think of dainty, little palace women, brown as smoked honey, lovely as *apsaras*, stirring secretively in these crowded cubicles. And those narrow streets of Pompeian silence passing between crumbling platforms of brick! Except for some workmen restoring the gateway of the city's three concentric walls the only other living things we encounter are birds and long-tailed, grey langurs with incredibly ugly old men's faces, gibbering rancorously at us. And then the

Common Market folk.

By now we have walked the length of the Gal Vihara and are staring at the reclining Buddha. He is in the posture of dying, Joseph tells us, the position of the feet reveals that, the left one slightly drawn back so that the toes of the right foot project further: the dying Buddha is always represented thus, as well as by the treatment of the eyes. There is an aura of ineffable repose about the figure, the great head slightly depressing the stone pillow while the pendulous ear lies along the jaw, taking the curve of the seraphic face. The pillow is embroidered with sun symbols, the wheel of the Universal Monarch, as are the soles of the feet. The Chakkra, or wheel symbol, derives from the sun lighting the earth during its circular course through the heavens, thus symbolising the spiritual domination of the Buddha as well as the doctrine set in motion by him during his first sermon. Joseph is explaining this, but as I have read it all several years ago I look around idly, sighting a freak.

A buddha freak!

He is past me and walking away when I first see him, but there is no mistaking what he is. In that gathering of bright shirts and bare knees, bare arms and gaily patterned skirts, sunglasses and guidebooks and expensive cameras he is conspicuous for his simplicity. Almost like Christ among the Pharisees. His sarong is a washed out red, his white shirt hangs about his hips, his feet are bare, his hair is tied behind his head: he has nothing in his hands. He is dark like David. And about David's height, while something about his bearing suggests David's strength, David's princely assurance and youth. Here at the Gal Vihara as Amos had predicted.

Without thinking I go after him, shouldering my way through the Common Market folk. They appear to be more interested in him than they are in the Buddha, turning to stare as he passes. He ignores them, walking serenely, as though he is alone in a wilderness. A young man focusses a camera on him. A young woman says something that bubbles throatily while the huge, black rounds of her glass-covered eyes glint above her mildly derisive smile. Then a fat, rubicund man wearing an inadequate straw hat, with a Leica dangling from his neck, accosts the freak. As I near them I hear the man talking in a foreign language. The freak is nodding.

It can't be David. David speaks no German or Dutch or French or Esperanto—no other language than English.

Bitterly disappointed I return to Martina who watches me approach. Joseph is explaining something else, pointing to the Buddha's face, moving a few paces one way, then the other.

"The eyes, Madam," I hear him say as I join them. "Always the eyes of the dying Buddha are carved so that when you approach from the feet the eyes appear to be open but if you come from the other way they appear to be closed. And the . . ."

"Not him, huh?" Martina greets me and I shake my head dumbly.

The Hun with the bull-horn starts roaring again.

We go on to the Vatadage.

"The Watadargie"—thus Joseph pronounces it as we alight from the car in the shade of some trees, leaving Gopal to have another snooze—"is quite old but its *dagoba* is before Christ."

And by Christ it looks it, I muse testily, perspiring profusely, deciding that this is our hottest day so far. The skies are no bluer than before, the sun no larger or closer, yet there is a baleful quality about its heat, as if it is disgusted by this race of humans it has sustained for so long and so is now setting about scorching them out of existence. Leaves hang motionless in the transparent density of the heat, but somewhere a coppersmith bird—so Joseph calls it—is tonking away with lunatic zest. Its enthusiasm makes me feel old. I glance at Martina: damp soaks darkly under her arms while the car seats have left a soggy patch above her buttocks. I think of them as I saw them last night, plump and bare, filling my hands delightfully. But it is too hot to think of that now. Mason, you are old!

The Vatadage enshrines a small, broken *dagoba*, certainly pre-Christian, a mouldering mound of child-sized bricks on a circular platform which is of later construction. Several rows of octagonal pillars surround it, those of the outermost ring being joined by a carved balustrade which contributes to the platform's drum-like appearance. It is approached by an oblong ramp which is detached from the platform, the empty space being bridged by a small staircase. The stairways are wide, their shallow risers decorated with kneeling dwarfs, corpulent beyond belief, resting their bellies on the ground. And the guardstones are superb, graceful, arrogant figures deeply incised, each with the seven-hooded cobra fanning over his head, a pot in his right hand, a sheaf of greenery in his left: each has a pair of dwarfs gambolling around his feet.

As we approach I see that the place is deserted, no Common Market folk, no gargantuan, queen-bee buses parked near, their airconditioning snoring petulantly. No Buddha-freaks either. I catch Martina watching me, eyebrows raised questioningly and when I shrug she shrugs. Apparently she is taking an interest in my search and that pleases me. Just then an attendant materialises from somewhere and motions to us to remove our shoes. What was it Amos said? "Any heap of stones has the Buddha-man's face on, it's holy." Barefooted, I feel the earth, hot and dank, as though I have placed my foot between a woman's thighs. Mother Earth?

Within the shrine four thick-limbed, black granite Buddhas sit, cross-legged, palm resting on open palm, back to the *dagoba*, staring broodingly out to the four cardinal points of the compass. There is something rudimentary about their workmanship, square shoulders as wide as crosstrees, hair delineated like a cap, clothing without folds while each bared right breast has a nipple like a baby's comforter, a disc with a teat. As I walk from one to the other of the figures I notice someone strolling between the trees. It is the Buddha freak from the Gal Vihara: I recognise the particular red of his sarong. My first thought is that he has made good time arriving on foot so soon after us, then I recall that we stopped at a coconut vendor's stall. Nevertheless I marvel at the hardihood of this youth, walking all that way, bare headed, barefooted, in this heat. They deserve to attain something, these boys, for they have a true penitent's lust for sacrifice.

It is even hotter here away from the trees, for the brickwork forms a cauldron in which the air stews. There is only a small hemisphere of shade thrown by one of the curving walls and we cluster in it jadedly. In the periphery of my vision something moves and I do not bother to turn for I have identified its red as the lad from the Gal Vihara stepping down into the well which separates the ramp from the shrine itself. The coppersmith bird tonks incessantly, a rich, mellow sound, like a copper bowl being beaten with a wooden mallet: it is its trip-hammer beat which irritates me.

Mopping his brow with a tartan handkerchief Joseph informs us that we go on from here to Sigiriya. Has Madam heard of Sigiriya, the Lion Rock? Madam hasn't, and she tells him so, listlessly. She glances enquiringly at me and I smile, and she smiles, and what flashes between us has nothing to do with Sigiriya. It has to do with our bodies, our senses, our memories of last night, savouring passion and tenderness and the cessation of loneliness. For we are lovers now, if that can be claimed after only one night, and though we haven't acknowledged that fact in so many words we have talked around it in the gamey, no-holds-barred dialogue of our own.

Oblivious of this, Joseph talks about the Lion Rock. He says we are scheduled to have *tiffin* at the Sigiriya Rest House and then visit the rock, after which we will travel on to Kandy. Kandy, he observes beguilingly, will be much cooler: it is in the hill country where the tea is grown. While I listen to him I see the lad from the Gal Vihara has entered the shrine and stands before one of the Buddhas, performing the *anjali*. Then he straightens and looks across the curve of the little *dagoba* and smiles, and in a blinding flash of recognition I hear his slow, amused, familiar voice, only slightly raised in surprise, rolling back the present as though I am standing is his mother's lounge room.

"Hullo, Mase! What are you doing here?" And in a pause of crashing silence he glances at Martina, adding: "Or shouldn't I ask?"

My first feeling, like a storm's eye calm in the centre of my shock, was annoyance with myself for not having checked him out properly back there at Gal Vihara, for allowing myself to be put off by the foreign gabble. But what the hell—he was here! And I was striding across to him through the muggy heat, wanting to throw my arms around my son, hold his strong, young body against mine. But Australian males, particularly the younger ones, abhor such displays of emotion so I grabbed his hand and began pumping all my joy and affection . . .

"Hullo, David! It's good to see you!" Pumping vigorously, I slapped his shoulder with my free hand, liking the muscled solidity of his youthful flesh which I was so sure was of my own. "I wondered if I'd run into you here. How are you, anyway?"

"Very well, thanks."

He disengaged his hand, smiling, those brown eyes twinkling with mild amusement at my senile exuberance: his teeth flashed whitely in a lush growth of beard that was jet black and glistening, but his face was thinner, cheekbones tending to jut out over the whiskers like those old temple stones in the lovers' grass.

"Did Mum send you?" he asked with a fleeting sharpness of tone and expression which reminded me of Janice—only for an instant, then his face softened.

"She didn't send me." I heard myself accenting the invidious word "send" a trifle defensively, at the same time mindful of Martina and Joseph listening in the background. "I always said I'd come back and write about this place. Now I have. Your mother merely asked me to keep an eye open for you. Where have you been?"

"Oh, around about."

Something seemed to shut down on his easy manner, something bland but impervious, what Janice used to call "clamming up". Not an original term perhaps, but appropriate, no change in his expression, just close-mouthed, giving nothing away. I knew I'd have to be careful with him. I saw him glance beyond me, at Martina.

"That's good," I beamed with an old-friend-of-the-family jollity, at the same time uneasy about the way he had looked at Martina. "It's lucky you met us. Another few minutes and we'd have gone. We're making for Kandy tonight and then we're going back to Colombo via the south coast. Come and meet a friend of mine."

Taking him by the elbow I led him across to Martina and Joseph. It wasn't far but I found myself falling into step with the coppersmith bird as though I was a sergeant-major escorting a defaulter to the beat of a drum. Martina watched us approach, smiling faintly, expectantly. Joseph, I could see, was prepared for anything.

When I introduced them David shook Martina's hand, if taking her fingertips as though he was accepting a puppy's paw could be called a handshake. Joseph was more forthright, brown hand extended and shaking manfully, a last, surreptitious glance disapproving of David's mendicant garb. All Joseph's status-conscious, sahib-trained standards were in that glance and I can't say that I disagreed with him.

119

"Hi, David," Martina greeted. "Nice to meet you. You're a student of Buddhism, I guess?"

She had looked him over interestedly, sarong, flapping shirt-tails, grimy, bare feet and all that hair, implying that she was only now guessing what she had known ever since she had heard of Amos and Red talking at Negombo. David looked at her guardedly.

"I follow the Way," he said with that staggering simplicity which earnest young people are often capable of. "I practise Dhamma."

"Do tell," Martina murmured. "Then what's this place all about?"

I expected him to stall. After all, he had only been here six weeks. Doubtless he had done some reading before leaving home but Buddhism is a very deep philosophy—men study it for years. David looked at her, suddenly smiling confidently, very much as a man smiles when he accepts a challenge.

"All this—." His hand swung outward, indicating the platform with pillars and Buddhas and *dagobas*. "All the basic principles of Buddhism are symbolised in this building. It is circular, which represents what you call Heaven—we think of it as Attainment. That, over there—" his gesture widened to take in the oblong ramp, the space which separated it from the platform and the four steps— "is the earth. When you cross that ramp you leave Samsara, that's the world, and you come up those four steps which represent the Four Stages of Deliverance, and arrive here, in Nirvana, which is salvation. You are at this *dagoba* then. Do you know what that means?"

His voice had strengthened, a more mature David than I had ever known: something was taking shape in him, developing him out of recognition. I remembered Janice dismissing the interest that had caused this change as a "Buddhist craze". I knew what Eric would have thought of it. The coppersmith bird was silent then and in the quiet I heard Joseph fidgeting, bare feet shuffling on the stone floor.

"The *dagoba*," David went on calmly, "represents the cosmos, or Buddha's Universal Body in Mahayanism. The square base is the torso, the dome is the head and this little knob on the top is the spiritual wisdom of the Enlightened One."

I was astonished. He was parading his knowledge to impress us,

120

Martina in particular, and being absurdly didactic about it, even enjoying himself. And Martina was impressed, watching him with that wide-eyed, enthralled expression I had seen at the Sri Maha Bodhi. The coppersmith bird began tolling once more, like applause. David nodded gravely, still talking.

"Mahayana is a sect of Buddhism. It means 'The School of the Great Vehicle of Salvation'. Actually Theravada Buddhism is practised in Sri Lanka. 'Theravada' means 'The Doctrine of the Elders', but this *dagoba* was built long before the original Hinayana Buddhism was broken up into eighteen sects, so the *dagoba* still represents the Body of Buddha."

Suddenly his sermon came to an end as though he had exhausted his knowledge, his voice trailing away and with it that quality which had charged him, leaking away into the muffling heat. Martina appeared to come down out of a private high like someone emerging from a dream, looking bewildered, as though something had also left her. I had the odd feeling that I had been left outside some sort of experience. Joseph's fidgeting had become more insistent and I caught him looking at me hopefully. Remembering that we were scheduled to lunch at Sigiriya I glanced ostentatiously at my watch.

"Yes, well, it's getting late." I paused, suddenly realising that my quest had ended. I'd found David and what the hell did I do now? "What are your plans, David? We're going to Kandy. Would you like a lift?"

He looked away, squinting through the midmorning glare as though he was searching for something, perhaps for that fervour which had sustained him so strangely. Certainly, without it, he looked young and uncertain once more.

"I'll take you up on that," he said slowly, "Actually I should finish my pilgrimage here but the local bus service is pretty rugged. I would be going back to Kandy anyway."

"To Pandy's," I queried sharply.

He glanced at me quickly. "Yes. How did you know?"

Once again he was the small boy in my life, the schoolboy truculently facing his mother, the young man, mulishly enduring one of Eric's tirades. I hoped I hadn't spoken out of turn.

"I met your mate, Red, at Negombo."

"Red?" David smiled the years away, retreating from me into the present, secrets in his eyes. "Red's a head."

What kind of head I wanted to ask —acid or pot? And how many other heads do you mix with at Pandy's? I wondered whether I was learning too much of their jargon for my peace of mind.

"Right then," I said brightly. "You've got yourself a ride to Kandy, if that's all right with Joseph."

It was all right with Joseph so we left the shrine by one of the external staircases because, David insisted, to return by our original route would be symbolically wrong. Once more he was the lad I had always known, affable, ready to please, explaining anything he thought might be of interest, almost as though he was trying to recover something.

"See this?" He checked us in front of one of the guardstones, hooking a thumb at the proud, graceful figure. "He's a naga-king. See the cobra over his head? And he's holding a *punkalasa*, that's the pot-of-plenty. Those two little fat guys are *yakkas*, servants I guess you'd call them. The one with the lotus is Padma and the one with the conch shell is Shanka. Interesting, isn't it?"

Interesting, yes . . .

The coppersmith bird was still tonking furiously.

Sigiriya Rest House was crowded. Two busloads of tourists from Kandy and a confederacy of Americans in private tour-cars had filled the dining room to capacity, spilling out to wine and dine at the little tables on the veranda where guests usually sat to drink aperitifs and admire the view. Someone was playing a button accordion and there was a lot of noise and frivolity and a good deal of steady drinking. I had expected David's unorthodox dress to cause difficulties but the staff were too busy to concern themselves with such conventions.

Waylaying a harassed waiter Joseph secured us a table on the veranda from where we could watch a tatty looking snake charmer who was alternatively fluting and provoking a reluctant cobra into performing aggressively for a gaggle of camera-toting tourists. After arranging to bring the car for us at two o'clock Joseph disappeared to wherever it was that he always disappeared at these places. Then Martina excused herself to go to the ladies' room, leaving me alone with David for the first time. On the way here he had said very little about himself, confining his talk to generalities and a discussion of Ceylon in which Joseph had joined from time to time. It was hardly the place for a heart-to-heart talk. As we sat down now I knew that this would be the only opportunity we would have to talk privately. I decided to let him make the opening bet and then follow up with my own. But he confounded me.

"Where did you pick her up, Mase?"

He spoke softly, smiling disarmingly, so that for a moment the import of what he had said eluded me in the babble of voices and the accordion's wail. Then the inference hit me and I felt a little spurt of anger warming my arteries.

"I didn't pick her up," I stated carefully, sparring for time to subdue my anger and think of a suitably dignified rejoinder. "We met at the airport. Our luggage was mixed up. We also shared a car into town. And we happened to be staying at the same hotel."

"Oh," he said softly, in such a knowing tone. "She's a bit young for you, isn't she?" And he smiled with that infuriating air of sexual superiority which young men adopt whenever they think of older men consorting with young women.

"I don't know." I tried not to sound annoyed. "Depends on your point of view. I would have said she was a bit old for you."

"Oh man, you don't know," he concurred enigmatically and wagged his head sagely. I wondered what it was that I didn't know. Martina? Or the extent of his interest, or disinterest, in her? Or my presumed flagging powers? I had the uncomfortable feeling that something eternal and very male had been brought out into the open between us. But I did know that Martina would return at any minute and I still hadn't talked to him about his mother.

"Anyway," I essayed tactfully, "how has it been for you, David?"

He hesitated a moment too long to be convincing. "I'm doing all right, thanks."

I tried not to smile sceptically. Did doing all right mean pigging it, commune-style, in that sleazy bungalow with earthen floors and *kadjan* thatching on the outskirts of Polonnaruwa village where we had driven him to collect his belongings? God knows he travelled light enough, a pack and a flight bag tied up with string because the zipper had burst. Did it mean mucking in with a gaggle of draggle-haired, rummy-looking, god-sotted weirdos? Several of them had drifted past while we waited for him, two bearded young men reduced to a state of saintly emaciation, and a young woman, heavily pregnant despite the camouflage of a voluminous caftan, and all of them so conscientiously unsmiling, so devotionally dour and depressingly unkempt. Damn it, I thought, I'm beginning to sound like Eric: but I had more right than Eric to sound like that. Janice had done it to me, made me Eric's surrogate, a second father without authority. David was looking at me, clammed up and resisting, that glass-hard serenity behind which he had always retreated from Eric. And that's how he sees me, I realised with misgivings. No longer as Mase, but as someone not very rightly assuming his father's role, asking questions which he had no intention of answering. Cagily I attempted another tack.

"Have you been doing any painting?"

His gaze slid away from me then to fix on the snake charmer outside, and he shrugged. I should have been warned by that shrug.

"Not much," he admitted too casually, adding, "None at all, in fact. All that seems a bit trivial now."

Trivial!

Three years of mounting tension and estrangement; of David's desperation — with which I had allied myself; three years of Eric's harangues and Janice's ditherings: not to mention the insults I had taken from Eric! Trivial! For what — this bare feet and piety bit? Baffled I looked away, devastated by the suddenness of the change which had swept us apart. Nackers and his girl friend were at an adjoining table with the camera between them like some sort of obscene, mechanical progeny. They had finished their lunch and were carrying on like a cover design for the *Karma Sutra*. Catching me watching them Nackers' square, battered face set belligerently. I turned back to David.

"It's your mother," I began disjointedly, feeling that I had no time for finesse now. "She's worried about you, you must know that."

"Yeah, I guessed that when I saw you." He spared me the briefest of uncommunicative glances before turning back to the snake charmer.

"I don't want you to think I'm prying, David."

"Of course not." Still he wouldn't look at me. "But I sure was knocked for a loop when I saw you with Mrs Gale."

"What's she got to do with it?" A tiny jealousy tweaked me: I didn't like his bringing Martina back into the conversation.

124

"I don't know," he admitted slowly. "I was just surprised, that's all."

"Don't worry about her," I advised briskly. "She's got nothing to do with this. I'll look after her."

He looked at me, his gaze coming up at me from under the lifting brows like something coming out of hiding. It was as if all his youth and vigour were being marshalled to oppose me, challenging me, ready to contest me in some way.

"D'you reckon you can, Mase?"

"Can he what?"

Martina's voice, Martina standing at the table looking down at us. Hastily I rose and dragged a chair out for her. At least David had the grace to pretend to rise, heaving himself up perfunctorily. Seated, Martina laid her handbag on the table and propped her chin on linked fists, looking enquiringly at David.

"Can he do what, David?"

"Can I get you a drink," I substituted smoothly.

She wasn't taken in, swivelling her head on her fists to look at me, eyes dilating slightly. When nobody spoke she settled her arms on the table and I noticed David studying her rings.

"I see," she said primly. "No telling, huh? A male conspiracy. Then I'll tell you something, David. Mason can cope with just about anything, can't you, Mason?"

This was getting too close to the bone. To cover myself I signalled to a passing waiter. Nackers and his girl were leaving now, he with the camera shouldered like a weapon, arrogantly walking his balls between the tables, she swanning pertly in his wake, waggling her trim little derriere. Catching my eyes she winked, flirting her hip in a cocotte's sexy twitch. Smiling I turned back to the table, feeling hugely elated, potent, equal to anything.

"Let's say I respond to challenges," I said lightly.

Yet the Lion Rock defeated me.

I had seen plenty of photographs of it but none of them show what it is really like. They cannot convey the fullness of its magnitude nor reproduce its brooding aura of history. The track winds through what looks like secondary growth, old paddi fields, pasture land grown over again and suddenly, there it is above the trees—Sigiriya, the "Lion Mountain" or the "Lion's Throat", whichever translation you prefer, both have awesome relevance—two hundred metres high, brown and grey and ochre red, streaked with the white of limestone solutions. Small trees and vegetation sprout from its seams and fissures, giving the appearance of a scruffy mane. From the distance it resembles the head of a lion; up close it is primeval and overpowering. Only a madman would build a palace and a fortress on its summit, but King Kasyapa had been just that—a psychopath and patricide.

Running the car into the shade of some trees, Gopal cut the motor. At once the soggy heat seeped in and there was a smell of the dust settling in yellow coils around us. Through the trees I could see a low lying area which might have been swampy, for the heat shimmer above it had the glimmer of ground glass. I looked at my watch, thinking wistfully of the other tourists sipping their beer in the comfort of the Rest House. They had more sense than to come out at this time of the day.

"King Kasyapa, A.D. 473," Joseph said, opening the car door for Martina, his free hand sweeping in an entrepreneur's gesture across the Rock. "He had his father walled up in a cave. Alive!"

"An enlightened guy," David murmured, sliding out of the other side of the car before I could answer.

Outside the full force of the sun settled like a heated metal plate on the top of my head, pressing on my shoulders, and I felt the exertions of the morning gathering heavily in my body. I heard Joseph telling Martina about Moggallana.

"He was the king's brother, not the same mother." His voice sank, skating with old fashioned delicacy over the indelicacy of polygamy. "In those days the kings—many wives. You understand?"

"A half-brother," Martina elucidated matter-of-factly.

"Ah yes. Half a brother." Joseph balanced the tale on an upraised forefinger. "Eighteen years he waited in India, then he came back with an army and a great battle was fought here."

"Who won?" Martina wanted to know with unexpected interest.

"Moggallana of course." The forces of right and order primed Joseph's tone and he looked surprised that she should even ask. "King Kasyapa's elephant turned away from a swamp and his soldiers ran away so the king stabbed himself, like this."

He proceeded, very graphically, to demonstrate the manner and agony of King Kasyapa's death, jabbing his throat with a brown forefinger, rolling his eyes horrifically. I set off after David who was walking ahead. Our talk in the Rest House had been most unsatisfactory and I was determined to re-open it as soon as I could. I had to push myself along to catch up with him, picking my way over some bricks in the grass for there was barely room for us to walk abreast on the path. He didn't make room for me.

"We've chosen the worst time of the day for this," I opened chattily, mopping my face.

"It could be worse." His tone was exasperatingly noncommital and I noticed that except for a light sweat under his eyes and on his brow the heat didn't appear to be worrying him. Abruptly he halted, looking back, waiting for Martina and Joseph to catch up.

"Have you been here before?" I tried again, one of those off-hand questions you throw into an awkward gap. He spared me a brief glance then looked away over the swampy area where the twisted, brown trees appeared to wriggle in the shimmer, like undernourished belly dancers. Just then Martina approached, calling to me.

"Hey Mason, you figuring to climb that thing?"

"Why not," I challenged jauntily, but out of the corner of my eye I saw David's white-toothed smile break through his beard.

Baffled, I looked up at the Rock, feeling something inside me hardening grimly. These things are of the mind of course, fantasies acquiring flesh and blood characteristics from our moods, but from that instant I felt that the Lion Rock was my enemy. Certainly everything about it was hostile to me.

From the very first steps, hacked narrowly through a towering rock, I sensed the presence of past violence—menace like the muffling heat reflected from the stones, the delusions of a deranged mind leading me upwards to a sinister grandeur which had been contrived as a refuge from retribution. If there are such things as old gods and ghosts they do their haunting at Sigiriya. Tiny grey lizards scampered, paused and watched me and scampered again, open-mouthed, their iridescent sides pumping hectically. I heard our footsteps grating on the stone like the rasp of steel in a scabbard while Martina's laughter, evoked by something David said, had the fickle sound of an odalisque's applause. The King is dead! Long live the King! What better place for that cynicism than here?

At the beginning of the climb there is a small audience chamber hewn out of the overhang, with a stone seat facing outwards. Higher up the rock has been levelled into an extensive platform, channelled at the edges so the rain runs off, with holes that suggest sockets which may have been for the poles of an awning, and here again is another throne, for such were the vaunting illusions and fears of that king. He must always have been looking out over the jungle, watching for the half-brother who drove him to do himself to death. Violence and terror cling to these stones. It is in the narrowness of the stairs, wide enough for a single spearman to defend, while the frequent and acute angling of their flights is surely designed to impede an attacker's rush. Between sloping brick revetments they climb to two successive terraces where there are remains of the walls of guardrooms and the barracks of the garrison. Now trees, and some bushes with blazing yellow flowers, grow in the corners where guardsmen lazed. A troop of monkeys startled us, hooting like foghorns, crashing wildly through the trees. On the upper terrace we were met by an old man and a boy selling Elephant Orangeade.

We rested there, drinking the carbonated stuff, tasting its spurious orange, and swapping comments about the ubiquity of soft-drink vendors. Yet I'm sure all of us were glad he was there. Martina sitting on the crumbling brickwork, daintily sucking her straw, fanning her face with a tiny handkerchief; David squatting, his sarong hitched above his knees like a native, tilting his black beard to the sky as he emptied his bottle in horse-like gulps; Joseph drinking in sensible, bird-like sips, pretending to understand our jokes. And me? The heat oppressed me, making my throat and temples pound while my legs ached dully. I drank very little for the cloying sweetness put a slime over my thirst, turning sour.

Yet this was only the Lion's shoulder. To reach the side of its neck below the ear we must ascend another staircase, as straight and as narrow as Jacob's ladder to Heaven, but unlike Jacob's ladder, this ended somewhere up against the sun-smitten expanse of precipitous rock. At its top I discerned a ledge, with a latticework like a ship's taffrail strung across the cliff to a narrow strip of smooth rock, unnaturally smooth and glistening like a newly healed scar. There the monstrous skull bulged ponderously like the wrinkled back of a fat man's neck, for at some time, aeons ago, part of the mass had fallen away, leaving a cavernous overhang. There I saw spiral stairs of contemporary steel, grey-painted, corkscrewing up into the shadows of the cavern. The ledge reappeared worming its way out of sight around the back of the Lion's head. I looked away, screwing up my eyes against the glare, feeling my ageing body protesting in anticipation.

David was the first to rise, stretching languidly, burping as if to show his disdain for the Rock. He appeared dauntingly young and tireless, eager to go on.

"Well, if you reckon you're going to climb this thing . . ."

The remark hung unfinished, somehow the more provocative for that and although he looked at us all it was on me that his glance seemed to rest longest. With it came the memory of him back there in the Rest House saying, "D'you reckon you can, Mase?" Rising stiffly I extended a hand to Martina, realising that my action hadn't been merely courteous, but also intended to show David something. But he was walking away, turning into the staircase, taking the first steps two at a time.

Determined not to be hustled I climbed slowly, doggedly lifting one foot after the other, all effort and movement fusing achingly in straining muscles, steps seeming further and further apart, steeper. Interminable heat, hot as the hobs of Hell, heart thudding, sweat trickling through my hair, air warm and surely depleted of oxygen, and smelling faintly of jungle rot. Joseph behind me climbing steadily, only a little bloke, but tough. Martina ahead finding the going hard, but David way up and going strong . . . Halting, I clawed at the balustrade, pretending to admire the view, panting heavily, vision wavering, green jungle, pale sky and angular hills overlapping, blurred by the heartbeat thumping behind my eyes.

"There's a wonderful view for you," I enthused groggily.

From far above David's voice came to me.

"If you want to see the view, come up here."

Angrily I began to climb again.

Cramp knotted my leg muscles and my heartbeat had reached a fearsome rate by the time I crawled on to the landing at the top of the stairs. It was an airy spot levelled at the foot of the precipice and from it the ledge with the guardrail led off across an expanse of bare rock. David was perched on the wall, nonchalantly swinging his legs in that tatty sarong, his bottom hanging over a magnificent view.

"How're you going, Mase?"

He had given me that greeting hundreds of times, smiling, a man-to-man equality which I had encouraged, yet this time I imagined an underlying smugness, a preening satisfaction with his youth which had enabled him to humiliate me. Nor did I miss his glance at Martina, who happened to be admiring the view. It was no use pretending, I was puffing like a winded steer and my face must have been the colour of a beacon light, my heart thudding ominously, so I played it wryly.

"Up here I'm closer to the angels than you think, laddie."

It was wasted on him. You have to be old enough to have glimpsed the tombstones on the other side of the hill or to have heard the rustle of dark wings a couple of times in your life to catch the implications of that one. Grinning David launched himself from the wall, hitting the ground with a look-at-me sound which caused Martina to turn and look at him. David look pleased with himself. Frowning, I sat down and began kneading my cramped leg muscles.

After that Joseph led us, reassuring Martina as she edged her way along the ledge, clinging to the rail and exclaiming unhappily. I didn't relish the crossing myself, all that sunny space dropping down to the ruined defences below. On the other side we found ourselves at the end of a parapet wall which enclosed a gallery under the overhang. Seen from below the wall it had resembled a newly healed scar, up here it was impressive, weathered to the colour of the rock, with a polish like marble. Joseph explained that it was all that remained of the Mirror Wall which had originally wound its way to the summit. Running his hand over the cement-hard, marmoreal surface he went on to say that it was called *chunam*, a process which had died with King Kasyapa's artisans—something to do with mixing their lime with egg whites and wild honey. Looking along it I wondered how many thousands of tiny Asiatic eggs had gone into the few hundred metres that survived. "All that souffle," was how Martina put it.

After that there were more steps, an iron ladder taking us up to an entrance barred with a grille, and another short climb which started me breathing heavily again, setting my overworked leg muscles twitching, and we were in the gallery behind the Mirror Wall. There, protected by the overhang from the weather of fifteen centuries were the Sigiriya Maidens.

I knew about them of course. Anyone who is interested in Sri

Lanka knows about the Sigiriya frescoes. Their reproductions are on postcards, batik, travel posters, and often seen as trademarks and costume jewellery and I think a set of Sri Lankan stamps also bears the likenesses of these intriguing ladies. They are to Sri Lanka what the Nefertiti head is to ancient Egyptian art.

Yellow, sienna, umber and green with never a touch of blue, bejewelled and ringed, with bangles and pins and massive pendants and turreted head-dresses encrusted with gems, they float in pairs, three-quarter length and waist-deep in clouds, noble ladies and their handmaidens bearing lotuses and crotons and frangipani wherever the Buddhist monks found a space on which to paint them. All face northward. In procession? The ladies have aristocratic, yellow skins shaded with warmer orange tones, while their handmaidens are dusky, with greenish flesh tints, suggesting a darker, subject race. Celestial maidens? Or the portraits of princesses? Incredibly sensuous, their voluptuous bodies sag with a studied languor, wide-hipped, slender waisted, with splendid swinging globes of breasts, while their fine-nosed, full-lipped Aryan faces gaze out of the enigma of their past with a slumbrous, heavy-lidded calm.

I am not the first to have fallen under their spell. The inner face of the Mirror Wall is covered with the scribblings and eulogies of enraptured wanderers of earlier centuries, the *Sigiriya Graffiti* they are called, the subject of almost as much controversy as the Maidens themselves. I had read some translations and although I could not recite any I remembered one in particular because of him who wrote it, "Poyal, the palace guardsman" who languishes for the "long-eyed maids of the mountainside," vowing that having seen them death no longer dismays him. A valiant sentiment. Yet the Sigiriya Maidens must have been something to see in Poyal's day, covering this cave and probably the entire wall of the gallery. The monsoons of a millenium-and-a-half have taken their toll so that now only twenty-one figures survive high up in the deepest concavities of the ceiling, where that spiral stairway takes you up to an observation platform that is screened with wire against the ravages of nesting birds and bees. The bees of Sigiriya were formidable, Joseph told us, big, ferocious *bambara* bees.

Martina wanted photographs so we ascended to the platform, the winding steel of the stairs vibrating under our feet, like climbing a tightened violin string. The paintings were worth the effort. Up close I was interested to see that they had been done in the true fresco style, the hand-ground earth colours brushed into the plaster while it had been wet. Seeing the broad, sure brushstrokes was like being in the presence of the painters while they worked. One figure in particular appealed to me. She was without an attendant, half turned as though protesting about that omission to her painter, one long hand gesturing towards her companions. What made her very real to me was the paleness of her exquisite shoulders and breasts compared to her lower arms and belly and narrow, aristocratic face. It was as if she had usually worn a bodice such as Singhalese women wear today, but had removed it to have her portrait painted.

There wasn't much room to take photographs up there on the platform so Joseph and I backed down into the stairs while David pressed himself against the furthest end of the cage and by crouching Martina was able to get my favourite lady into her viewfinder. At once David moved in, "to give an idea of its size", he explained. The flashlight sizzled and in its instant's garish glare I saw David smiling, reaching out as though to take my lady's outstretched hand. His clowning irked me, seeming to deliberately intrude on my fantasy.

Returning to the gallery I declared another rest period while Martina changed the film in her camera. The path was narrow, the rocky floor bulging unevenly so that I was able to find a comfortable projection on which to seat myself. David was restless, staring at the way ahead. When he heard Martina close her camera he turned to me.

"Ready, Mase? I suppose we'd better get on our way."

Again I felt a mulishness rising in me. I'd had enough of him. He had tried to hustle me all the way here, even pushing himself in beside my lady. Besides, I was comfortable, the sweat drying on me, not unpleasant, creating the coolness of evaporation over my skin. I thought of the way ahead, more stairs, exertion, heat, with David punishing me for having followed him here. I'd had enough of him and the Lion Rock as well. Looking away I saw the graffiti on the inner side of the wall, and thinking of Poyal, the long dead guardsman, I mused grimly: Oh long-eyed maids, I have climbed your mountain and the thought of dying on it dismays me.

"You go on if you want to," I said quietly. "I'll stay here and have a smoke while I'm waiting for you."

I felt David's surprise focussing on me, his mind turning over all he knew about me, setting it against my refusal. He was baffled and that pleased me. It was so quiet that I heard the leafy stirring of the mountain airs and a little bird twittering somewhere, then David's voice, faintly incredulous.

"You mean you're giving up?"

"That's right." I nodded woodenly. "I know when to stop."

"There's plenty to see up there," David began cajolingly. "There's the palace — what's left of it — and the throne and the king's bath. Just around the bend there's the real entrance, great big brick paws with stairs. You can see Dambulla from up there."

"You've been up there before, haven't you?" I said sharply.

"Well, yes, I have." He smiled, boyishly contrite. "I was here a week ago with some mates."

"Why didn't you say so?" For some reason his admission troubled me.

He shrugged, smiling blandly. "I didn't think it mattered."

But it did to me. It mattered because he had deliberately deceived me in a way which was part of his resentment, and that hurt. But I wasn't going to let him see that.

"Well then," I said dismissively, "now's your chance to see it again. Away you go. I'll wait for you here."

For a moment I thought he was going to decline then I saw his lips tighten in his beard and I knew that he had decided to bluff it out. However I didn't expect him to call my bluff the way he did.

"What about you, Mrs Gale? You'll come with me, won't you?"

This is it, I thought dully. This is what it is all about — Martina. She was to be the instrument of his retaliation. His covert challenge back there in the Rest House, his smile as we stood at the foot of the Rock, the way he had pushed me so hard. And this was when she would sort the man from the boy. I happened to be reaching for my pipe just then and my fingers froze, clamped on the bowl. Without looking up I knew that she had moved closer to me because I heard the rustle of her dress.

"Thanks, David, I'd like to, but I think I'd better stay with Mason."

Dragging my pipe from my pocket I clamped my teeth on the mouthpiece. She had made her choice. Yet there was little satisfaction in it for me. "I'd better stay," she had said. Not that she wanted to stay or that she was too tired to go on, but because she felt that she had to stay. I looked up at the mass of the Lion Rock feeling that it had defeated me. Oh long-eyed maidens, I am doubly dismayed!

As Joseph had predicted it was cooler in the hill country. Much cooler, in fact cold. We hadn't climbed very far out of the lowlands before Martina was asking for the windows to be closed and lamenting—not complaining—but wishing wistfully, over and over again, that she'd had the foresight to leave a cardigan unpacked. Finally, when she was shivering unrestrainedly and snuggling, not very surreptitiously, against me, Joseph got the message and had Gopal stop the car while she got out and dragged a blue woollen garment from her suitcase in the boot. Back in the car, sleeved and buttoned and huddling more cheerfully, she smiled beguilingly at Joseph, wrinkling her nose outrageously. "Thanks Joe, you're a doll. And so's your friend." Joseph looked absurdly pleased with himself. I don't know how well the compliment came over in Singhalese but when it was relayed to Gopal he laughed so uninhibitedly that I suspected Joseph of including interpolations of his own. Of course I had long since unrolled my shirt sleeves. I think David also felt the cold in that shirt and sarong, although he steadfastly refused to admit it.

He said very little after leaving Sigiriya, just slumping in his corner, not actually sulking but withdrawn. Several times Martina endeavoured to include him in our somewhat desultory conversations but his replies were off-hand, discouraging. I doubt that he was ashamed of what he had done on the Lion Rock, more likely annoyed and trying to justify his action to himself. I had seen him in many a bad mood during the course of his growing up, but none quite like this one. Of course in the past we had never been in competition: I had always been his confidant and partisan, sustaining him through his depressions. Nor had there ever been anyone like Martina to complicate our relationship.

For my part I welcomed his silence, consoling myself with the thought that we would soon be in Kandy and rid of him. Yet it troubled me that I should think like that. His behaviour had hurt rather than angered me. I suppose I flattered myself that my place in his esteem should exempt me from childish retaliations. Most of all I found it hard to excuse him for having tried to use Martina against me. For the first time I began to regret having accepted Janice's commission. The best that I could say was that I had humoured her to satisfy my own romantic whims. What had I hoped to achieve? His renunciation of Buddhism and return to take up that very thing which I had always encouraged him to resist—Eric's mantle at Australasian Industries? Viewed dispassionately my presence in Sri Lanka must appear as a betrayal to David. Disconsolately I concerned myself with Martina and her delight in the passing scenery.

The hill country was fascinating—green vistas as delicate and as finely detailed as a Japanese print. Always we climbed, worming our way, low-geared and twisting back on ourselves around valleys and the dizzying edges of gorges where the gossamer haze of tumbling water conjured rainbows in the spray. On the highest places jungly stands of sombre trees showed like unclipped curls on a poodle's flanks: for this was tea country and all but the steepest slopes, the most inaccessible hilltops, had been cleared. Tea, hectare upon hectare, hillside folding into hillside, rows of low, shrubby bushes winding like contour lines on a map, looking like crumpled miles of suburban hedges, all neatly nipped and topiarised by the fingers of dark, anaemic Tamil women with golden studs in their nostrils and rings in their ears and baskets of "only the tenderest of tips" on their backs as they laboured up those murderous slopes. Men supervised them, checking the level of the bushes with long, white wands. On the bluffs and ridges the factories stood, white and sprawling, turreted with chimneys like the chateaus of medieval robber barons, overlooking their domains.

Just before sunset we ran into rain, not a tepid, tropical downpour, but dismal and skin-pimpling, cold hill rain that soon had freshets cascading down the slopes and gushing off the road in rills. Within minutes the rear window began to leak, an unpleasant trickle channelling down my back, soaking my shirt. Joseph was apologetic and Martina was concerned, but there was nothing I could do other than finish the journey leaning forward, shuddering.

And there was more than the chill to make me shudder for the hazardous driving conditions didn't worry Gopal. We were on the downward slopes above Kandy then and he bowled along that narrow, winding road at an unvarying speed, riding horn and brakes, chuckling whenever he shaved another existence from the quota of reincarnations allotted to some dilatory fellow Buddhist: and he had an aversion to using headlights, preferring to wind and swoop around those murky bends in the will-o'-the-wisp glimmer of parking lights. I wasn't sorry when Kandy came at us out of the darkness, cars with headlights like bleary eyes in the drizzle, a bullock cart, unlit, a near miss, and pedestrians skipping, hooded and bare-legged, through the misted streetlights. Gopal had to slow down. Then David heaved himself out of his corner, leaning forward to speak to Joseph.

"Will you ask him to drop me at the railway station, please?"

That shocked me, not so much because we were about to part, although that was a jolt no matter how I felt about him, but his speaking to Joseph without a word to me. I wondered whether it had been deliberate, whether he felt that he no longer owed me anything, not even the courtesy of a few words before he made his farewells. A sense of futility swept over me. I had found him, but what had that accomplished? Nothing—worse than nothing—resentment, estrangement, our relationship never the same again. In a few minutes he would be leaving me to go back to Pandy's no doubt, to the hippies and Buddha freaks and other vagrants. I had to talk to him, had to have something to take back to Janice.

"What about coming to our hotel?" I suggested, remembering, with the hopeful half-cunning of desperation, that we had only met that morning, a few frustrating hours of stalling and animosity with Martina or Joseph always within hearing. "We haven't had much chance to talk and it will be the last I'll see of you for a while."

He made a little sound, faintly derisory, exasperated, hidden from me in the darkened corner of the car. Then the glow of a passing streetlight lapped the interior, splashing us all with fleeting shadows and in its pallid wash I saw Joseph's big, rough head turn quickly.

"Sir!" His tone was agitated and I knew at once that he was thinking of arrangements, his budget, the added expense of another person. "Our hotel, the Rubaiyat—it is a first class hotel. They will not take—" there was a flutter of a darkened gesture like bat's wings in the gloom—"besides, I have only booked two rooms."

136

"They'll have others, surely," I rasped testily. "And don't worry about the expense. I'll pay."

Again the bat-wing flap of Joseph's hands as he started to protest, saying, "But sir, but . . ." But David cut him short.

"I think he's trying to tell you," he offered sardonically, "that it's a very straight hotel, the Rubaiyat. Like the man says, it's a first class hotel, very square. That means no freaks allowed, so they wouldn't have me in this gear."

"Damn it," I burst out but at that moment Gopal took a corner tightly and along with the swish of wet tyres and the whine of changed gears I heard Joseph saying very precisely, relievedly, "Yes, that is right."

"So you see." I knew that David was smiling in the darkness beside me, thankful for Joseph's intervention. "I'm sorry, Mase, but thanks all the same. Anyway, no worries. I'll be all right. I've got a pad to go to."

"Pandy's, I suppose," I said sharply.

He didn't answer and since there seemed to be nothing more to say we sat in silence. What the hell, I thought aggrievedly. It was useless trying to persuade him to come to the Rubaiyat Hotel, he had made up his mind to give me the slip. The rain had ceased and in the light of the street lamps the buildings looked like cliffs riddled with shadowy clefts and openings. We were passing along a thoroughfare lined with spreading trees and drops of water fell from them on to the roof of the car with drum-like sounds. I saw Martina's profile sharp against the glow, half turned away from me. Joseph and Gopal were talking softly. I shivered in my damp shirt.

I recognised the railway station at once. Despite the flower beds it had the impersonal look of public places, governmental architecture, colourless, governmental paint, dim lighting, a few people and a clock. And it smelt like a railway station, coal smoke, humanity and public conveniences. A policeman, looking like a boy scout in his khaki shorts and slouch hat, slowed his ambling to watch us pull up between the sheets of light-starred water on the asphalt. David turned to me, his face a pale shape in the dimness, or what I could see of it above the beard, no face at all.

"Well, goodbye, Mase." I realised that his hand had come out and I took it, feeling the lack of conviction in his grip. "It was good to bump into you again. I'm sorry we couldn't have a real talk but that's the way it goes. Give my love to Mum. Tell her I'm fighting fit and having a ball."

"Write and tell her yourself," I growled. "And not just a postcard this time. Make it a proper letter."

"Yeah, yeah, I will," he muttered and his hand slipped out of mine. Then he was reaching across me to Martina, finished with me.

"Goodbye, Mrs Gale." Martina's shoulder stirred against mine and there was a moment while they fumbled and found each other's hands, shaking. "Been nice to meet you. I hope you and Mase enjoy your trip."

"David." She ignored the innuendo, her hand holding his overlong, detaining him, I imagined. "Why don't you come with us? This Rubaiyat place—I'm sure we could get you in. As for a room—you can have mine. Mason and I will be sharing."

"Oh!" To say that David was surprised was an understatement. And so was I, surprised and startled, then delighted, not merely because she intended to come to me but because she had said so to persuade David. She felt enough for me to do that.

"Well, thank you, Mrs Gale." David was quick to recover his aplomb. "It's very nice of you to offer but I wouldn't"—the slightest pause, sufficient to be insolent—"I wouldn't want you to compromise yourself for me."

Then he was gone, the door handle rattling, the door slamming, bare feet slopping through a puddle around to the rear of the car.

"David," I called, groping for the door handle.

He had the boot open when I reached him, the pack slung on one shoulder, the flight bag hanging from the other: something was hanging out of it and he was stuffing it back, not looking at me.

"Look, David," I began but he tried to divert me.

"Half your luck, Mase. She's some bird, that one."

I ignored that. "We've got to talk."

He shrugged, slamming the boot closed. "What is there to say? You've found me. I'm healthy and happy. So tell Mum that."

"That's no good." I was angry, his manner to Martina, his lack of concern for his mother. "Your mother's worried, David. You've got to give me some idea of what you intend to do."

"Now?" He was stalling, I knew, debating whether to defy me.

I shrugged grimly. "Or tomorrow. Anywhere, any time you like."

He regarded me steadily for a moment longer, head tilted, his face clear now in the outer radiance of the station light. I noticed that he had put the flight bag down.

"Okay," he conceded and there was more than a touch of resignation in his voice. "Tomorrow, huh? I'll tell you what—you'll be going to the Temple of the Tooth, won't you? All the tourists go there, it's on the circuit. I'll meet you there, ten o'clock, at the gate."

"A bloody temple," I burst out exasperatedly. "That's no good! How the hell can we talk there? There's sure to be a crowd."

"You said anywhere, man, and that's where, or nothing." He dropped into freak-talk, grinning hugely, pleased with himself, yet a hardness in his tone warned me that I had pushed him to his limit. "The temple, tomorrow, ten o'clock. *Ayubowan* and"—again that merest of pauses underlining insolence—"have a good night's sleep."

Picking up the flight bag he sauntered off, carrying it the full extent of its strap, almost skimming the puddles. The darkness closed about him lingeringly, a ghost figure, then nothing. Somewhere a locomotive hooted derisively.

Climbing into the car beside Martina I thought of the Temple of the Tooth and Pandy's and then, for some reason, of the Rubaiyat Hotel. The Rubaiyat, for God's sake! A line came glibly to my mind. "But come with old Khayyam and leave the lot . . . !"

"He's not much like you, is he?"

Martina came to the bathroom door, barefooted, rubbing wet hair, a towel as brightly patterned as an Oriental prayer mat wrapped around her. The rest of her was flushed, bare shoulders, legs and thighs as pink as that steamed-up, pink and black bathroom. And a most exotic bathroom it was too—sunken bath in the lotus design, lotus pattern sand-blasted on the shower screen, lotus-shaped light shades, everything in black and pink. And a bidet! The best of the mystic East and the hygienic West. For the Rubaiyat, understandably, went in for Moslem decor, mini-Taj Mahal arches, wall hangings covered with hooked Islamic script and lacy Arabic grilles like a harem, along with h & c, airconditioning and piped music—only television missing. That much is spared the mystic East in Sri Lanka.

"What do you mean, he's not like me?" I pretended affront.

Still towelling she said, "I don't know, just different."

"Well, he's my son all right," I insisted. "I'm as sure of that as I am of you being with me now."

"Yeah, well don't bet on that. Any more stand-offs like this afternoon and I might dump you both."

She had paused in her towelling to deliver that one, head tilted, eyeing me with some sourness from under the arch of upraised arms and hanks of damp hair. Muzak came to me softly from the nightstand between our beds, Bacharach or the Beatles or one of those other groups young people seem to need to fill their silences these days. I knew I would have to get used to it for Martina had switched it on almost as soon as we had come into the room, leaving it like a bleeding heart trickling its sentimental gore. I closed my notebook and turned to her.

"I'm sorry about that but he did push me. You saw the way he tried to run me off my feet."

"Why would he do that?"

"Because he wasn't very happy to see me. And because he disapproves of you being with me."

"Disapproves of me! Thank you!"

"Correction. He doesn't disapprove of you personally . . ."

"Thank you again, sir!"

". . . in fact I think he likes you. But he disapproves of me taking up with you, if I may put it that way . . ."

"It doesn't matter which way you put it, it doesn't sound nice."

"Of course, if you're going to keep on interrupting me . . ." I protested loftily.

"Enlighten me, O Guru." She pulled a gamin face at me.

"You see," I found myself frowning as I thought about it, "I have an idea that David thinks of me as family. It's all mixed up with his mother and father and memories of his early life, and when he thought of what we might be doing together he was shocked. He might even feel that I've betrayed him in some way, the image he has of me. So he decided to punish me, show me up in front of you."

"Why me? He doesn't know me." This time she halted her towelling to glare at me out of a tangle of damp hair.

"You're a woman. That's enough," I pronounced sagely.

"The eternal triangle yet!" She withdrew into a renewed frenzy of rubbing, presenting only the top of her head. "Two men in my life I can take, but three...!"

Three? Stephen, of course. And myself. And the third? David? The idea didn't appeal to me at all. She was stalking flat footed across the room, to halt in front of the mirror. It was large and oval with a shaded light shaped like an Aladdin's lamp that gave off a soft glow that enclosed her, raising the faintest nimbus over her shoulders. She watched me in the mirror, her movements slowing, arms sinking until the towel was draped over her head like a cowl, her reflection, rather like an ikon, staring out at me. Muzak seemed to rise around us, flooding us with sentiment, and I wondered what life would be like with her. I don't know if that was love, certainly it was the body and senses taking over. Abruptly I snapped myself out of it and went to the bed, sitting down. One of us had to break that silence and I found myself picking resentfully at the memory of David.

"You think back to this afternoon on those stairs."

She giggled. "Will I ever forget? I thought you were going to throw a coronary."

Score one to David, I thought bitterly. Why is an older man's humiliation always amusing. I shrugged wryly, sheering away from the memory of what she had said up there beneath the Sigiriya Maidens.

"I know David," I told her, our gaze meeting in the mirror, talking to her reflection. "He doesn't brag. He's not a show-off. Yet he started talking his head off when he met you at the Vatadage."

"That was interesting." She ignored my charge, eyes deep in shadowed pits, her voice livening. "All that stuff about enlightenment, leaving the earth and rising by the Four Stages of Deliverance. I really dig that, Mason, really, really."

"So he's a full bottle on Buddhism," I agreed with a trace of sarcasm. "But can he live it? He didn't this afternoon."

"He'll learn to," she assured me with a simple certainty.

Score two to David. He had convinced her of his sincerity. Baffled, I didn't answer, remembering her after the Sri Maha Bodhi ceremony, her euphoria, her craving for serenity . . . "just float and float and never be. hassled again." Without realising it I reached out and stemmed the Muzak to the merest murmur.

"You're too touchy," she said and for a moment I thought she was referring to my dislike of piped music.

Again I shrugged. "I wasn't until I met you."

"Meaning?" She was very still, staring at my reflection.

"That I wouldn't like to lose you."

"To David! For God's sake . . . !"

"No, for my sake."

She wheeled sharply, the towel slipping to her shoulder, sliding heavily to the floor. She was transformed from a Madonna-like ikon to a very real woman. I liked the way her freshly washed hair hung thickened and gleaming.

"You're not for real, are you," she demanded tautly. "You're not saying that kid's got the hots for me?"

The expression irked me, yet put that way, and in the intimacy of this room, the idea did sound absurd. She must be twenty-nine or thirty while David was twenty-one, and by life's standards, by the measure of female development, he wasn't much more than a boy. Yet at the age of twenty-one I had been through an economic depression and gone to a war, taking part in two major battles and two evacuations, killing at least three men that I know of, as well as bedding more prostitutes than I cared to admit. Had that made me a man? My mind swung uneasily away from that reckoning.

"If I'm touchy it's because he's my son."

"Oh Mason!"

She came to me quickly, hurrying around the end of the bed to stand in front of me. Gently I laid my hands on her hips, feeling the hardness of bones under the flesh as I drew her closer, between my knees. This close I could smell her hair and the soapy, bathroom breath of her skin. Placing her hands over mine she pressed them hard against herself.

"Did you mean that, Mason—about not wanting to lose me?"

I nodded, feeling the intensity of her gaze on my face, and knowing her loneliness, I knew the intentness of her question.

"And did you mean what you said up there on the rock, when David asked you to go to the top with him?"

"What did I say?"

"You don't remember?"

She shook her head very slightly, more like a tremor, still watching me intently. "What did I say?"

"That you thought you'd better stay with me."

"Did I say that?"

So she didn't remember. It had meant nothing, just a carelessly used word. I nodded, relieved. Something of that must have showed in my face for she took me by the hair and pushed my head back, her body curving away from me, knees spread slightly between my thighs.

"And you thought . . . you ding-a-ling!"

I laughed shakily. "Like you said, I'm touchy."

"Oh Mason." She shook her head slowly, smiling sleepily. "There's two guys there inside your head. One is an old guy who treats me like I'm his daughter at times. The other is my devoted companion and lover. Which one is really you?"

"Which would you prefer?" I offered, head back, still in her grip.

Lips pursed, she considered, brows drawing together thoughtfully.

"Both, I guess." Nodding. "Yeah, both."

And she drew my head against herself, pressing my face against her tummy, against the soft tension of its muscle-wall, against a warmth and sweet, flesh-smelling richness. It was as though a boundless contentment enfolded me then, taking me into its comfort.

"You love him, don't you?" she said, not releasing me.

"Who? David?"

I felt her nod, and still clinging to her I examined my feeling for David very frankly. Men are shy about using the word "love": it has been debased so often, but whatever the reason they are loth to use it readily, the sincere ones, and then only under stress.

"Yes, I do," I murmured against her, conscious that I had evaded the word again. "That's why this business troubles me."

"Not his showing off, surely?"

"It's more than that. He resents me, Martina. He thinks I'm spying on him for his mother. Why didn't he tell me he'd been up there before? I can't explain it but that means something, I'm sure."

"Maybe he didn't want to spoil it for you."

"Oh yes? Well, I don't think he'll turn up tomorrow."

"He said he would."

"In a pig's eye! You believe that, you'll believe in Santa Claus."

"Just the same, I think he will."

"I'll bet he doesn't."

She pushed my head away, hands clamping my temples.

"What'll you bet? Come on, money up or shut up."

I considered her slyly over the towel-covered swell of her bosom.

"I'll tell you what—if I win you come to me tomorrow night. If you win I'll go to you. Fair enough?"

"Mason, you shyster!"

She began to rock my head between her hands, but I grabbed her wrists and somehow the towel came off and we went down into the bed, tusselling.

I heard the drums as we alighted from the car. Gopal had parked under a banyan tree beside the Sacred Lake and the drumbeat reached us there, thudding through the traffic noises. Even at that distance it burred my nerves and I knew that it came from the Temple of the Sacred Tooth, or as Joseph called it, the Temple of Dalada Maligawa.

I had seen a picture of it in a tourist brochure, a section of a heliotrope coloured building which had looked like a cross between a banking establishment of the Victorian era and a medieval Japanese castle. There had been an elephant in the foreground of the picture, caparisoned and painted blue around the eyes, standing with trunk raised and one forefoot lifted like a society lady dallying with a cocktail. That picture maligned the Temple of the Tooth.

Seen in brilliant sunshine the heliotrope is really a gentle, immaculate pink and although the building is massive the architectural embellishments dispel any likeness to the utilitarian ugliness favoured by the Victorians. The surrounding wall, with its distinctive pyramid crenellations, as well as the moat, gatehouse and squat, octagonal towers with pavilion roofs, was what had made me think of a Japanese castle. Of course there were no elephants posing for us that day for they only appear on ceremonial occasions when the golden reliquary which contains the hallowed tooth, rescued from Buddha's funeral pyre, is borne through the city in the *perahera* procession. Across the road in front of the Temple is the Sacred Lake, square, surrounded by similarly crenellated walls, reflecting the heavens, Nirvana. All around are the steep, luxuriantly covered little hills which appear to rise out of the very streets, for Kandy is embowered in green hills.

David was nowhere in sight at the gatehouse but there was a beggar who moved me with a weepy glance that cost me a couple of rupees. People were streaming in and out of the temple and I spied a blond young man in a faded sarong accompanied by a frail looking girl. I looked at my watch. It was a few minutes after ten o'clock. Consulting Martina I decided to wait for a while. The drums were insistent, drumming up a ceremony, Joseph said, something about the tooth reliquary being on display. He went on to tell us about the library of Buddhist writings housed in one of the towers, and about the corpulent, verdigris coloured carp that drifted majestically in the verdigris coloured water of the moat. And all the while the crows swooped around us and the sunshine beat on those stark, pink walls while the beggar lifted his hand every time he caught my eye. By twelve minutes past ten Joseph had no more to tell and Gopal was beginning to stamp around, hitching his sarong high in his crotch and rubbing his nose with blubbery sounds. After another five minutes I decided to leave David to his own devices. Janice would have to be content with what information I had. Glancing at Martina I leaned close to her.

"That bet we made—it looks like you'll have to pay up."

She smiled enigmatically behind her sunglasses and brushed her hip against mine.

To enter the temple was to walk point blank into the racket of the drums, taking it on the face and chest, feeling it reverberate inside your head. I put my hands to my ears but the cacophony came through, pacing the stolid lub-dubbing of my heart. I saw Martina mouthing wordlessly. After the glare outside it was dim, a great columned hall, shuddering with noise, with a stairway where people crowded in restless coils and there was a table of flower offerings as well as four, white clad, turbanned kettle drummers and a trumpeter. I looked around, expecting to see more of them for it was difficult to imagine that five men could raise such a din. Joseph mouthed and beckoned, attaching us to the tail of the crowd.

After that it was a matter of queueing and moving slowly up the stairs and out on to the gallery of a two storey building which stood like a tower in the centre of a courtyard. By then the drumming had become more bearable. I was on the watch for David and I wanted to talk to Martina about him, but there was no opportunity, standing in line with Joseph between us and all those Singhalese families around us dressed in their best and carrying flowers while coveys of children watched us solemnly. There were a number of freaks in the crowd, coteries of earnest young people costumed in the uniform of the vagrant generation, beards and beads and caftans and that preposterous, preternatural gravity.

Their sedateness saddened me. They seemed to have bartered their youth for piety, abandoning laughter in their search for enlightenment. I saw Joseph studying them interestedly and once, as our line shuffled along, he asked me if they were gipsies. Baffled, I searched for a simple explanation. I know, I understand, I sympathise with the revolt of the young, and whenever I think of the world as I knew it in my own youth I envy them their ability to rebel. But try to explain to a citizen of the Third World why so many young people in our affluent society renounce the comfort, the safety, the social equality and the abundant food to live without status or dignity, like beggars. How do you explain the dubious nature of the benefits of our society to someone who lives in the presence of want, surrounded by ignorance, class distinction, infant mortality, hookworm, anaemia, malaria and all the age-old evils of poverty? I heard myself expounding unconvincingly. Joseph's face puckered, his sincere eyes searching mine bewilderedly. "But they have so much," he protested. I shrugged, wanting to say that perhaps that explained everything, that the seeds of dissatisfaction might lie in inexperience, but Joseph confounded me. "They even have television," he murmured. Over his shoulder I saw Martina's eyebrows arch expressively.

The casket containing the tooth of the Buddha is in a tiny receptacle set on the tip of the spire of a gold-plated replica of a dagoba which stands almost two metres high. The whole thing is enshrined in an alcove lined with blue silk and protected by twenty-five millimetre thick, bullet-proof glass, donated by Japan. A monk is always present to lay hands on the sick, comfort the poor, bless the babies and accept offerings from the devout as they file past. Subdued lighting glows richly over the golden dagoba, bringing out the sensuous lustre of the metal, while the kings of every Buddhist country have presented the thick ropes of pearls and rubies and sapphires and diamonds that drape its rotundity like the braid on a general's chest. Their profusion drugged me with an emanation of immense wealth. It required an effort to remember that to become the Buddha, Siddhartha Gautama had renounced jewels like those, and much more, to embark on a life of asceticism under the bodhi tree. Beside me a string-haired hippie girl was murmuring reverently.

Outside the drums took us back into their foundry din. There seemed to be more people in the courtyard now, while at the entrance a cluster of monks shamed the pink of the walls with their vivid saffron. Once again there was no sign of David at the gatehouse . . .

. . . but he was waiting on the footpath, smiling as he watched us approach.

It was a moment before I took in his transformation, jeans, fresh shirt and even sandals. His hair was tied behind his head while his beard appeared to have been oiled, every hair glinting sleekly. I had the feeling that he was dressed for something special. And his smile was so wide and white and disarming.

"I thought you'd forgotten me, Mase."

"Ten o'clock, you said. My watch must be gaining."

"Good old Mase," he murmured, looking past me to Martina. "Good morning, Mrs Gale. I trust you had a good night?"

"Yes thank you, David." She was untroubled by the gibe. "I took something to make me sleep."

"I thought you might," David purred and I could almost see the sparks of that thrust and parry flashing between them in the street.

"Where shall we go to talk?" I broke in, not liking the undertones of that exchange.

"The car, I think." David turned to me, suddenly in command of the situation. "I stashed my gear in it. You see" —he looked around us, smiling— "I thought I'd go on with you. If that's okay?"

"To Colombo?" Suddenly I didn't relish the prospect of his company on the remainder of our tour.

"Well, not quite," he demurred. "Colombo's not my scene. To Matara, please. You can drop me off there. D'you know it?" He swung that question to Joseph who nodded vigorously.

"To Shangri-La," I hazarded tersely and had the satisfaction of seeing David's eyes widen.

"You know your way around," he said softly.

"I ask questions," I told him and this time the cut and thrust was between us.

147

"I should have known, shouldn't I," he conceded graciously. "Well, there's a vihara there I want to see." And a colony of no-hopers I almost said, but Joseph began to speak.

"We get to Matara not tomorrow but the day after. Tonight we stay at Ella Gap. Tomorrow we are at Tissamaharama to see the wild life at Yala sanctuary and the next day we are at Matara."

"Fair enough," David conceded regally. "That'll suit me great."

As we moved off Martina brushed her shoulder against mine. "About that bet — who's paying who now?"

PART THREE

When in the lowering sky thunders the storm cloud's drum,
And all the pathways of the birds are thick with rain,
The brother sits within the hollow of the hills
Alone.
Psalms of the Brethren, adapted from translations of C. A. F. Rhys Davids.

Before leaving Kandy we were taken to see the sights, one of which was to watch the elephants—or "ellyfonts", as Joseph called them—bathing in the Mahaweli Ganga. Ellyfonts, he explained, were only worked until midday, after which they were taken to the nearest river, thoroughly scrubbed with pieces of coconut shell and then allowed to wallow in the water for several hours.

Apparently it was standard tourist practice to view the ellyfonts at their ablutions, for overlooking a small cove with a sandy beach there was a well defined area where parked cars had long since flattened the roadside grass. The river was wide and unruffled, flowing between banks of vivid green and in places bright squares of cloth had been spread out to dry. Women were doing their washing, beating it against rocks with flat, pistol-like reports. Some were washing themselves, ankle deep in the water, rinsing their hair, or dunking themselves, their white cotton bathing cloths transparent on glistening areas of brown flesh. But we had come to see the elephants.

In the shallows below us three of them lay on their sides, partially submerged. It was difficult to gauge their size for only the wrinkled mounds of their bellies, their knobbed foreheads and baggy haunches showed, so many disembodied elephant parts awash in the pea-soup coloured water. Occasionally a leathery ear would flap lazily, or the wavering tip of a snorkelling trunk would blow a spumy exhalation and if you looked carefully you could make out a little eye here and there, blinking somnolently. They looked blissfully content, luxuriating like corpulent old men and women enjoying a mineral bath.

Martina opened her camera and took a light reading and at once a driver, or mahout, or whatever they are called, a scrawny youth in dirty shorts appeared and waded into the shallows, splashing and hallooing. Reluctantly the elephants sat up, blowing and uttering disgruntled squeaks, whereupon the youth mounted the neck of one, chirruping and rubbing it with his heels. Resignedly, lugubriously, the beast waded ashore like a dinosaur quitting a primeval swamp, water streaming from it as it plodded up the beach to the road, the great stumps of its feet making a scuffling sound like rubber soled shoes. It was quite small, the colour of dried moss, with pink splotches on its trunk and tattered ears and around one small, shrewd eye. Reaching us the youth heeled it into a sitting position, one forefoot, like an antique umbrella-stand, uplifted, its mottled trunk curled over its forehead in salute. Martina photographed it whereupon, again at the youth's urging, the elephant reached out its trunk, the pink and rubbery, fingered tip, with twin nasal orifices snuffling moistly, feeling around beseechingly.

"He's asking for rupees, Mase," David prompted.

I was slow to catch his tone for I happened to be thinking, not very favourably, of the men who taught noble animals such ignoble tricks. Elephants have a majestic dignity, comporting themselves like kings in their wild state, taking whatever they fancy with a lordly arrogance, never needing to be servile. To train them to beg is to degrade them. Yet that was part of the Sri Lanka I was discovering. Then the irony in David's tone stung me.

"Okay, give him some," I invited.

"Eh?" He glanced at me quickly, taken aback, which pleased me.

"Give him some," I repeated, rather more sharply.

Recovering, David shrugged, saying offhandedly, "It's not my show."

"No it isn't, is it," I agreed smilingly, for suddenly I was enjoying myself, enjoying humiliating him for being so righteous, for what he did at Sigiriya, for being so cocky and priggish and young. He must have guessed my mood for his eyes met mine in a hard, blank stare while the elephant stirred restlessly, shifting from one foot to the other, its tiny, absurdly long-lashed eyes blinking listlessly as though it was unaware that its trunk was wavering hopefully between us. The slap of washing came to me like a fusillade.

There was a flurry of movement, Martina moving briskly past me, opening her bag. Conscience smitten I went for my pocket but she forestalled me, reaching up to the youth on the elephant, a note fluttering from her fingertips. Taking it the young man touched the note to his brow, hoorawing the elephant which made a soulful little sound and saluted us again, curling its drooling trunk. Out of the corner of my eye I saw that David was smiling.

"You shouldn't have done that," I murmured, leaning close to Martina.

"Done what?" She looked at me uncomprehendingly, the camera lifted to her face, the incident at the elephants' bathing place forgotten.

We were in the orchid house at the Peradeniyia Botanical Gardens, on the outskirts of Kandy. It was steamy, smelling of leaf mould and voracious plants, the exhalations of all that foliage misting the glass of the hothouse, like being clenched in a giant gardener's sweaty fist. At Martina's request David had gone ahead to pose among the rank, massed green, one arm raised to a group of carnivorous flowers. At least they looked as though they were carnivorous. All that sultry, waxen beauty nourished on mulch and insect juices, rapacious, more invasive than the Triffids, tiger-striped or leopard-pelted or jug-shaped fly-eaters and some yellow beauties that pouted like petulant blondes. David shifted restlessly, calling, "Is that how you want me?"

Martina lowered the camera long enough to call, "Terrific." Hard on the shutter's clash I tried again.

"You shouldn't have butted in like you did back there."

"You think not, huh?" Lowering the camera she cranked film with that deft wrist movement which was so characteristic of her briskness. "Really Mason," she chided lightly, "telling him it was your show! You came on a teensy weensy bit heavy, didn't you?"

I shrugged. "It was he who said it. I merely agreed."

"And how!" Slinging the camera she looked at me defiantly. "It's my show too, you know."

"You made that clear too."

"What did you expect? The two of you backing off from a lousy tip like that."

Her scorn seemed to devour me like those insect-eating orchids and I wished I hadn't broached the subject. Mason, you're a gig, I reproved myself. You can't leave well enough alone. But I didn't like the thought of her getting David off the hook back there. Suddenly I realised that I was thinking of him as an adversary to be outmanoeuvred and blocked, and that made me uneasy.

"That wasn't what it was about and you know it," I began defensively, but she left me as I began to speak, stepping briskly, hips swishing between the benches of drooping leaves. I followed, not liking David's half smile as he watched me approach.

After that we didn't speak until we were looking at the cacti. They also were in a hothouse but it was different from the orchid house, no humidity, only a dry heat that kept the glass panes clear of mildew, and those spiney, pulpy forms that looked like plant life culled from the cosmic wastes of the moon. I dawdled, more concerned with my own thoughts than cacti. Having come out of that confrontation rather poorly I decided to let the matter drop. Perhaps she was right, I had come on a bit heavy back there at the river. But in these cogitations I had reckoned without Martina. She drifted close to me, smiling enigmatically under those huge, dark glasses.

"Still sore at me?"

"Never." And I wasn't, just then. Looking down I smiled, once again seeing myself reflected, distorted in the glistening black ovals of her glasses. Then she giggled unexpectedly.

"You should have seen yourselves—like a couple of roosters shaping up over a worm."

"Hullo worm," I greeted dryly.

That stung her, her smile fading under the glasses, suddenly prickly, like the cacti. Then she walked away, not far, but far enough for me to have to raise my voice if I wasn't going to follow her. Halting, she pretended to study a grotesque, towering cactus, one of those fleshy, Andean monstrosities, paddle-shaped and bayonet-spiked. I followed her, standing so close that our shoulders brushed.

"I'm right, you know," I said softly. "You are the worm."

"And you think you're the early bird, huh?" She shot a resentful glance at me and turned back to stare at the cactus.

"No," I said slowly. "I think I was the only bird at the time."

"You're too touchy." This time she didn't turn.

"So you keep telling me," I commented sourly. "Like I said, I think he's made you the worm so that he can punish me. You think about it. Why didn't he stay with his scaley mates in Kandy? We didn't invite him to come with us. And now he's carrying on like an avenging angel, and a rather juvenile one at that."

She shrugged, still not turning. "So he's a silly kid and he's trying to take a rise out of you."

"For God's sake," I growled exasperatedly. "Don't tell me you're defending him?"

"He'll learn," she predicted ambiguously, then as she turned away she touched my hand lightly. "Anyway, early bird, I'm a free agent, you know."

We departed from Kandy as we had entered it, with thin rain sweeping down from the hills, pervading the car with its damp and its chill. Fortunately Joseph had done something about the leaking rear window so I was spared the discomfort of another wetting, but he could do nothing about the depression that settled upon me. David was in fine fettle, in no way abashed by the incident of the morning, riding high and ignoring my taciturnity. He talked blandly across me to Martina, choosing the only subject they had in common.

"What did you think of the Temple of the Tooth, Mrs Gale?" His politeness sounded a trifle exaggerated to me, an undertone of mockery somewhere in its smoothness, particularly in the way he came out with the "Mrs Gale".

"Very interesting." If she noticed anything in his manner she showed no sign, whereupon David went on about the Buddhist ethic, the Buddhist Way, instant Buddhism. It would have been amusing but for his sincerity, that same feeling of conviction which I had noticed about him at the Vatadage, as though he was drawing strength from his new beliefs. I had the uneasy notion that Janice wouldn't see her son for quite a while and that when she did he would be a different person. Martina appeared to be impressed but I didn't know whether it was by what he said or by the extent of his knowledge.

"This Buddha," she broke in. "He was strong on poverty, wasn't he? I mean no materialism, give your bread away, the simple life and all that."

"Right on," David agreed. "The monks own nothing but three yellow robes and their alms bowls. Earthly possessions are a load to the true believer." Putting his hands together he began quoting solemnly. "May I not be selfish and self-possessive but selfless and disinterested! May I be able to sacrifice my pleasure for the sake of others!" He looked around, smiling selfconsciously. "That's one of the Perfections."

155

"Then what about all those jewels back there in the temple?" Martina came back at him.

He shrugged and pulled a face, countering adroitly. "Everything is relative. Each gives according to his means. Kings of every Buddhist country gave that stuff. Relative, like I said."

Martina looked thoughtful but said nothing and when David didn't elaborate the conversation lapsed. Then Joseph, sensitive to his clients' silences, began to talk about the Sri Lankan Government's intention to nationalise the tea plantations which Martina deplored, as any good American would, while David, like any good adherent of the counter culture, approved whole-heartedly, saying some harsh things about Big Business fattening on cheap labour, and going on to cite a report he'd recently read about the high incidence of malnutrition among the Sri Lankan tea-pluckers and their chronic inability to support themselves even if they worked every hour of the day and every day. I was surprised, for except for the customary student radicalism, he had given no indication of these feelings. Joseph looked worried and began to protest and so the discussion became an argument on human rights.

Stifling a smile I stared out at the thousands of dripping tea bushes. The rain had brought the pluckers out in force for that, Joseph had informed us, was when the sap rose in the plants, making it the optimum time for gathering. We passed groups of them, thin, bedraggled, shivering women with bags or pieces of plastic over their heads, scurrying dejectedly through the rain. Others were already pawing over the bushes, nipping and tweaking. It was like the television advertisements for tea, except that the advertisements didn't show the rain or the cold or the bone-thin, hungering, servile bodies. I found myself thinking of poverty and Buddhist abstinence and tea plantations and malnut-rition and those wretched Tamil women hurrying head down through the drizzle.

By mid-afternoon we ascended to Ella Gap, climbing out of the rain, above the clouds, emerging in a fresh-washed, golden world of sunny voids between bald peaks or tree-furred hillsides and stretches of rankly grassed, cleared slopes which Joseph called *patna* land where, he added, deer and bears were sometimes seen. Below us mist was streaming along the valleys, looking more like one's idea of Scotland than of Sri Lanka.

As the name implies Ella Gap is an opening high in the hills where a Rest House stands on an elevated point, looking down a mountain corridor. The place is not large, but quite adequate as Rest Houses go, while from a railed lookout point on the bluff the view of the upland plains below is magnificent.

There were a couple of people on the lawn and several more were bunched within the rails of the lookout: as we drove up to the porch their pale faces turned to watch us, but since they were too far away to distinguish clearly I took them for Common Market folk. One of them had a movie camera which put the usual tourist's 16 mm to shame, as big as a small portmanteau, with twin film containers like Micky Mouse ears, very professional looking. I also noticed one of the girls in the group, black hair, pale, straight, slender legs under a short skirt, and she was carrying a clipboard. It was an unusual item for a tourist to be carrying but then tourists encumber themselves with some peculiar things. Yet it wasn't the camera or the clipboard or the girl in the skirt that interested me, so much as the way they stared at us, even after we had alighted from the car. Then Joseph was leading the brace of boys who carried our bags up the steps, followed by Martina, then me, with David, as junior and supernumerary, bringing up the rear. At the entrance of the Rest House I looked back. The party in the lookout had turned back to the view, with the exception of one man who was talking animatedly to the girl with the clipboard, pointing in our direction.

Joseph's inspection of our rooms was thorough, prodding beds, flicking light switches, testing hot water taps like the veriest martinet. Without consulting us he ordered Martina's bags to be put in the same room as mine. Also without comment David slung his pack and flight bag into the adjoining room.

Later, showered and changed, we strolled out to the porch to look at the view. The other guests had also retired to the porch, sitting around a table with drinks, laughing and chattering like a flock of birds. Even before I emerged among them I heard their voices and knew that they were Japanese.

For some reason I was disturbed, not shocked or surprised, but something I had taken for granted, something I hadn't thought about for many years, was rudely shaken. Thirty-three years before I had been brought to this island to take part in its defence against the Japanese. For a moment the intervening years were gone, leaving a sharp sense of failure. An old hostility flared momentarily and with it a resentment, not so much against the Japanese as against history and that supreme exercise in futility which is called war, with its subsequent events which proved me to have wasted two years of my life fighting the Japanese. Of course it was a pointless preoccupation with the past, but what man who has risked his life in a war has not felt as I did at some time? Then the feeling subsided, commonsense accepting the inevitable, but a restraint remained like a bruise.

At our appearance the Japanese fell silent, an air of expectancy seeming to settle over them as though they had been waiting for us. There were six of them, four slender, vital-looking young men with smooth, smart, Oriental faces, and two exquisite young women who looked as dainty and as fragile as blown-glass figurines. They all looked so young and sophisticated and contemporary, children of this nuclear age, so unlike the stunted, haggard, malarial wretches we had come up against during that last year in New Guinea. That much has to be said for General MacArthur's post-war reconstruction programme—it has produced a race of super Japs.

Then I saw David rising from his seat among them, coming to us in long, eager strides. Behind him one of the girls was also rising, moving around the back of the group towards us.

"We've been waiting for you," David greeted effusively. I noted his use of the plural and realised that he was excited.

"You didn't waste any time settling in," I commented.

"Why not?" He tossed his head, laughing elatedly. "They asked me to join them. They're a television crew from Tokyo and they're making a documentary on Sri Lanka."

"Fine," Martina approved brightly and she would have said more, but just then the Japanese girl joined us.

David turned to her, bringing her forward, a svelte, sylph-like figure admirably displayed by Western dress, a carefully cosmeticised, doll-like face smiling its stereotyped, geisha smile and those lovely legs. All that good Australian beef, all that good American enlightenment, all that money and technology and liberation. Catching my eye she bobbed her head, all that was left of the traditional submissiveness of the women of old Japan.

"This is Micky," David was saying. "She speaks English."

"My name is Meiko," the girl corrected gently, looking up at him appraisingly out of almond eyes. "We are from Nippon television and we would be honoured if you would permit us to photograph you here."

Her English was faultless, and except for a certain sibilance, without accent; certainly no trace of the usual difficulties which most Japanese have with our pronunciations. She was representative of the new Japan, one of the phoenix generation risen out of the heat of nuclear explosion.

"Isn't she groovy?" David enthused.

"Yeah, groovy," Martina conceded with rather less enthusiasm.

The girl ignored her, acknowledging David's accolade with an upward smile, cool, without coquetry. When she looked at me I had the feeling of an ageless, Oriental woman considering me speculatively with an understanding which we Westerners are slow to grasp.

"He is your son, I think," she pronounced with an almost oracular innocence.

That jolted me, cutting right through my precious pretences. I glanced at David, aware that Martina was looking at me intently and I knew that the girl hadn't missed the exchange and was including it all in her speculation. It was as though some sort of web had dropped over the three of us with the girl, Meiko, caught in it momentarily. Oblivious of that communion David was laughing, embarrassed, yet pleased by the girl's attention, quite under the spell of her miniaturised, Japanese beauty.

"Don't tell him that," he clowned. "Do you know, when I was a little kid I used to tell people he was my second father."

"And I used to think I was," I amended, suddenly finding that I enjoyed taking that risk. Meiko nodded, still studying me out of narrow, knowing, black eyes.

"I think so too," she agreed ambiguously, then her beautifully manicured, pale hand swept out, indicating the lookout and the scenery. "You will help us, please? Our director wishes to film this place for Nippon television. He would be happy if you would allow him to include you in our picture."

"They want a shot of us looking across the valley," David hastened to elaborate. "You know the kind of thing, tourists from all over the world coming to Sri Lanka, British, Germans . . ."

"Australians," Meiko interjected gravely and somehow her slight bow to me seemed to transform the word into an honorific.

"What about it, Mase?" David urged. "I told them you were a

big-shot Australian author. How does that grab you?"

"Not very much," I demurred dryly, not liking the thought of him misrepresenting me to the Japanese. And to please Meiko. Also there was something petty about the deceit which I couldn't condone. An Australian author, yes, but a big-shot . . . ! He meant well of course, but I didn't have these young people's slavish admiration for television, nor their craving to be seen on it, believing that it was the ultimate in recognition. And least of all did I want to be seen on Japanese television. It was something I couldn't explain, something deep and unrelenting, left over from the past.

"I'd rather not, thanks all the same," I declined gently.

"Why not?" David was surprised, nonplussed.

"He's camera-shy, that's why," Martina broke in briskly. "He won't even let me photograph him."

"Ah so," Meiko murmured softly, glancing slantwise at her. Once again I marvelled that so little yet so much could be read into that utterance, a question, resignation, or polite regret. Certainly that boundless female understanding which Eastern women have developed after centuries of submission to their men. Martina was oblivious of it, smiling thinly at me. I was on the point of capitulating when I saw one of the young men at the table lift the camera to his knees, smiling confidently as he checked its controls. Something about that smile stiffened my resolve. It was so Japanese—arrogant and confident—like the Japanese I had known.

Looking at David I shook my head. "You go. I'll wait here."

"You're sure?"

Still he hesitated. I could see him mulling over my refusal hurriedly, warily, just as he had been put out by my refusal to finish the climb with him at Sigiriya. He wasn't used to me backing out on a thing: in the past it had always been me who had urged, opening his mind to new possibilities, leading him. He suspected me, and more than ever I knew that we were in competition, pressuring each other, manoeuvring, taking advantage of every shift of circumstance. Suddenly conscious of Martina at my side I wondered to what lengths he would go in that competition.

"You go in my place," I invited softly. "I'll delegate you to stand in for me. You be the big-shot from Australia, David."

It was a senseless gibe compounded of my mood of that

moment—David, Martina, our tensions and my own historic grudge, utterly without justification. He stared at me mutinously, his chin lifting aggressively, then, just as he had done at Sigiriya, he turned to Martina now.

"What about you, Mrs Gale? You'll be in it, won't you?"

"Of course she will." I was unable to resist that one also. "She's a free agent, isn't she?"

And that one registered. Martina gave me a hard glance, not answering. Opening her handbag she brought out a tiny mirror and studied her reflection, mouthing the lipstick she had put on not ten minutes before.

"Hows about we knock off the Mrs Gale bit, huh," she suggested briskly. "After all you're just about one of the family, second father and all that." Again her sidelong glance burned over me. "Anyway, 'Missus' always makes me feel like something out of the deep-freeze. What about 'Martina'?"

Taken with Meiko as he was, David was slow to realise what she was saying, then his eyes widened delightedly, his smile opening whitely in his beard.

"Sounds great! Tina. Like in 'concertina', eh?"

I looked at Martina, waiting for an outburst: in Colombo she had warned me against calling her 'Tina'. Pulling a little face she dropped the mirror back in her bag, closed it and looked up at Meiko, smiling brightly.

"Yes, well, I guess if we're going to be in this movie we'd better go down there while the light is still good."

We are travelling again, encapsulated in the car, enclosed in a bubble of upholstered steel and glass that whirrs and grinds and bumps occasionally, yet always keeps us dry and at one remove from the realities outside, from the rain and the chilly, tea-girt hillsides and the dejected women who work on them.

This is the third or fourth day we have been travelling—the fourth I think—and this feeling of timelessness, of time and myself becoming static entities, steals over me before I have been in the car for very long.

Paradoxically it is time that stands still while we are travelling, arrested hours during which we sit lumpishly while the countryside streams past. We are static, it is our surroundings which are flux, villages, people, traffic on the road, the endless downward sweep and dip of the road itself, coming into our consciousness, registering varying peculiarities, then whooshing past, back out of sight into that limbo which is a jumble of images. The road of today is so like the road of yesterday and the day before.

It is only when we stop —"comfort stops" Joseph calls them for obvious reasons —that I have the feeling of time again. Because of this events that occur during these halts have a brilliance, multi-faceted and often hard-edged, like jewels studding the green belt of the day. There is the night of the Sri Maha Bodhi ceremonies and Martina drinking bourbon; being in bed with her at Polonnaruwa; meeting David at the Vatadage; David at Sigiriya; events at Kandy and lastly, and most hard-edged of all —the Japanese at Ella Gap. That one has a significance which I have not yet determined, but I have a feeling that whatever it is it is detrimental to me, something to do with my long-standing ill-feeling for the Japanese. Martina has not commented on the incident, not even when we went to bed, which is unusual for her. I feel that she also has sensed a significance in the episode and is trying to understand it herself.

Of course we talk as we go along, for in the presence of Joseph and Gopal we are three congenial travellers, but our conversations are superficial, burgeoning out of comments on the things we see, circling aimlessly and subsiding, exhausted. Yet under the banter there is an undercurrent of feeling which is anything but congenial. I know that David is watching me, listening for anything that can be used against me. This is proved by what he says when we resume our journey after having been conducted over a tea factory.

It is like any other factory, bustle, machinery pounding, belts flapping, but what is different are the baskets of wilting green leaves, "only the tenderest tips", that are being brought in, and the all-pervading aroma, sappy, slightly acidic, but unmistakeably of tea. Dark, barefooted women and girls peep at us, giggling, from behind the frames of grading machines. Martina photographs several of them solemnly lined up beside dusty mounds of tea. One of them writes the address of the factory and asks that a copy of the print be sent to each of them. Then the young man who has shown us around tells us that we are each permitted to send home a two-and-a-quarter kilogram packet of tea. I suggest to David that he send a packet to his mother, and I despatch another to Clare. Whatever it is between Clare and me is not strong, yet it means

162

enough for me to want to send her something unusual, something inimitably Sri Lankan. So what better than tea? I pay, both for my own consignment and for David's, and it is I who writes both addresses in the book which the manager keeps for that purpose. David watches, smiling, patently humouring me. Not so, however, when we return to the car.

"Who's Clare Dalley, Mase? I thought I knew all your girlfriends but I don't know her."

"You don't know everything David." How bloody juvenile, I explode inwardly: how pathetically small-minded! "Clare does my typing, has done for years. We're old friends."

"Seems like it." He turns to Martina, grinning hugely. "He's a dark horse, is Mase. I often wondered what he was up to when he went off up north each year."

"Business," I say, trying not to sound cross.

"Yeah, monkey business." He cannot resist that hoary old one, or perhaps he is so young that it is new to him. Anyway, he thinks he has me on the rack and is pleased with himself. "What do you think, Tina? Where did he get the experience to write all those love scenes in his books?"

Every author has that said to him, but coming from David it is an affront, clumsy, lacking in originality and with malice aforethought. Martina shrugs but I know he has made his point.

"I don't think anything, David. I'm keeping out of it."

At least she professes disinterest and I am glad of that, so to keep it light I recite the standard reply which I have for that question. "All characters are fictitious and any likeness to the author is coincidental."

"Oh sure," he agrees sardonically.

By midday we are out of the hill country with its winey air, its mists and its clammy chill. The rain is still with us intermittently, but we are back in the land of palms and paddi fields. The air is noticeably warmer. Joseph tells us that we are not far from the coast and that soon we will reach Tissamaharama, where we will have lunch at the Rest House before a Land Rover from the Wild Life and Game Preservation Service arrives to take us around the Yala Game Sanctuary. I welcome the thought of wild animals for a change. At least they are uncomplicated, without deceit or malicious ploys.

Yet when we pull up in front of Tissamaharama Rest House

monkeys are playing on the roof. Martina scrambles out to photograph them and when she has done so I borrow her camera to look at them through the telescopic lens. They are big and lanky, with pepper-and-salt coloured fur and sooty faces like vaudeville comedians, clownish yet shrewd, with a haunting sadness in their huge, round eyes: they carry their tails in the shapes of question marks. The Ramayana, that great Buddhist epic, tells of Monkey Soldiers assisting Rama, the young Indian prince, in his battle against Hanuman, the Demon King, and it is no wonder that they play such a large part in the folklore of Asia—they are such caricatures of ourselves. Or are we the caricatures of monkeys gone mad, pompous bipeds raising ourselves upright on Darwinian pretensions to superiority? I get the answer to that question from one of the monkeys. As we watch, David and Martina laughing and gesticulating, the terribly scarred elder of the troop takes umbrage, first herding his females and infants and frisking youngsters away, then coming down the roof to the very eaves, jabbering and grimacing, with much yawning and baring of yellowed fangs, and then turning, and with a dignity which no human being could hope to emulate, defecating on the Rest House steps in front of us.

The Land Rover spluttered chronically, idling raggedly, loosing frequent noisy eructations of grey smoke that smelled of burned oil and unburnt fuel. It was old, British army flotsam by the look of it, washed up here at the end of the war and used hard ever since. A framework had been added to its rear section so that tourists could stand safely to view the wildlife, and although the bodywork had been recently painted and the Wild Life and Game Preservation Service stencil renewed I doubt that much had been done to the engine since some British Ordinance corporal had handed it over on Independence Day. Listening to it draw up in front of the Rest House I diagnosed its malaise as either dirty fuel, or worn or improperly set electrical points. I remarked to Martina that I didn't like the look of it, but she astonished me by murmuring "I think he's dishy!" It took me a moment to realise that she was referring to the driver.

He would have rated that reaction from most women, for he was young, with that startling, androgynous beauty which you see in

Hellenistic statuary such as the *Ludovici Ares* or the bust of *Antinous Mondragone*, an almost Greco-Roman effeteness. Tall and thin, his brown hands and bare forearms drooping from the steering wheel with an elegant languor, he reposed rather than sat in the driving seat, his long body curved bonelessly, knees bent, big, booted feet filling the limited space. His self-absorption was unshakeable. Even when David climbed into the seat beside him, while the rest of us disposed ourselves along the uncomfortable benches behind, he disdained to look at us, presenting his cameo profile for our admiration, comely and knowing it, driving himself single-mindedly through his narcissistic world. It was like being chauffeured by the ghost of Adonis.

Our journey to the sanctuary wasn't without incident for the engine misbehaved at frequent intervals, back-firing and missing, whereupon the driver would tread the accelerator pedal with brutal force, as though he was chastising an obstreperous beast. Once, despite this rugged treatment, the engine coughed itself into extinction and the Land Rover coasted impotently to the edge of the road. This time the driver alighted, rangey limbs unfolding languidly, and lifting the bonnet he removed the air-cleaner and puffed mightily down the fuel line, all with a beautifully vexed disdain which wasn't without a certain histrionic virtuosity. I wondered whether we would end up pushing our sickly vehicle to the sanctuary.

However, we finally reached the sanctuary. At the entrance, which had sentry boxes and a boom-gate like Checkpoint Charley, there was a pavilion-like building into which Joseph disappeared to report our arrival to the chief warden. With David and Martina I strolled around the small museum, viewing the skeleton of an enormous crocodile, pairs of yellowing elephant tusks set up like bridal arches, a couple of snarling, glassy-eyed leopards' heads, several pairs of massive buffalo horns with wickedly sharp, discoloured tips, some glass cases of stuffed lesser creatures and birds, and an Honour Roll bearing the names and photographs of wardens who had given distinguished service. Four of them had died in fights with poachers.

"Give me animals any time," Martina murmured when I drew her attention to the fact.

Just then Joseph emerged from the warden's office with a leaf-brown, barefooted, buck-toothed little man in a stained khaki shirt and shorts. Joseph explained that he was the tracker who would accompany us to see that we came to no harm and to ensure that we left the sanctuary before dark. Headlights disturbed the animals, and elephants were prone to charge when frightened.

"If he's supposed to protect us why hasn't he got a gun," David wanted to know.

"Oh no, sir," Joseph explained hurriedly. "In the sanctuary animals are never shot."

David laughed. "Does he bare those teeth at the elephants? Is that why he doesn't wear boots—in case the elephants won't be scared?"

I wondered whether the tracker understood English, but he merely rolled his bright, brown, red-veined eyes and bared his protruding teeth in a hideously amiable grin.

Much of Yala Sanctuary was bushland. There were a few small tracts of jungle, but the rest was open grassland or patches of thickly timbered scrub interspersed with pools and wallows and swampy places "all set around with fever trees", as Kipling puts it, and all penetrated by a maze of haphazardly winding, muddy tracks. At least they were muddy that day, for the rain had not gone away, still no more than drizzle yet unpleasant to drive into. Martina, who had been accorded the place of honour at the framework because of her photography, had tied a scarf over her hair and steadfastly kept the lens of her camera turned into her bosom. I stood behind her rather more precariously, arm spread around her, gripping the framework. Standing thus the upper parts of our bodies soon became wet. Joseph and the tracker huddled under the meagre shelter of the partial canopy. Only David and the driver remained dry. I had a gloomy premonition that we wouldn't see a leopard under these conditions—cats have much more sense than tourists.

If our first sighting wasn't spectacular at least it was unusual, giving me a look at a creature that I had only seen mentioned in the clues of crossword puzzles. It was a pangolin, often confused with "palanquin" by crossword puzzle enthusiasts. Unfortunately it was dead, its head having been rather messily removed. The tracker sighted it first, trilling what sounded like bird songs at the driver who brought us to a halt alongside the carcass. It lay in a welter of dirt torn up by a much larger animal, a sad, mustard coloured, little cadaver that looked like an oval section of venetian blind, all overlapping plates with horny legs and a long armour-plated tail. Where the head had been there was just a macerated stump trailing wisps of white tendon. Without alighting the tracker studied the signs and pronounced that a leopard had chewed the creature's head off, and not very long ago since the rain hadn't yet obliterated the spoor. It might even be lying up in the scrub watching us at that very moment. I looked around uneasily, suddenly aware that the Land Rover was idling like a winded rickshaw coolie, only bullied into continuing by repeated stabs of the driver's boot.

Our next sighting was a pair of wild pigs that hurtled across the track like four-legged torpedoes before Martina could bring her camera to bear. However about four hundred metres further on she had her chance. A herd of dappled deer were feeding in an open space in company with a lone boar, while in the branches of a scrawny tree a peacock roosted, a teardrop of midnight blue with a drooping sheaf of folded tail. Slipping the clutch the driver let the Land Rover roll quietly to a halt, whereupon the engine coughed asthmatically and died. Nobody moved except Martina, whose camera clicked twice, so loudly that I expected the deer to take fright but they remained feeding calmly, so close that I could have counted the chocolate spots on their buff coloured hides. A mossy-horned buck lifted his head and took a few irritated, pencil-legged steps towards us, chewing like a rabbit, and the boar looked up, red mouth champing with piggy gusto, long white teeth like a dog's. There was an Eden-like unreality about it, the peacefully feeding animals, the weepy quiet of the overcast, the grey-green, untropical looking scrub—more like the Australian bush. Then the peacock screamed like a harridan and at once the boar took off like a rocket leaving its launching pad, while the deer departed more sedately, nervously twitching their scuts. The driver alighted and began leisurely going through the procedure of removing the air-cleaner and unscrewing the fuel line. Joseph and the tracker lit cigarettes so I brought out my pipe. Martina cranked her camera. David watched her.

We were ten minutes there, departing at last in a scud of needle-pointed drizzle. Still in the drizzle, we halted to look at a crocodile lying, in all its antediluvian repulsiveness, on a sand spit which projected into a soupy looking swamp. This time the scene was primeval, the sludgy water spiked by slanting slivers of rain, the mis-shapen trees and a fan-shaped palm that looked like those imprints sometimes seen on coal, and the crocodile. White egrets stood in all the perfection of a Chinese vase painting while an obscenely wattled, stork-like bird walked the edge of the swamp, probing the mud with its beak. Then the driver revved the snuffling motor whereupon the crocodile jacked itself up on bandy legs and launched itself into the water with scarcely a ripple. I rubbed my hand over my face, noticing that the drizzle had stopped.

After that we saw deer, so many that Martina didn't bother to photograph them, and buffaloes browsing in herds or luxuriating, embedded like monstrous raisins in Christmas-cake wallows. Lone bulls swung away at the Land Rover's coming, snorting, fearsome horns laid across their backs, snotty filaments trailing from pimpled, black muzzles. And there was a peacock strutting belligerently beside the track, fanning his gorgeous spread of eyed feathers and screaming stridently at Martina's camera. Once, in a jungly patch, we came upon a family of monkeys, the infants riding on their mother's hindquarters, the males clustering, hurling monkey vituperation at us until the clash of Martina's shutter put them to flight, still screaming and carrying on like hooligans. We even met a white and scarlet tour bus, the largest thing we'd seen until then. It halted for our drivers to converse, shouting to make themselves heard above the diesel's throb and the Land Rover's cough and the throaty purr of the airconditioning, while pale European faces stared at us through the tinted windows. I began to feel like a species of animal myself by the time we parted. Soon after that we saw the leopard.

Again it was the tracker who saw it first, croaking sibilantly, pointing a scrawny arm. I had no difficulty in distinguishing the beast, the speckled yellow of its coat like a blaze against the murky tints of scrub. He was prowling regally across open ground but when he saw us he halted in his tracks and I swear I saw a look of blank surprise on his vicious, triangular, catty face. Then he started off, loping, belly close to the ground, crossing the track no more than thirty metres in front of us, looking like an exotically marked tom cat furtively returning home after raiding someone's chickens. Martina's camera followed him, clashing frantically.

"I got him! I got him," she exulted.

Twisting within the shelter of my arms she swayed against me as

168

the Land Rover bucked in and out of a puddle and her arm went round my waist so that I thought she was going to kiss me. Her excitement was infectious, Joseph chortling, the tracker baring his lichened teeth in a proud grin, while even the driver turned to accord this gabbling tourist woman a supercilious glance. Still clinging together we swooped around a heavily timbered bend with Martina still ecstatically babbling about the leopard so that I gave no heed to the tracker's sudden outburst until Joseph's awed voice cut into my excitement with a single word.

"Ellyfont!"

The driver hit the brakes, bringing the Land Rover to a bucking halt that threw me against Martina and jammed her against the rail. It must have hurt because I heard her gasp. Then the motor slackened to its worrisome dot-and-carry-one beat. Joseph and the tracker were conversing in low, urgent tones and pointing away to our left. It took me a moment to pick out the elephant. There was a lot of trees and scrub ringing an open space in which a large, luxuriantly foliaged bush was growing some hundred metres, or less, from the track. Perhaps it was several bushes or a clump of saplings, I don't know, but the elephant was feeding on them. I seemed to take in every detail of the beast with frightening clarity; its bulk and rotundity, the backswept dome of its great skull and the humped, posterior ridge of its spine, the pillared legs with mushroom feet and half-moon toenails, and the batwing ears that flapped slowly. The brute disappeared while I stared at it, gliding behind the bushes. It was frightening the way that ponderous mass of flesh could move so effortlessly.

A bubble of trepidation started to swell in me and I shivered with a chill that had little to do with my drenched shirt. Glancing at Martina I saw that she was untroubled by the elephant's presence, examining her telly lens—apparently it also had taken a bump. David was leaning out of the cabin while Joseph and the tracker were silent. The driver revved the ailing engine, not with his usual elan but gently, almost stealthily, and I remembered Joseph saying that frightened elephants usually charged. I hoped this one was accustomed to hearing motors backfiring. Overhead a brahminy kite skidded sideways across the sky, screeching unpleasantly.

"Why won't it come out?" Martina asked plaintively.

She had the camera at the ready, the long, weighty tube of the telly lens slanting slightly. I found myself regarding the thing sourly. If it wasn't for that camera we'd be tootling blithely down the track, leaving the elephant to its repast. Just then the Land Rover emitted more sounds like subdued burps and again the driver revved it cautiously. Tensing I glanced towards the elephant.

"It will come out in a minute," Joseph promised nervously.

David looked around, grinning. "Lets see if he'll show himself when I whistle."

And he whistled, a prolonged, low, monotone note repeated twice more at regular intervals, like kangaroo shooters do to tempt their quarry to sit upright and look around, for kangaroos are very inquisitive creatures. But elephants aren't: they charge without waiting to investigate. Uneasily I watched the saplings, imagining that I saw movement through the leaves which may have been ears flapping. I tried to remember all that I knew about elephants but the only thing that came to me was that flapping ears was a sign that a charge was imminent. David whistled again, three or four low calls that penetrated to the very core of my nervous system.

"Let up, David," I commanded tersely.

"What's wrong, Mase?"

He looked up at me, surprised, innocent, guilefully guileless, enjoying my apprehension. Just then the motor coughed and for a breath-taking moment I thought it was going to cut out completely.

"Just shut up, that's all," I snapped.

"Yes, shut up, David," Martina joined in, but she was smiling and I had the unpleasant feeling that she was merely humouring me.

Shrugging David turned in his seat and stared at the saplings.

And then, because I happened to be looking at David, I saw the driver's brown left hand go out to the dashboard and twist the ignition switch. The engine died with dramatic suddenness, a last soughing throb and instantly the silence rushed in, bringing leafy, wilderness sounds and the insane, high-pitched, muted shrilling of insects. There is something maddening about the sound, all those millions of disinterested insects screaming mindlessly.

"My God," Joseph intoned hollowly. "He shouldn't have done that!"

The bubble of fear in me felt as large as a balloon, constricting my breathing. The tracker leaned forward, gabbling at the driver, cantilever teeth bared, no longer a bird song but deep-throated gutterals, castigating savagely. Turning, a look of great hurt passed over the driver's beautiful features and somewhat sullenly he reached again for the ignition switch.

In the quiet the grind of the starter motor sounded as loud as a circular saw ripping into a log. Fearfully I stared at the saplings, suddenly possessed of X-ray vision that could distinguish the elephant's outline through the foliage, seeing something large and brown like a fishing boat's sail, something pendulous and fleshy curling ominously. I also made out something curved and ivory-coloured that hadn't been there before. With a shock I realised that I was looking at the elephant's head. It had moved around the bush until it was looking at us.

Again the starter motor sawed loudly, advertising our helplessness. The elephant fanned its ears, curling its trunk petulantly, and simultaneously I found that I was taking note of every tree within hop-skip-and-jump distance: they all looked so stunted and deplorably frail. I wondered whether Martina was agile. Languidly the driver uncurled himself from his seat, banging the door of the Land Rover shatteringly, and strolling round to the front, opened the bonnet, letting it clatter hideously against the windscreen. Removing the aircleaner he produced a spanner and proceeded to disconnect the fuel line. He seemed to perform every action in slow motion, and my hearing must have been abnormally acute because the rattle of the spanner on the copper piping sounded horribly alien and provocative out there, with a wild elephant watching us and those crazy insects cheering him on. Then the tracker went over the tailboard like a monkey, so suddenly that I almost followed instinctively, but he merely scampered around the front of the vehicle. There followed a spirited exchange, the tracker hissing angrily, the driver answering in offended tones. Catching my eye Joseph shrugged apologetically: it didn't ease my mind to see that he was worried, particularly when I recalled that he had been a Forestry Officer and knew the caprices of wild elephants.

"The circuit bungalow," he said desperately. "There is a circuit bungalow a couple of kilometres from here. When we get there we will fix the car properly."

When . . . ? If! Anxiously I turned back to the elephant. It was turning its ears inside out like wind scoops and curling and uncurling its trunk over its brow like a small boy thumbing his nose. Martina, unperturbed, had the camera to her eye studying the beast through the telescopic lens.

"He's big, isn't he," she remarked in that syrupy tone women use when they're admiring babies. "I wish he'd come right out and let me get a good shot of him."

"Oh no, Madam," Joseph pleaded, showing a lot of the whites of his eyes. "He is a charger. He has a short tail."

In the vague, distracted way of such moments I wondered why a short tail would predispose an elephant to mayhem, what quirk of animal psychology found cause for resentment in that feature, but I was never to ask because just then I was aware of David getting out of the Land Rover. I thought he was going to join the tracker who was perched on the bumper bar, teeth and head bowed over the engine like a scruffy bird. The driver had laid his spanner on the mudguard and was now puffing into the fuel line like an Arab with a hubble-bubble pipe. Instead, to my horror, David advanced three or four steps from the track and stood staring at the elephant. I swear my hair stood on end. I don't know what he hoped to accomplish unless it was to provoke a charge in which he would distinguish himself with a Walter Mitty gallantry. It was sheer bravado, calculated to show me up and impress Martina, all with that blind faith in his immortality which is the courage of the young.

"Sir! Come back!" Joseph was leaning far out over the side of the Land Rover, frantic with worry. "Watch out, he will charge!"

"David! Don't be a bloody fool," I rasped, trying to keep my voice low yet still project authority.

He heard me, the toss of his head, the lift of a shoulder, then he turned and gave me a wild, defiant, even contemptuous smile, delaying several heartbeats longer to show me that he wasn't submitting, that he wasn't to be coddled by his mother or me any longer. Nonchalantly, with a cockahoop lift of his bearded jaw, he strolled back, not to his seat but to the driver and the tracker. Behind him the elephant thumbed its trunk at him, flapping big ears irritably. I was shaking, white knuckles gripping the framework like claws, the bubble of fear in my guts pushing up under my heart, making me sick. Suddenly I felt old.

"Bloody young fool," I growled feelingly.

"Don't get so uptight," Martina chided smilingly.

I could have hit her then, slamming my affronted older man's outrage against her head. She was no better than David, too unthinkingly ignorant to recognise danger, easily carried away by excitement without thought of consequences. David would preen and strut and she would admire and David would strut all the more. That was the pattern that ensured the continuity of all species. Women, I thought in the furious calm at the back of my mind, they incite us to the ultimate stupidity, first me and now David. Yet he and Martina had one thing in common, they were young. I drew a harassed breath, intending to blast her back to some commonsense appropriate to her age and experience — marriage, divorce, unhappiness, surely they had some maturing effect — but Joseph forestalled me, gently but sternly reproving her in an old fashioned, gentlemanly manner of which I was totally incapable at that moment.

"Madam, I don't think you know how dangerous that ellyfont is." His vowels were clipped, never more British, yet with that full-mouthed, Singhalese intonation which rolls the words over you. "All old tuskers are chargers. They have been driven out of the herd by younger males and so they are bad tempered and very dangerous. We must not do anything silly."

Martina took it meekly, a trifle taken aback, her camera held halfway to her face. I wanted to applaud Joseph but what he had said about old tuskers disturbed me. The whine of the starter motor cut across the thought. The driver was back in his seat, hopefully tramping the starter, while the tracker had his hand over the throat of the carburettor, making it suck air with a loud hissing. After a few ineffectual turns there was silence, only the insects and the elephant, and the driver making an exasperated gesture. Elbowing the tracker aside David took the spanner from the mudguard and tapped smartly on the diaphragm of the carburettor.

"You've got dirt in the jets," he pronounced, rapping the carburettor again. "Now give it a go."

Again the motor turned over, once, twice, firing, backfiring, then taking hold and revving staunchly. Without hurrying David put the air cleaner back in place, tightened the wing-nuts and closed the bonnet with a hearty slam. As he scrambled into his seat I heard him say above the engine noise: "I don't know why you old blokes get so jumpy."

The circuit bungalow stood in a clearing in the bush, looking more like a farm house in the Australian wheat country than a circuit bungalow in a Sri Lankan game reserve. It had verandas all round, a low, white-painted, paling fence and a vine that climbed a post and dripped blue flowers from the gutters. All around was the same bushland that had once been cleared and was growing up again, long grass, a few big trees and clumps of scrub. Away to our left, white driftsand was banked against large granite outcrops with a few hardy plants sprouting from their cracks. Beyond was a suggestion of the sea, no trees, just the murky sky coming down to the rocks. It was difficult to be sure because we reached the place during the heaviest shower of the afternoon, rain beating the canopy, leaking on our huddled shoulders. Fortunately it wasn't cold. As we splashed to a halt at the bungalow I saw people on the veranda, a couple of women, a child, a man standing beside one of the posts. They were Singhalese, the women in saris, their features very dark and fine boned. One of them rose to receive us as we rushed on to the veranda, heads bowed and shaking ourselves like dogs.

"Hullo, hullo," she greeted affably. "What a pity you weren't here ten minutes ago. You would have seen the elephant."

Elephants didn't turn me on just then, but I got the impression that our hostess was as responsive to them as she was to every other experience, a woman who took an interest in everything, elephants being the sensation of her day. She was small and plump with a charming smile and the pleasant, placid face which time brings to a pretty woman who has matured in contentment and good living. Her sari looked expensive and she wore some solid, knuckle-duster rings while the child, a little boy, looked not only well dressed, but pampered.

I started to thank her for giving us shelter and would have introduced our group but Joseph took it out of my mouth, assuming that near-Prussian formality which he reserved for such occasions, heels together, head inclined, speaking in Singhalese. His deference suggested that these were not ordinary folk.

"This lady is Mrs Gunawardena," he began like a master of ceremonies but at that point the lady, in her turn, took the introduction away from him.

"And this is my mother-in-law." A wave of her hand to the other woman, much older, grey-haired, fierce black eyes and a

174

nutcracker chin, a massive bosom filling out her sari like a trade-wind filling a tea-clipper's sail, flaccid, elderly woman's forearms resting on the arms of a canvas camp chair. "And this is my husband." She indicated the man who looked on silently, slightly stooped, pinch-faced, a sickly yellow under his brown. Since he showed no sign of wanting to shake hands I stood my ground and we exchanged the minimum of conventional grimaces and meaningless words consistent with civility. I sensed a professional detachment about him. Doctor, academic, business man? I began to understand why Mrs Gunawardena took an interest in elephants.

"You will have tea," she pronounced rather than invited.

Her voice was mellifluous, the usual singsong Singhalese cadence noticeably absent. She clapped her hands peremptorily, bringing a black-eyed serving girl out of the bungalow to be subjected to a rush of snappy Singhalese that set her ferrying more chairs from somewhere before disappearing inside on silent bare feet.

We sat in a group except for Mr Gunawardena who slumped in his chair slightly apart, and Joseph for whom no chair had been provided and who stood just outside the pale of our social congress. I sensed the barrier of class, or perhaps caste, relegating him to the status of hired help and I felt sorry for him. The child stood at his grandmother's knee, fidgeting petulantly. The rain had eased and I heard the driver and the tracker getting out of the Land Rover. I noticed that David looked bored.

"Tell me," Mrs Gunawardena commanded sweetly, "have you seen any wild animals today? It is such a pity about the rain."

Martina and I exchanged glances while David smiled lazily. I looked up in time to catch Mrs Gunawardena senior regarding us speculatively. I guessed that she had placed David as my son but Martina—ah! Obviously she was too young to be David's mother and by generally accepted standards also too young to be my wife. I could see that Martina had the old lady intrigued. Meanwhile her daughter-in-law was rushing on, a compulsive talker which wasn't surprising when you considered what life must be like with Mr Gunawardena.

"You've just missed the old elephant. He likes to stand there on those rocks. He comes every day—if the leopard isn't there, that is. There's also a leopard, you see, and it likes to sun itself on those rocks too so, of course, the elephant doesn't come then."

I murmured something about a gentleman's agreement but she didn't hear me because just then the maid arrived with the tea and a plate of water-like confections rolled in delicate scrolls which she set upon a gate-legged table. Mrs Gunawardena sat up, rearranged all the cups on the tray, peered into the teapot and began to pour, in between telling us about the elephants which foregathered around the bungalow at night, silent and well behaved—and my goodness, didn't they look ghostly in the moonlight!—and asking who took milk and who didn't and how much sugar, one lump or two? The little boy stared fixedly at the wafer-like confections while his grandmother laid a seamed brown hand on his head and murmured endearments in a mannish voice which boomed mutedly from caverns deep in her body. Mr Gunawardena said nothing. Indeed but for him and Joseph it was all very cosy and sociable and eerily British, only vicar and the muffins missing. It gave me another insight into the extent to which the British way of life and standards had penetrated the upper social echelons of this island. They were like a fragment spun off the Victorian era and left to rusticate, insulated and insular.

"Is that the sea over there?" I enquired, not because I was interested but because so far we visitors had said little, David sitting like a dummy, Martina interposing American accented "my goodnesses" and "fancy thats" which jarred against Mrs Gunawardena's elegant, markedly Anglo-Saxon diction. Besides, I had the uncomfortable feeling that the old lady had reached a conclusion for she was looking at Martina disapprovingly, and at me with undisguised contempt.

"Oh yes," Mrs Gunawardena nodded. "The sea is on the other side of those rocks. We don't go bathing of course—the animals, you know. But being so close to the sea is what keeps this bungalow so lovely and cool. It is by far the most pleasant of them all."

Despite myself I felt my eyebrows go up and I wondered how they came to be here, holidaying in a circuit bungalow which, I understood, was for the use of rangers caught out on patrol after dark. It smelled of good connections, old family wealth, the class and caste thing which had put poor Joseph on the outer. Mrs Gunawardena had passed the tea around and was about to take up the plate of confections when the little boy pounced, snatching one and ramming it into his mouth.

"Wilfred!" His mother wheeled, her plumpness stiffened voluptuously, splendid eyes huge with outrage. "Where are your manners, sir? You know it's rude to snatch. You're a naughty little boy!"

The wilful Wilfred stared at her, his eyes also splendid, but huge with mutiny and glee, the scroll-shaped wafer sticking out of his mouth like a grotesque cigar. His grandmother made indulgent, clucking sounds, again touching his shoulder and darting a bright, beaky glance at her daughter-in-law so that for several heartbeats the silent tension of confrontation was stretched embarrassingly over us all. Then Mrs Gunawardena junior capitulated, turning to us, pretending, knowing that she had been defeated again.

"You must excuse him," she cooed maternally. "Since we have come back the servants"—a glance at the old lady belied that word—"have spoiled him shockingly. And I think he's missing all his little friends in New York."

"New York?" Martina perked up at once.

"Yes. You're an American, are you not?"

"Texas," Martina stated succinctly and I heard echoes of Belle Starr, Calamity Jane and all the other lady outlaws of the Wild West. "How old is he?" I recovered myself, realising that she was asking about the little boy.

"He will be four this year," Mrs Gunawardena supplied fondly. "He was born in New York. We have lived there for four years. My husband is a lawyer with our Sri Lankan delegation to the United Nations. He has been very ill so we have come home on furlough."

United Nations! And a lawyer. That explained much—the circuit bungalow, the smell of wealth, Joseph's deference. A big wheel in a land of so many little wheels within wheels. Mr Gunawardena continued to look sick and smug and aloof. Mrs Gunawardena senior looked proudly at her son. Wilfred munched the last of the wafer. I found myself listening to the voices of the tracker and the driver and the occasional clatter of tools as they worked.

"Is this your first visit to Sri Lanka?" Mrs Gunawardena asked Martina, who nodded and glanced sidelong at me for some reason.

"I'm a journalist doing an assignment on the tourist potential."

"How nice," Mrs Gunawardena remarked ambiguously: she was looking Martina over with that critical intentness which women turn on one another, doubtless thinking of all she had heard about lady journalists. "And you, sir, you are not an American, are you?"

I realised that she was addressing me, having picked my accent for a maverick. "I'm Australian." As I spoke I knew that she would be putting one and one together and coming up with a juicy twosome.

"Ah, an Australian." She looked at me rather coyly. "We have had your cricketers here recently. My goodness, didn't they give our lads a trouncing! Our papers say that we must learn to play cricket the Australian way. They say we are too gentlemanly."

There it was again. Ye Olde Mother Country. Damn it all, man! Australian cricket is just not cricket! She played it up, dimpling prettily, but nonetheless I was being reproved for my countrymen's ruthless sportsmanship.

"And this is your first visit to Sri Lanka?" She kept at me, gently and with a pretty insistence.

"I was here for a few months many years ago."

"During the war," Martina interposed quickly.

I don't know why she had to mention that but it had a peculiar effect on old Mrs Gunawardena. She snorted and sat bolt upright, fixing me with a renewed interest which I found disquieting. Young Mrs Gunawardena glanced at her and smiled serenely.

"I was only a little girl then, a wee baby," she told me primly, stressing her "weeness" as if it gave her considerable womanly comfort. "But my mother-in-law remembers the Australian soldiers."

Nodding I pretended to appear interested. Somehow she had made me feel as though I had just crawled out of a time machine, hoary, prehistoric, a survivor of an earlier, fallacious age. Bracing myself I faced the old lady, finding myself subjected to a fiercely bright-eyed scrutiny, that boney blade of nose and witch's chin tilting towards me imperatively. A powerful, matriarchal personality turned pitilessly on me like a searchlight.

"In which province were you stationed?" she rumbled.

"All over the place really." I jerked a hand perfunctorily, hoping to imply a ubiquity which made me in no way responsible for the misdemeanours of the rest of my countrymen and then, because there was no resisting her interrogatory state, I had to be specific. "Bentota, Horana, Udugama . . ."

178

"Ah!" She impaled me with that exclamation. "I remember you fellows at Udugama."

Her tone suggested secret knowledge of old misdeeds, making me search my conscience frantically. Which of us there in those days had got drunk or made advances to the village girls or run over a dog or omitted to pay for his washing? At the periphery of my vision I was aware of Martina watching me, while David was also looking interested.

"I wasn't stationed with the other troops at that time," I pointed out, not only for old Mrs Gunawardena's edification. "A couple of us were on a detachment, working with the local Justice of the Peace, a Mr Jayasakewa. He was our interpreter."

"I knew him," the old lady declared in a voice of doom. "My husband was also in the legal profession and he had many dealings with Mr Jayasakewa. We knew the family."

Anula, I thought, dumbfounded, yet suddenly cautious: she had to be at the core of this. Nothing else would cause this old woman to act like a sort of female Angel Gabriel consulting the Doomsday Book. Certainly the lapse of time made that simile feasible. Udugama of 1942 was almost like another life now, while I was certainly another man. Yet it was fantastic, unbelievable! Of all the people to meet it had to be this grim old matriarch who held some unspecified grudge against me. Why? I had nothing on my conscience as far as Anula was concerned. We had held hands occasionally and she had kissed me goodbye when our marching orders came through and although she wept a little she hadn't asked me to write to her. Apparently she felt she had no claim on me. Casting around for words to ask about her I decided to do so circumspectly. Work on the Land Rover must have been completed for I could hear no sounds from that direction.

"Mr Jayasakewa was very kind to us."

"I know." The old lady cut me short implacably as though Mr Jayasakewa's kindness was related to my crime, whatever that might be.

"He took us into his home and made us welcome."

"Mr Jayasakewa died twenty years ago."

"I'm sorry to hear that."

"He was old." She shrugged with the resignation of one whose time has not long to go.

"And what about the rest of the family? I remember a daughter,

Anula. I suppose she's married."

"Anula is dead."

"Oh."

I suppose I looked stupid just sitting there gaping, but for a moment I couldn't take it in. Anula dead! Not even thirty-three years could soften that fact. We think of people as we last saw them and remembering Anula as she had been made the thought of her death very difficult to accept. I looked away, wanting time to think. Rain was coming in from the sea, drifting greyly across the scrub.

"I'm very sorry to hear it," I said slowly for suddenly I was reluctant to talk about it any more. Something had ended for me here, something sweet and romantic, echoing gently from my youth, had terminated abruptly, rather brutally, leaving me with a poignant sense of loss. Anula and the memory of her had been so closely interwoven with my association with Janice and Eric that I had come to think of her as part of the fabric of that life. Without thinking I fumbled for my pipe, saw that nobody else was smoking and pushed it back into my pocket. Martina was watching me closely, but David was looking away at the rainstorm. Mrs Gunawardena junior was genteely sipping tea.

"Anula died in February 1943," the old lady went on remorselessly and something about her tone told me that she expected that date to have a special significance for me: she even repeated it more fully. "The twenty-fifth of February, 1943."

Still it meant nothing to me except that Anula had died after we had left Ceylon in June '42. Glancing at Mrs Gunawardena senior I was repelled by her beaky features, her coal-hot stare, her direful sibylline relentlessness. I knew that she was telling me something, trying to get it across to me with a maximum of dramatic effect. February '43 and June '42. There had to be a relationship between those dates. I should have realised that something old and shameful was involved when I saw Mr Gunawardena look at his mother and gently shake his head, but I was preoccupied by thoughts of Anula and her death. The old lady spoke again, her tone accusing.

"Her baby was illegitimate. The father was an Australian soldier!"

Baby! My God, so that was what it was all about! Anula and an Australian soldier! And this old harridan thought . . . The enormity of it overwhelmed me, sweeping me back all those years, thinking confusedly. Of course she was wrong. Wrong in a way that I could never prove and that she would never believe. Few things in this life are certain but of one thing I was very sure. Anula's baby wasn't mine . . .

. . . which left only Eric!

"It must have been Eric," I muttered distractedly, opening the door of our room and motioning Martina to precede me.

She went past me into the bedroom without a word and switched on the light. The sudden brightness hurt my eyes just as the enlightenment of the afternoon had hurt me. Let there be light, I mused bitterly. And there was light — stark and searing, illumining the darkest corners of my ignorance, revealing Eric and Anula . . .

It obsessed me, thoughts tumbling in the dark wilderness of my confusion just as we had jolted through the night and the jungle back to Tissamaharama Rest House. We had been late getting away from the circuit bungalow, what with young Mrs Genewardana covering my very obvious shock with hasty sallies of small talk alleviated by more cups of tea and then, after a decent interval of genteel chitchat under the cloud of the old lady's condemnation, gushing farewells, so that the darkness had caught us still in the sanctuary. I wouldn't have cared if we had met another old, rejected elephant, short-tailed and cantankerous, ready to charge. As it was the most dangerous animals we had encountered were a herd of buffaloes congregated in the middle of the track, their rotund, black bodies milling in the headlight beams like tadpoles in a bottle. The Land Rover, its pipes purged and carburettor cleansed, had behaved impeccably and there had only been one light shower of rain to inconvenience us.

"You'd better get those wet clothes off," Martina advised.

She had dropped her handbag and camera on the bed and was unbuttoning her blouse. I fumbled absent-mindedly with the buttons of my wet shirt, still unable to get my mind off Eric.

I had always pitied him because I believed him incapable of siring a child. All those years of living with that conviction and now this — Anula bearing his child! And the child? A girl, old Mrs Genewardana had said, adding with dark disdain that it was alive somewhere. Somewhere! Eric's daughter growing up in a Sri

Lankan village, a woman now, probably with children of her own. Eric's grandchildren! The issue of his loins. While I had . . . David? Yet Eric had fathered Anula's child, hadn't he? I stood for a moment, pondering that thought, feeling the dampness of my shirt unpleasant on my back. No, I decided, it was Eric's final obscene joke, mocking me from beyond the grave. From beyond two graves. Eric laughing at my naïveté all those years, titillating himself with the memory that he had taken Janice from me by implying—cunningly implying—that I had done the very thing of which he now stood proven.

"It must have been him," I insisted doggedly.

"You're sure, huh?"

Martina had removed her blouse and hanging it over the back of a chair she kicked off her damp shoes: without them she looked much smaller, and standing there in only her slacks and bra she reminded me of one of those little clay figures of the half-naked, Minoan fertility goddess. Then she turned away, bare ivory back, quartered by the straps of her bra, bending over her suitcase. Distractedly I tossed my shirt aside.

"Of course I'm sure. There was only the two of us on that detachment. The rest of our company was thirty kilometres away."

"I didn't mean sure in that way." She didn't look up, hands carefully turning over folded clothes. "I mean are you sure you're levelling with me. Did you ball her?"

"Dammit, I tell you I never touched her," I shouted.

"And so you're blaming your buddy, huh?"

Her calm was infuriating. She took something from her suitcase and without so much as a glance at me crossed to where the water carafe stood and gathered up the two glasses. Still angered by her scepticism I didn't realise what she was doing.

"It must have been Eric," I argued resentfully. "An Australian soldier, the old lady said. Well, he was the only other one there."

She didn't answer and looking around I saw that she had the bottle of bourbon, or what was left of it after the night of the Sri Maha Bodhi ceremony. Surprised, I eyed it dubiously, not welcoming its reappearance. It augured ill in some way that I couldn't define. A return of the Martina of the gem shop? Suddenly uneasy I watched her pour the remainder of the liquor, two modest drinks, carefully apportioned to the very last drop—no tears tonight, thank God, no maudlin heart-searchings and invocations of the ghost of Stephen. Raising the empty bottle she wrinkled her nose ruefully. Then she was coming to me with the glasses in her hands.

"You need a drink. It's just not been your day, has it?"

There was a brusqueness about her that irked me vaguely. I thought about the day—that lonely, old, rejected elephant, David's bravado with Martina secretly urging him on, and old Mrs Genewardana's revelation—and I wished I could think of something clever to say, something that would purge me of my shock and bitterness and make me equal to Martina's unconcern. Instead I raised my glass in a toast.

"To posterity," I proposed bleakly. "Eric's—and mine."

"To David," she responded ambiguously.

Startled I looked at her sharply but she was drinking so I emptied my glass, gulping the silken burn in one swallow. To David? To posterity—Eric's and mine? My mind shied away from that doubt, disturbed by the thought that she was being deliberately provocative. A bubble of frustration began to swell in me: her cynicism was becoming hard to bear. Perhaps she was tired. Tired of me and my drama?

We were standing nursing our empty glasses, regarding one another intently. I was conscious of the softness of her shoulders, the way her damp hair curved in dark sickles behind her ears, and her pointed chin lifted challengingly. Suddenly I wanted to kiss her, wanted to press down and smother her cynicism, forcing her to acknowledge my distress. Instead I laid my hand on her shoulder. She twisted away quite violently, ostensibly to put her glass on the dresser but I knew that was a pretence, for I had felt her tense at my touch. Backed against the dresser she watched me, dark eyes not hostile but wary. Piqued I made no attempt to touch her again.

"Why, Martina?"

"That girl." She made a shuddery little gesture. "It's creepy, her coming back like that."

"It bothers you?"

"It's like you've lived another life."

I let a few moments tick by loaded with her unease: she was on the defensive, evasive, while I was calm, in control.

"You think that child was mine, don't you?"

Her gaze met mine then swung away uneasily. "There's another you, Mason, a guy who's lived half his life before I was even born."

So it was out at last, that thing which had haunted me all the time I had known her, and somehow it was the worse for having come from her. Suddenly the difference in our ages was open between us, a void of years in which lurked the ghosts of Anula and her baby. And Eric. And Janice also, in a nebulous way. I drew a deep, despairing breath, feeling frustrated and suddenly old, glancing at the glass in my hand, seeing that it was empty. Empty! Through the window I heard the sounds of dinner being prepared, the clatter of kitchen utensils and the buzz of servants' voices. The village dogs were barking, a yapping concert keen with doggy melancholy. The muffled hiss of a shower came to me through the wall of David's quarters. David seemed always to be within earshot these days. David who had a half-sister somewhere here?

"That's what it's all about, isn't it?" I said.

She looked at me, brows wrinkling worriedly. "It's like you've got ghosts," she said carefully and I knew she was searching for words with which to express herself honestly without hurting me. "The Buddhists say we've lived before—right? Well, that's what I mean about you. It's like you've lived before, seen things, done things, things that are a part of you I'll never know."

"That's understandable, I'm—" I faltered, reluctant to put words to this thing between us then, suddenly desperate, plunging on—"I'm older than you. But that shouldn't worry you."

"But it does," she insisted vehemently. "It's like you come back from the past at times—the other you—like when you wouldn't let the Japanese photograph you. That was the war thing, wasn't it? Okay, I can dig that, but do you have to hate them after all this time?"

I stared at her, dismayed to realise that she had seen through my reluctance at Ella Gap. So that was what had started her thinking this way. More of my ghosts. She was impatient of what my generation thought of as The War, not at ease with it, disparaging. For her it had no reality, no meaning, no credibility. Wanting a moment to think I put my glass on the dresser.

"You don't understand, Martina. I don't hate the Japanese, not now. It's just that I don't want to have anything more to do with them. There's been too much between us in the past."

There it was again, that word "past". For me, in this particular context, it meant accounts of Changi Prison, the Burma Railway, the Sandakan death march, nurses beheaded on a tropic beach. And more personal and harrowing, so much blood in the mud; palm trees circled by deeply trodden tracks where tethered prisoners had provided bayonet practice; wounded crying out to be brought in out of the stinking nights where land crabs gathered and the Japanese waited for restraints to snap; Indian prisoners crucified with bayonets; the bodies of butchered native women rotting in a storm-water drain. That was the past and a changing world required me to forgive, but I would never forget. Feeling more than ever at a disadvantage I gestured helplessly.

"We're all influenced by our past, even you. What about your marriage and divorce—don't you think that's affected you? Every experience we live through is a link in the chain of what we are now."

"Big deal." She hunched a bare shoulder sullenly. "So I've had a bad marriage. But there's part of you always lives in the past, all mixed up with David's old man and David's mother and the war and that girl and her baby. You've got so many spooks, Mason."

Spooks! The word angered me. It was flippant, irreverent, typical of her generation who had never known adversity, took everything for granted, had demanded and been given everything.

"What about Stephen?" I demanded harshly. "Isn't he your spook?"

"Damn you, Mason," she raged. "Leave him out of this, d'you hear! We're talking about you and that girl. D'you realise that her child is four years older than me?"

"Are you telling me you're young enough to be my daughter?"

"I didn't say that."

She turned away, once again presenting her rounded, bare back, so smooth and firm. And young! I wanted to hold her and press her youth against myself, but that was impossible now. Through the wall I heard David turn his shower off, the squeak of the tap and the clank of back-pressure in the pipes.

"I'm sorry, Mason." Still turned away, her voice bitter, scarcely contrite. "It's the past that bugs me. And your baby!"

"Correction," I slammed back harshly. "Not my baby!"

"That's what you say!"

Swinging away she crossed to her suitcase and snatched up her negligee, dragging it on, arms windmilling, much shrugging, fists clutching it closed in front. Decently covered once more she faced me scornfully.

"I've got to hand it to you, Mason. You've laid a few dollies in your time—that girl, David's mother, me. And who's that one you sent the tea to—Miss Clare Dalley? Is she another of your lays?"

That infuriated me. Clare of all people, the least involved in this horrible affair. Hardly knowing what I was doing I grabbed Martina by both arms. She jerked back, wrenching with a lithe, young woman's strength, getting in at least one hefty, bare-footed kick to my shins, but I bore down, applying pressure with my thumbs to the insides of her elbows, at the same time walking her backwards until the edge of the bed was against the backs of her knees. She almost broke free there, managing to drive a sharp elbow into my ribs, but I shoved her hard and she sat down heavily on the bed. Even then she continued to struggle, writhing, elbows thrashing, knees jabbing wickedly at my groin, even trying to get an arm up to bite my hand. Holding her relentlessly I bore down until the pain of my gouging thumbs made her cry out. She was panting, head tipped back, sobbing with pain and humiliation, a straggle of black hair whipped across her eyes. Still holding her I eased some of the pressure on her elbows but kept her knees pinioned between my own.

"Let's get this straight," I ground out grimly and the words seemed to beat against her face for I was bending over her, our faces close. "I didn't fuck Anula! Never! Got that?"

"You bastard, Mason," she hissed, then a shudder ran through her and suddenly she seemed to hang in my grip.

Ashamed of my violence I released her and stepped back quickly in case she lashed out at my groin again. But she remained sitting slackly, glaring at me, crossing her arms over her breasts and rubbing the insides of her elbows. I don't know how long we remained watching one another, then to my surprise she smiled thinly.

"It was your buddy, huh? And you didn't know he was screwing her?"

"What difference would it have made if I had known?"

She didn't answer at once, just sitting still, staring at me and rubbing her elbows. The negligee had slipped off one shoulder and a strap of her bra had been broken in our struggle, peeling down. Seeing me looking at her breast she covered it quickly with a movement which seemed to reject me completely.

"Good old Johnny-Walks-Alone," she jeered softly. "Well, you go on thinking that if it makes you feel good."

The bubble of frustration burst in me, leaving me spent, inadequate, without hope. I would never convince her. Defeated I turned and walked off into the bathroom.

The Buddha of Matara was huge. More than thirty metres high he sat in the lotus position, looking down on a courtyard with a lotus pool. The enormous face was enigmatic, the hair and spiritual topknot painted black, the long feet resting one on top of the other, soles upward and flattened. Around him a nine storey construction was growing up, its skeleton of steelwork putting on grey concrete flesh which would eventually enclose the great figure on three sides and roof it over.

"I'd love a shot of him," Martina yearned, glancing at Joseph, the camera already halfway to her face. Joseph glanced around nervously, but except for the construction workers, high up and ant-like on the scaffolding, there was no one in sight.

"Quickly," he hissed and the Pentax clattered, recording the Buddha of the Purvaramaya Temple for the curiosity of prospective American tourists.

"One day you'll get caught," David predicted disapprovingly.

He was wearing his sarong, David the neophyte once more, all abnegation and piety, shirt hanging out and barefooted, even before the rest of us had removed our shoes at the temple entrance. I wondered what he thought of the incident at the circuit bungalow.

He must have known what Mrs Gunawardena was talking about. He had often listened to Eric and me reminiscing so he knew of our asssignment to Udugama and of Mr Jayasekewa's hospitality. But not about Anula—her name had never been mentioned in David's home. Yet the old lady had made no secret of her suspicions and David, being an astute young man, must surely have pieced the rest together. I felt a tremor of guilt, guilt by association, guilty of not knowing what Eric had done. Not involved, Martina had said. Johnny-Walks-Alone. Looking up at the tranquil face of the Buddha I remembered that David wouldn't be with us much longer, for just as long as it took us to look over this temple and drive the remaining five kilometres to his precious Shangri-La. And suddenly I was glad, looking forward to being rid of his censorious presence. With that thought came another guilt—that I should contemplate parting with David with such relief. David who had been the lodestar of my life.

Martina had lowered the camera and was looking around apprehensively. Her glance passed over me, a tiny hostility flaring in her eyes, then she turned back to David.

"What'll they do if they catch me?"

"Probably take your film," he hazarded dryly.

"You're kidding! So I took a photo of their Buddha. That's what I'm here for—to give the place some exposure. That's a damn good picture, magazine-wise." She swayed closer to him, smiling up beguilingly. "I couldn't pass that one up, Davey boy, just couldn't."

His hands moved impatiently, as though warding off her blandishments. "One may conquer a million in battle but he who conquers himself is the greatest conqueror of all," he intoned unsmilingly and I guessed that he was quoting the Enlightened One. Nevertheless he sounded a trifle smug for someone who had yet to fight most of his life's battles. Yet the change in him troubled me, the smiling young man of yesterday so abruptly transformed into the zealot today. Martina didn't appear to have noticed it.

"Don't come on so heavy, Davey," she chided laughingly. "That pic will make a super cover spread. Can't you see it? The big boy there and our name, *Odyssey*, above him in script and underneath in solid blocks, 'Sri Lanka—Island of Buddhas!'"

She was kidding him openly now, a sweep of her arm tracing that title and subtitle across the sky over the Buddha's head and over the lotus pool at his feet. The movement exposed the inside of her elbow and I saw the suffusion there, too dark to be anything but a bruise. I must have gripped her more tightly than I thought last night. Last night! I shuddered.

The remainder of the evening had been only slightly less ghastly—dinner had been little better than a wake. And the deceased? Anula? Or had it been the troubled thing which had existed so briefly between Martina and me? I had watched its corpse stiffening there on the table between us and I had mourned despite my better judgement. It was David who had carried the evening, which was why I was so surprised at the change in him this morning. If he had felt the tension that had fairly crackled between Martina and me he gave no sign, talking easily about the afternoon, recalling the monkeys and the deer, joking with Martina about "her leopard". At no time, however, did he mention that elephant. I had admired his aplomb and was grateful to him, hoping that he attributed our poor responses and brittle politeness to the shock of the old lady's news. And then had come the final charade, Martina and me walking stiffly, side by side, back to our room, undressing in complete silence, avoiding one another's eyes, apart, yet intimate in the bitter tricks of sexual antagonism, before finally retiring to our separate beds. I don't think we exchanged more than two dozen words all evening and probably even less this morning. There was just nothing more to say.

"Don't rubbish me, Tina," David was saying doggedly. "This Buddhism is real for me."

His sincerity seemed to get through to Martina for she turned to him, laying her hand on his arm, almost a caress, her tone apologetic: suddenly she was talking to him in the funky dialect of their youth.

"I know, Davey, I really know. I feel for you, believe me, I do. I'm not trying to hassle you, really I'm not. This is no fun thing for me. You've got to believe that. This island wants tourists, Buddhists and everybody—they need the bread, really they do—so I'm taking pictures. Where's the sin in that?"

"No sin," he conceded patiently. "Buddhists believe there's no such thing as sin, only evil. And this tourist crap—that's evil! Materialism, greed, a big rip-off, that's what it is. D'you think they'll come here to follow The Way. Not a bit of it! They'll gawp at that picture and maybe smile and tell themselves how much better they are than the poor natives who worship idols. I know, I've watched them and listened. Intolerance. That's what's bugging the world today. Intolerance and greed. Look at the Negroes in America, Vietnam, Hitler and the Jews. Racial intolerance, religious intolerance, false views. Your Island of Buddhas stuff is evil, Tina."

I was astounded, not quite sure how we had come around to Hitler and the Jews and Vietnam. Garbled, dedicated stuff which could be the prelude to a fanaticism which would shut out that reason he was trying to promote. Glancing at the Buddha figure I silently saluted the power of that ancient faith which could stir young men like David. Yet he was becoming a little overpowering and besides, there was no shade in the courtyard and the sun was burning through my shirt. Nor do I endure homilies patiently at any time, much less from a twenty-one year old who has had nothing more than his father's intolerance and his mother's affection to make life hard for him. Perhaps if he had lived a little longer . . . But that doubt is the particular intolerance of age. Yet I remembered that Siddhartha Gautama had been a pampered young man before he had discovered his vocation. Baffled I wiped the sweat from my brow.

"I'm sorry to interrupt you," I began, ignoring Martina's cool glance, "but we want to see the rest of this temple so if we're going to get to this Shangri-La place of yours we'd better keep moving."

"Sure, sure." David came down from his proselytising high looking abashed, turning from me. "Come on, Tina. We got to get going."

Even without that enormous Buddha the Purvaramaya temple would have been unusual. I don't know whether there were caves there originally, which had been enlarged and extended, but we were conducted through a complex of underground chambers which must have honeycombed much more than the area of the courtyard above us. With that realisation in mind I pondered the weight of the Buddha overhead. We were met by Gopal in company with an English-speaking monk from Thailand, an angular, skinny, affable young man, boney as a garfish. His black eyes watched us astutely through steel-framed spectacles and he carried a furled umbrella which he used to point out objects of interest: from time to time he passed a knuckly hand over his shaven poll, producing a grisly, bristling sound.

Happily he showed us a gilded Buddha in a sanctuary smelling of incense and damp, then on to see the temple treasures, proudly pointing out a miniature jade dagoba which had been his present to the abbot. Finally he led us through chambers painted with the Jataka stories. Painted from floors to ceilings and over ceilings, every millimetre of space covered with pictures, highly coloured, often crudely executed, but always vigorous, each enclosed by a narrow saffron border. The effect was like rooms papered with the Sunday comics in colour. Martina studied them, asking questions that seemed to amuse the monk immensely. I lagged behind, interested in a series depicting the birth of the Buddha. There was a mother on a couch, nursing a remarkably adult looking baby, attended by a trio of kingly personages with worshipful menials keeping their distance and some animals in the background. It was like the Adoration of the Magi in comic strip. Engrossed I wasn't aware of David's presence until he spoke.

"Sorry about sounding off up there, Mase."

Surprised I could only shrug. "I'm sorry I broke it up, but the heat was getting me down. I haven't got your youth and stamina."

"Yeah, I guess I get carried away at times." He nodded, tilting a diffident, sidelong smile at me. "I hope Tina wasn't bored. She does seem to go for it, doesn't she?"

"She's interested in it," I conceded dryly.

He seemed uncertain how to answer, shuffling his feet, looking away to Martina who was listening to the monk explaining something in clipped English. David's eyes swung back to me, very direct.

"She's very unhappy, isn't she?"

"She's getting over a bad marriage," I said, wondering what he was leading up to, and not particularly wanting to discuss Martina.

He nodded gravely. "I thought so. Stephen, wasn't that his name?" And he paused as though considering his next words carefully. "I heard her going on at you about him last night. I couldn't help hearing. I was in the bathroom. Those walls are pretty thin."

My heart missed several beats, a terrifying sensation of my life force faltering then thundering on, panic rampaging through me. Desperately I tried to recall exactly when I had heard the shower being turned off, but all that came was a confused memory of the ugliness. Yet he had heard her "going on" at me . . . "you leave Stephen out of this!" And what about: "You've laid your share of dollies, that girl, David's mother" . . . ? And then all about the paternity of Anula's child and my denunciation of Eric. I watched David's eyes for some indication of what he had heard, but his eyes looked steadily back at me, such clear, dark eyes with a troubled, youthful intentness in their depths. The silence had expanded around us like a bubble tinged with the garish colours of the paintings, with the monk's precise tones coming as though from far away. I made a little embarrassed gesture, noticing that my hands were trembling.

"Yes, well, I'm sorry about that. We were having a row."

"Yeah, I heard."

But how much, I wondered uneasily. About Eric? About your mother? I shivered, the subterranean cool of this picture-bedizened cavern chilling the soles of my stockinged feet. Martina and the monk had moved into another chamber, their voices coming to us, echoing hollowly. David smiled yet somehow it didn't quite reach his eyes.

"By Christ, you guys must have had a ball over here," he said softly, but with a subdued passion that startled me. "That girl—was it really your kid, Mase? Or was it my old man's?"

"I don't think it's got anything to do with you," I said stiffly, pretending an offended dignity which was neither dignified nor offended, just base, on the defensive.

"Hasn't it, by God! He was my old man, wasn't he? I've got a right to know."

His voice had thickened, that passion which I had noticed in him erupting now. It was like something familiar and trusted blowing up in my face. Had a right to know . . . whether he had a half-sister, whether his father was a seducer? But Eric wasn't his father. Despite the doubts which the old lady's information had roused I couldn't quite give up that belief—it had sustained me for so long.

"It happened a long time ago," I began temporisingly, but he cut me short impatiently, almost accusingly.

"He was with you, wasn't he? I've heard him talking about that place. Matagama, wasn't it?"

"Udugama," I corrected, grabbing at that futile respite. He wasn't to be distracted, relentlessly tearing away my evasions and prevarications, pinning me down.

"And my old man was there?"

"Yes, he was with me."

"So it could have been his kid."

"It could have been anyone's."

"For Christ's sake, who are you kidding?" he raged. "You said the rest of your company was thirty kilometres away! And that old dame—she might be a hundred years old or whatever—but she's got all her marbles. She knew. An Aussie, she said, so"—voice dropping, words coming out dramatically—"that leaves only you and my old man. So whose kid was it, Mase? Yours or my old man's?"

Eric's or mine! The choice was simple. Yet was it? There was an anguish in David's eyes now that moved me, a ruthless, youthful righteousness waiting to pass judgement, waiting to accept and punish himself for the sin of his father. I had an uneasy memory of the fanaticism I had seen in him this morning. In his present mood of piety David was capable of imposing some penance on himself, seeking absolution in his father's name. Yet should I accept the blame for the very act which had been used against me? I thought wildly, the truth tolling mockingly in my brain, but all I could think of was Anula and Eric, Janice and myself and . . .

"Mine," I said tersely and with the word a terrible sense of defeat swept over me, a chagrin, so that I couldn't resist adding testily, "I can't think what difference it makes after all this time."

"Can't you?" David queried softly and for some reason I found this calm more disturbing than this rage. "You really don't know, eh? You think it doesn't make any difference, huh? Well, he was my old man, wasn't he?" He broke off, watching me narrowly, letting the pause draw out, something retributive and implacable and triumphant seeming to gather in him, pouncing. "Or was he?"

So . . . ! I think I had sensed all along that this was what it had been all about, the change in him this morning, even his tirade up there in the courtyard, part of the turmoil which must have been seething in him ever since he had overheard us last night. Suddenly the deceits and subterfuges of thirty years had risen around me, like spectres hemming me in, with the ghost of my most precious illusion accusing me. Yet now that it had come I was calm. The deception, the hypocrisy, the artifices and ploys with which I had protected my secret, and with them, the constant need for vigilance, had been stripped from me. A feeling of sheer relief raced through me and I felt free, bursting out into the thin, pure atmosphere of truth. So strong was it that I was tempted to shout. No, he wasn't your father! He was the man who took your mother from me! Then the sight of David's face humbled me and again I dissembled.

"I don't think I understand you, David."

"Oh, come on, Mase," he snapped, white teeth showing savagely in his beard. "Don't shit me, man! You know what I'm on about. Am I your son? Did you do my mother over like Tina said?"

Like Tina said! That girl, David's mother! So she was back between us! Damn her to hell! Her hang-ups might very well change my life. I could accept the blame for Anula's child, but I couldn't bear to lose my son. Why should I renounce that belief now? I had relieved him of the embarrassment of a sister. Surely that entitled me to claim my own. A word would be sufficient, even a nod. I hesitated, thinking of Janice . . .

"David"—the words came slowly, winding up out of an emptiness—"your mother and I were in love long before she married your father."

"Hold it!" His hand went up peremptorily. "You called him my father. Is that your answer?"

Taken aback I stared at him, regretting my stupid slip of the tongue, but before I could answer there was a sound nearby, footsteps on the echoing stone, Martina's voice breaking the bubble of quiet.

"Are you two going to stand there rapping all day?"

Martina, I thought hotly: always her! Without taking his eyes off me David jerked his head in her direction as if acknowledging yet dismissing her. His curtness made me wonder what he really felt for her. Then his voice was boring into the thought, demolishing it.

"What about it, Mase? Like was that the answer?"

And so help me—I nodded.

"David! Mason," Martina called again, beckoning impatiently.

Looking at her I had the feeling of standing amidst ruins. Not David Mason, I thought despairingly: David Coleman. No matter what I believed I had given him back his birthright. I turned away but he fell into step with me, speaking quietly, bitterly.

"You know, I should knock you down, messing around with my mother like that. But I can't. For why? Because you're Mase and you showed me how to be myself, not David Coleman, materialist, but David Coleman, follower of The Way. I guess I'll always remember you might have been my old man—if my father hadn't come along. But this is where I split that scene, Mase. This is where I do my own thing for real. So you tell my mother when you see her."

"What do you intend doing now?"

His own thing! I didn't like the thought of that. His calm bothered me, somewhere in it that zeal, a renewed dedication, an objective. His own thing. Martina was watching us quizzically as we neared her and I knew that all that was left to us were these last few steps together. I wanted to touch him.

194

"I guess I'll just hang loose," David was saying thoughtfully. "Maybe I'll go to Adam's Peak, maybe I'll just stick around Dobradulla and meditate."

"Dobradulla?" Martina queried brightly, for by then we were close enough for her to hear what was being said. David grinned at her, once more becoming the David of yesterday, flip, young, talking that jargon of their own. I had the feeling that it would be the last I'd see of him like this.

"Like Shang, kiddo. Shangri-La, like that beach village I was talking about. Maybe if you drop me off at the Rest House there I'll even sport you a farewell lunch."

He did just that, not only paying for Martina's lunch and mine but also for those of a couple of freaks we came upon lounging, with no purpose that I could see, in the lounge of the Rest House. They were acquaintances of David's and out of the babble of their greetings, unusually exuberant on the part of the girl, I heard enough to learn that they had just completed a pilgrimage to a place called Kataragama. It must have been a weird, even grisly experience to judge by their wide-eyed references to fish hooks, skewers and bloodless wounds. I wasn't sure that I liked them.

Both were Americans, the boy drawlingly so, tall and beanpole thin, with chestnut hair flowing to below his shoulders and a chestnut beard streaked with blond around the mouth. It gave him the look of a youthful seadog that accorded well with his grey eyes and austere, bony face, so that despite bare feet, sarong and peace beads he made me think of a Viking. When he talked he looked over your shoulder as though he was searching for new horizons. David called him Yitzo.

The girl's name was Collie, which was short for Colleen. And a colleen she might have been, but for her twangy accent and her Irish complexion which had been cured to a mahogony blush by the Asiatic sun, and for the gold ring which she wore through her left nostril. As it was, with her tousled black hair and lively blue eyes and that preposterous nose ring, she looked more like a bouncey gipsy. Bouncey because she had loose, round breasts that always seemed to get in her way—the front of her granny-dress was soiled by smudges where her forearms brushed their undersides. Far from being ascetic she was totally uninhibited, as friendly as an over-indulged collie bitch.

Lunch was sere fish, thick cutlets curried to a point of sweat and tears, along with curried beans, curried beetroot, curried potatoes, all somewhat inadequately tempered with grated coconut and followed by slices of papaya and slivers of lime. The freaks ate ravenously and as I watched them wiping their plates with pieces of grey Sri Lankan bread, scraping their papaya down to the rinds, I understood their delight at meeting David.

"So you guys're cuttin' out?" Collie said, addressing the question to Martina and me, yet looking at David for confirmation.

Behind her a white-jacketed waiter was reaching for her plate and eyeing her nose ring with fascination. In Sri Lanka it was Tamil women who wore rings and plugs in their noses. Around us I could feel the decaying British decorum of the old Rest House; the tall windows that offered a view of the sea and a garden where an old man was lethargically raking leaves; the dining room with its near-white napery and spotty silverware and somnolent waiters standing against the walls; the bar with its rump-sprung leather chairs; the whole columned and grubby mausoleum of a place, weathered and run down, with thick-stemmed vines clawing up its walls and jagged cracks beneath its cornices. Dilapidated as it was it struggled to preserve those traditions and standards that Collie and her kind were revolting against.

Leaning back David placed his hands, fingers linked on the top of his head. "Not me. They are." The toss of his head indicated Martina and me. There was a certain brusqueness in his tone which made me wonder whether he was bored with Yitzo and Collie.

"Where you-all headin' then, Davey?" Yitzo turned from staring out the window, his glance sweeping the room like a searchlight beam.

"Here." David stamped the floor lightly.

"Whyn't you go to Kat, Davey," Collie came in quickly.

"Wolfgang'n'Pedersen're here." Yitzo ignored her, watching David.

"Gas," David pronounced without much enthusiasm.

"So's Smitty'n'Doreen'n' coupla others." Yitzo's drawl became syrupy, persuasive. "An' Looey the Frog. You-all know Looey. Little Frog guy, goin' off to Adam's Peak last we saw him. Maybe we get together for a rap session, huh?"

"Go to Kat, Davey," Collie urged winningly.

"Kat?" Martina asked.

She was shaking out a cigarette and I noticed her jerky movements, as though she was nervous of breaking into their talk. She tossed the pack on the table amongst us and at once Collie's troublesome breasts surged flaccidly over the tablecloth, a brown arm going out, gipsy fingers abstracting a cigarette.

"Yeah, Kataragama, that's where." Still lolling, the unlit cigarette flopping between her lips she answered Martina with a barely concealed insolence.

"Where's Kataragama?" Martina asked, her crisp tone overriding Collie's veiled hostility. Again I noted her movements, the way she snapped her lighter into flame, thumbing it forcefully, jerking her head down to it, and the way she tossed the lighter to the girl, as though she was dispensing largesse.

"Long way down, out in the boondooks," Yitzo explained and I got the feeling that he wanted to discourage Martina's interest.

"It's far out, I tell you," Collie enthused, grabbing the lighter and flicking flame behind the screen of her untidy hair that tumbled dangerously close when she lowered her head. She puffed smoke and excitement, blue eyes glittering, even her nose ring quivering. "It's wild, that place! Spo-oo-ky! There's these guys, see, an' they want something, I don't know what, but they want it real bad so they make a vow to this little ole god at Kat. He's not the Big B of course, not Gautama Sidd, but he's mucho grand just the same. An' when he delivers these guys gotta ante up, like make with this vow thing. So they stick spikes an' skewers through their tongues an' right through their cheeks an' hang hooks with weights in their ears."

She broke off, sucking hungrily at her cigarette, not inhaling, just puffing smoke distractedly, lost in rapturous contemplation of skewers and spikes and mutilation. I wondered what rites they had stumbled on out there in the jungle. The little ole god of Kat. Probably Hindu, like the processions of penitents in India. It was horrible to see its effects on Collie. She was looking around us, speaking in fascinated tones.

"There was this guy—he stuck fish hooks through his skin. For real, I tell you. Fish hooks! An' they hoisted him up an' let him swing an' he prayed an' sung an' we talked to him, didn't we, Yitz. An' he didn't bleed one little bit, did he?"

"You're a grade A vampire," Yitzo denounced flatly, turning his slightly disgusted, slightly bored, bony face to the rest of us. "I tell you-all I swear she near on creamed her jeans when she seen this guy hung up on hooks like a side o' beef in a ree-frigerator. Jest no knowin' what turns this chick on."

"Not you, that's for sure," Collie snapped.

"Try me, whyn't ya," Yitzo invited.

"You've had your chance, buster," Collie told him warmly.

They had forgotten us, their gazes locked in a purely sexual confrontation. I saw Martina watching them intently. Her face was turned away from me so that I couldn't see her expression, but she was sitting very straight, the cigarette burning away between her fingers. I sensed her involvement with these young people, if involvement was the right word—perhaps identifying would be more correct. The realisation disturbed me for I remembered her vulnerability. It was a long step from the Sri Maha Bodhi ceremony to these gamey waifs, but Martina was making it. From outside I heard crows cawing loudly.

"Sounds groovy," David said suddenly and removing his hands from his head he smiled. There was something about it I didn't like, such a secretive smile with a quickening of excitement in his eyes like a decision suddenly taken. This was a new and baffling David grown out of the lad I had known and encouraged. Collie had disentangled her sullen gaze from Yitzo's, turning eagerly to David.

"Whyn't you go, Davey? I'll go with you."

"Like hell you will!" Yitzo's impassiveness left him completely, his lean Viking face tightening, his hand clamping possessively on Collie's wrist. "You-all haul ya little ass anywhere it's with me, Pussy. Davey wants to go to Kat let him take the old guy'n'the dame but you'n' me stay together. Collie'n'Yitzo. Happy ever after like the books say."

For a moment I thought Collie would claw him. There was more than a little hate in the way she glared at him, her gipsy face rebellious, all her pretty sunburned youthfulness stretched tautly over the features of the shrew she was bound to become. It was another embarrassing moment, fraught with the echoes of old confrontations and silent except for the crows and the drowsy murmur of Singhalese voices from the kitchen regions. I looked away at the beach, noticing the pink sand, the blue of the sea and the green and graceful tilt of palms. Some fishing boats were out on the salty glitter, their bellying sails, with upturned tips, reminding me of open purses, purses opened to receive the silver of the sea. "He's right, Collie," David said placatingly.

"Aw, shee-it!" Pouting she wrenched her wrist from Yitzo's grip and shrugged, then popping her cigarette into the dregs of her teacup she shot a venomous glance at Martina. "You wanna take that dame, doncha? I know. You got the hots for her."

It came out so flatly, catching us unawares. Somewhere in my surprise was the memory of David at the Vatadage and Sigiriya and at the elephants' bathing place. And I found myself silently saluting Collie's perception. Stiffening, David bunched his hand into a fist on the table. Martina had paled, pointed chin lifted angrily, and she was savagely jabbing her cigarette into her saucer, mashing it. She was the first to recover.

"You stupid little bitch," she said scathingly.

"Yeah, Pussy, you-all mouth 'n'tits," Yitzo agreed, grinning.

"Hey, no!" David snapped out of his tension, clenched first opening into a brisk gesture, checking Yitzo. "She's got something. I hadn't figured on going to Kat, but maybe it's a good idea. What about it, Tina? You be in it?"

Dimly through my surprise came the realisation that he had ignored me, that he wasn't asking me to go to Kataragama. That it was deliberate, no spur-of-the-moment invitation, to be belatedly extended to me. He was looking at Martina, turning the full blaze of his youth and charm on her, making it seem as though there was no one else at the table, only himself and her. I knew then that everything that had ever been between David and me had ended at this moment, here in Dobradulla—in Shangri-La, the goal of the ever-youthful—in the harsh clear burn of the midday sun that was filled with the flicker of yellow blossom and banyan leaves and the cawing of crows while the purse-shaped sails of catamarans netted the silver of the sea. I was aware of Martina turning to me, her voice, that American accent which I hardly noticed any more, coming to me as though from a distance.

"What about it, Mason?"

"Please yourself. You're a free agent."

I didn't know why she bothered to defer to me. Perhaps it was because of Collie. Anyway I came out of my daze shrugging, once again quite calm, as though I had crossed some watershed of decision, looking back at the way I had come with relief and not a little repugnance. Why had I ever become involved with her? Involved! That was a touchy word now. But not for much longer. After last night at Tissamaharama it was over between us and I had no intention of resurrecting it, certainly not among the fish hooks and superstition of Kataragama, with David in attendance. He was looking from one to the other of us, eyes bright above his beard, breaking in before Martina could speak.

"Come on, Tina, you'll get some good stuff at Kat. Lots of gory photos, first-hand stories, bloody rites of jungle god sort of thing."

"Weren't no blood," Collie muttered petulantly.

"Well then, there's your angle," David urged, leaning back, hands spread expansively, looking as innocent as Lucifer. "Wounds but no blood. Is it voodoo or is it for real? Mystery of faith and all that crap. You'll be on a winner."

"Don't hassle me," Martina protested, looking at me.

Perhaps if I hadn't been so preoccupied with David, or if I hadn't been so sure that everything was dead between Martina and me I might have drawn an inference from her indecision. It was so unlike her, the woman I had drunk with in the Hotel Taprobane, the scene in the gem shop . . . I thought of the moonstone pendant then, the lotus, flower of enlightenment . . . my bitter enlightenment! Suddenly I knew that I must save what was left of my pride, get free from these young people who had no feeling for anything but their youth, no commitment to anything but themselves, so I avoided Martina's eyes, finding myself looking at Collie's nose ring and vaguely wondering what it must be like to go through life with a ring through your nose.

"Mason?" Martina's voice was soft, penetrating my obduracy.

Turning, I found David, sitting beyond her, watching me. There was an intentness in his eyes that startled me, a concentration of will focussed on me, with Martina between us of no consequence at that moment, a thing to be used against me. For that was what this was really all about, I realised—David and me—David growing up, David knowing about his mother and me. He had declared it at the Purvaramaya Temple this morning and this was the final act of what had begun more than twenty years ago, when I had gone to Janice at that beachside motel. He was avenging himself and proving his maturity by taking Martina. As Eric had taken Janice . . . Eric who had also taken Anula, whose

200

ghost had risen against me last night, making it easier for Eric's son . . . ! For David *was* Eric's son. I knew that now with all the blinding certainty of a biblical revelation, and the knowledge made me feel old and deluded and wasted. For a moment that frightened me, the futility and the emptiness, then there came to me once more the only line of the Buddha's teaching I could remember. "One is one's own refuge. Who else shall be the refuge?"

"Count me out," I said tersely, not taking my eyes off David. Martina's expression didn't change, only her eyes widened slightly. Angered? Elated? Or merely glad to be rid of me?

"So what?" She shrugged, turning to David. "I'll go with you."

Rising I pushed my chair back noisily, drawing Yitzo's interested glance and a brief flicker of Collie's attention. I already had David's—David in that faded red sarong, bare feet and beard—watching me, smiling.

I left the dining room walking stiffly . . .